This is a work of fiction. Names, characters, organizations, places, events, and incidents are either products of the author's imagination or are used fictitiously. Any resemblance to actual persons, living or dead, or actual events is purely coincidental.

Text copyright © 2020 by Paige H. Perry

All rights reserved.

Chapter 1

Anna Hartman pulled into the office parking lot and shook her head at the blue jeep that was already there.

"How does he always get here before me?" she chuckled to herself before popping the car in park and opening the door. She hurried around to the passenger side to retrieve a large box from the seat.

Balancing it on one arm, she used her free hand to pull her purse and a grocery bag from the floorboard before locking her car and heading to the office. When she reached the front door, she caught the handle with her fingers and flipped it open just enough to wedge her foot in the opening.

She shoved the door open and squeezed herself and the items in her arms through it. Once the door closed behind her, she let a puff of air escape her lips and looked around the lobby.

Hearing the doorbell chime, the young woman sitting behind the desk closest to the door looked up at her. She took in Anna's disheveled appearance, an amused smile forming on her face.

"What in the world are you doing?"

Anna sat the box and grocery bag down on the woman's desk and shook out her arms. "Biting off more than I can chew. That was heavier than I thought it would be."

"What is it?"

Anna grinned. "That, dear Allie, is a cake. We are celebrating."

"What are we celebrating?"

"Today is our official six-month anniversary of opening this law firm of ours," Anna said with a grin. "I figured we should celebrate with some cake."

"Six months?" Allie said. "Already? I can't believe it's been that long!"

"I know! I had to do the math twice to convince myself."

"That's worth celebrating."

"I'd say so," Anna said. "It's been a mostly successful six months, too. We've averaged a case every month and only had that one loss. But I guess you can't win them all, right?"

"Definitely not."

"And we couldn't have done it without our faithful paralegal," Anna said, sending a warm smile in Allie's direction. "I'm glad we didn't run you off."

"Are you kidding me?" Allie replied. "I have the best coworkers in the world, and I get to see my boyfriend every day. What more could I want?"

"Well, when that boyfriend of yours gets here, make sure you send him to the conference room for a piece of cake, and don't forget to stop by and get some for yourself too."

Allie laughed. "That thing is so big we'll be eating on it for two or three days."

"What can I say?" Anna said with a laugh of her own. "I like cake."

Anna hoisted the cake back into her arms and headed off toward the conference room. One chair was facing away from her when she entered. When it didn't turn after she sat the cake down on the table, she shook her head and rolled her eyes.

"Is there ever going to come a day when I get here before you?"

The chair swung around, and an unfamiliar face smiled back at her. Anna narrowed her eyes at the man and his smile widened, his green eyes twinkling. He ran a hand through his disheveled blonde hair and winked at her.

"You are not Joe."

"Honey, I'll be whoever you want me to be."

"Ugh," she said. "Who are you and what are you doing in Joe's chair?"

"Derrick," a voice suddenly said behind her. "That's Derrick."

Anna turned around and raised an eyebrow at the dark-headed man, who was now leaning against the doorframe behind her. "Derrick?"

The smile on the man's face grew until his amusement made its way up into his blue eyes.

"You have a Claire. I have a Derrick."

Anna turned back to look at Derrick, who grinned at her, causing her frown to deepen. "Joe, why has it taken you six months to introduce me to your best friend?"

Joe laughed. "I just figured we have enough of your best friend that we didn't need to add mine to the mix."

Anna flipped her gaze back in his direction, gave him a playful glare, and swatted his arm.

"Are you not going to introduce her to me?" Derrick asked, turning Anna's attention back to him.

Joe laughed. "This is Anna."

"Ahh, the famous Anna Banana."

"Absolutely not," Anna said.

Derrick laughed, leaned back in the chair, and gave her another glance before sending a wry look in Joe's direction. "You're right, Joe. She is pretty."

Joe rolled his eyes and shook his head. "Stop it, Derrick. Her boyfriend would eat you for lunch."

"Hmm," Derrick said. "Is the best friend as pretty as this one? Does she have a boyfriend?"

Anna shook her head, groaned, and turned to look at Joe again. "Please tell me this will not become a thing. He is leaving soon, right?"

Derrick stood up and walked around the table, eyeing Anna's box. Anna glared at him and pulled it closer to herself to protect it.

"He's just messing with you," Joe said. "Do you think I'd be friends with a guy who treats women like that?"

"All right," Derrick said. "Enough of this. I'm dying to know what's in that box."

When he reached for it, Anna swatted his hand away and shooed him back around the table. "Stop that! Joe, make him stop!"

Joe laughed when she jerked the box further away from Derrick. "Behave, Derrick. What's in the box, Anna?"

"It's a cake," Anna said, still glaring at Derrick and blocking his view of the box. "And if the two of you will behave for five seconds, I will open it and cut us some pieces."

"It is way too early for cake," Derrick said with a laugh.

"It's never too early for cake," Anna and Joe said in unison.

Derrick laughed again, and Anna got busy opening a package of party plates and plastic cutlery. When she opened the box, Joe peered inside and whistled.

"That looks good," he said. "But what's the occasion?"

She smiled, but before she could reply, the front door chimed. Within moments, she heard heels clicking down the hallway and looked up just in time to watch a blonde-haired woman sweep into the conference room.

"Anna," the woman said, ignoring Joe and Derrick when she walked in. "What in the world do you have me out here at this hour for?"

"It's nice to see you, too, Claire," Joe chuckled.

Claire frowned at him and then pivoted her eyes to Derrick. He raised his eyebrows at her. "Who are you?"

"Derrick," he replied.

"Who's Derrick?" Claire asked, looking at Anna.

"So far, he's a pain in the ass," Anna said.

Joe laughed. "Derrick is my best friend. He lives in Chicago."

"I didn't know you had friends," Claire said.

"Ah, you have cute disses and everything!" Derrick said. "How adorable!"

"Cake!" Anna said with a groan. "I brought cake."

"You called me here at 8 in the morning for cake?"

"I called you here at 8 in the morning because I knew you had a full schedule today, and I didn't want you to miss the celebrating."

Anna smiled and put a plate in Claire's hand. Claire looked down at it and then frowned back at Anna.

"What are we celebrating?"

"We have been open for exactly six months today!"

Claire's eyes lit up. "That's awesome!"

Joe shook his head. "Six months. That's crazy. It seems like we've known each other forever."

Anna smiled and turned back to the cake, cutting a piece for herself and Joe and putting a third on a plate for Derrick. When she slid it across the table in his direction, he grinned.

"And here I was beginning to believe we would not hit it off," he said. "You do like me."

"Don't get ahead of yourself," Anna said and sat down at the table. "But since you're here, I guess you can have cake."

Claire took a bite of her cake and sat down at the table next to Anna. Derrick watched her take another bite and smiled when she looked up at him.

Noticing her curiosity, Joe sat down in one of the remaining chairs in the room and said, "Derrick comes down every year. He spends Thanksgiving with my family and then heads off for a week with his family before heading back home after the new year."

"Wow, that's a long vacation," Claire said. "That must be nice."

Derrick shrugged. "We run the finances for some high-valued people. They all take off for the last month of the year, so we take a couple of weeks, too. Of course, if they need me, I'm still available, but most of the time it's pretty quiet."

"Speaking of Thanksgiving," Joe said, turning his attention back to Anna. "What's on your agenda?"

Anna shrugged. "Well, Claire heads off to visit her mom here in town on Thanksgiving Day and then drives up to spend the weekend with her dad in Philadelphia."

"Chestnut Hill," Claire corrected.

"Sorry," Anna laughed. "Chestnut Hill. My sister is meeting up with her best friend for the day and then spending the weekend with her fiancé's family."

Joe laughed. "You seemed to leave Anna out of either of those scenarios."

"Anna is cozying up with an enormous bottle of wine, a fluffy blanket, and the Thanksgiving Day Parade," she said and took another bite of the cake.

Joe laid his fork down and narrowed his eyes at her. "Come again?"

"I said—"

"No, I heard you. You said you spend Thanksgiving by yourself."

Anna shrugged. "Everyone else has plans. So, yeah. By myself. It's peaceful."

"What about the big strong boyfriend who would eat me for lunch?" Derrick asked. "He leaves his girlfriend alone on Thanksgiving?"

Anna shook her head at him and laughed. "He's a police officer. He works on Thanksgiving. As does my dad, who is in Boston right now."

"Every year?" Joe asked. "By yourself."

Anna laughed. "I think we've established the fact that I spend Thanksgiving alone."

"No turkey?" Derrick asked, a horrified look on his face. "Or mashed potatoes? Or pumpkin pie?"

"Sometimes I order in if that makes you feel better," Anna said with another laugh. "It's fine. I'm used to it."

"Yeah, that will not work this year," Joe said. "You now have plans. Dinner's at 3. Mom will not let you bring a thing."

Anna shook her head. "Joe, no. I am not invading your mom's house and inviting myself over for Thanksgiving dinner. She has enough things to worry about—"

"You aren't inviting yourself over," Joe said. "I am. And you're coming. How many times have you been to my house in the past six months? Like seven? Do you think my mother would let me live if I told her I let you spend Thanksgiving by yourself?"

"Who's spending Thanksgiving by themselves?" a voice suddenly asked from the conference room door.

Anna smiled up at the man in the doorway. "Bryant, tell your brother he's being ridiculous."

"Anna," Joe said, ignoring her. "Anna thinks she's spending Thanksgiving by herself. Bryant, tell her she's not allowed to do that. She's not listening to me."

"Does she ever listen to you?" Bryant asked as he cut two pieces of cake. "For once, I have to say I agree with my brother on this one, Anna. You should come to our house."

"Guys!" Anna argued. "I'm totally fine. You don't have to go to all this trouble!"

"Oh, for crying out loud," Joe said, reaching for the phone on the desk. "Quit talking."

Anna continued protesting as he ignored her and dialed a number on the phone. When it started ringing, he put it on speaker and Anna sat back in her chair. She groaned when Joe's mother answered the other end of the line.

"Hey, mom!" Joe said. "What're you doing? Just so you know, I have you on speaker with Derrick, Anna, and Bryant...oh, and Claire."

"Thanks," Claire mouthed at him.

"Hi, everyone!" she said. "Joe, you know what I'm doing. I'm grocery shopping."

"For Thanksgiving Dinner, right?"

"Of course."

"Good. That's what I wanted to talk to you about. I just found out something interesting that you will want to know."

"What's that?"

"Anna spends Thanksgiving by herself every year."

"Excuse me?"

"She seems to think she's spending it alone this year as well."

"Well, she's not," his mom replied. "You tell her...wait, you said I was on speaker. Anna, honey, you can't spend Thanksgiving by yourself. Please come to our house tomorrow. I won't feel right all day knowing you're by yourself."

"See, how can you say no to that?" Joe asked, grinning at Anna as she chuckled and shook her head at him.

"Fine," she said. "I'll be there, Beth. Thank you so much for the invitation."

"Good!" Beth replied. "And Anna, bring that boyfriend of yours if he's free. And your sister and her fiancé. And Claire, of course. I'm dying to meet the men who belong to you two."

"I'll see if they are available," Anna said. "But they usually aren't."

"Well, bring them if they are."

"Love you, mom," Joe said, still grinning at Anna. "Bye!"

"Bye, honey!"

Anna shook her head at him again and turned her attention back to her cake. "I can't believe you just added five people to your mother's Thanksgiving guest list while she's out grocery shopping."

Joe shrugged. "Mom always fixes enough food to feed thirty people, anyway. It's not like it's that much of an addition. And she was serious about you coming, too, Claire. If you are available, of course."

"You know," Claire said with a grin, "I don't have to leave to go to my mom's house until tomorrow evening, so maybe I will come by and hang out for a while."

"That's perfect!" Derrick said. "Joe, we can take them out in your jeep and spin up a little mud. Be back in time for appetizers and cocktails."

Joe laughed. "The last time we did that, we almost missed dinner and mom about killed us because of all the mud we left on the porch."

"What do you say, Anna?" Derrick asked, throwing the adventure in her direction. "Are you up for a little back road adventure before lunch?"

"That sounds like a horrible idea," Claire said.

Anna laughed. "You're right. That does sound like a horrible idea."

"Man, just when I was starting to like you, too," Derrick said.

"Wait for it," Joe said, smirking at Derrick as he took another bite of the cake.

"Oh, I didn't say we weren't going to do it," Anna said with a grin. "I was just acknowledging that it's probably a bad idea."

"Lord, help me," Claire muttered.

Chapter 2

Anna took a sip of her coffee, sighed, and closed her eyes as the warm liquid slid down her throat. With a yawn, she looked down at the paper in her hand and flipped through the pages half-heartedly. When the bedroom door opposite her own opened, she looked up and frowned at the woman who emerged.

With a sigh, the woman smiled at her and ran a hand through her brown hair before shuffling to the coffeepot. After she'd filled a mug, she took a seat at the table next to Anna and propped her head on her chin.

"Anna, it's seven in the morning," she said. "What are you doing up?"

Anna laughed. "They have summoned me to the Malone house for Thanksgiving dinner."

"And you're up and planning to behave today? I'm impressed!"

"Marie, you've been my sister long enough to know better than that," Anna said with a snicker. "Joe and one of his friends are taking Claire and I mudding this morning before dinner."

"Oh, brother," Marie said. "I should have known."

Anna looked down at her sister's pajamas and frowned. "Speaking of which, shouldn't you already be on your way to meet Frankie?"

Marie shook her head. "She's not going to make it."

"Well, that's too bad," Anna said. "Is everything all right?"

"I don't know. She sounded a bit upset but rushed off the phone before I could get anything out of her."

"Let me know when you find out what's going on," Anna said with a frown. "What are you going to do today, then?"

"I don't know," Marie said. "Eddie and I don't have to head out to his folk's house until tomorrow morning."

Anna laughed. "From the conversation I had with Beth yesterday, she would be ecstatic if you brought Eddie to her house so she could meet him. She invited all of us, even Alex and Claire."

"It would be nice to have an actual family Thanksgiving dinner for a change," Marie said with a soft smile.

Anna smiled at her. "It would."

Anna's phone chirped on the table, and she glanced at it. "Is it 7:30 already? I need to get ready! Joe will be here at 8."

She rushed off into her room and started pulling off her pajamas and flipping through the outfits in her closet. She pulled on a pair of jeans and a long-sleeve t-shirt before rummaging through a drawer for a pair of socks. She was sitting on the edge of her bed and pulling on an old pair of boots when Marie walked into her room.

"I just texted Eddie," she said. "He's fine with going to the Malone's house for dinner today. What time did Beth say to be there, and can we bring something?"

Anna laughed. "Beth told me she would refuse to serve it if I brought anything. All she wanted me to bring is an appetite for dinner, which is scheduled for three."

Marie chuckled and shook her head. "She certainly loves to cook, doesn't she? We'll be there."

Anna returned to her closet and pulled out a sweater, a second pair of jeans, and another pair of shoes, which she tossed on her bed.

"Great! It sounds like everyone will be there," Anna said with a smile. Her boyfriend's face flashed through her mind and the smile faded. "Except Alex, I suppose."

Marie grimaced at Anna's sudden sadness. "I'm sorry, Anna. I'm sure he would be there if he could."

"I know," Anna said, turning her attention back to her closet. "I just wish things were different sometimes."

Before they could talk more, their doorbell rang, causing them both to jump. Anna hurriedly threw a few more items in the bag while Marie went to answer the door. Anna stepped out of her bedroom and pulled the backpack around her shoulders, and smiled when she saw Joe standing in the living room.

"I hear we are having more guests for dinner," he said in greeting before turning back to Marie. "I'm glad you and Eddie can make it, Marie, but I'm sorry to hear your plans with Frankie got messed up."

"Thank you," Marie said. "I'm sure it's nothing. I'm going to check on Frankie later to make sure she's alright."

"Good idea," he said. "Let us know if she needs anything." He turned to Anna and said, "You ready to go, Anna? Derrick is chomping at the bit to get out there in the jeep, and mom would love to get him out of the house so he'll stop snacking on everything in the kitchen."

Anna laughed. "Yep, just finished getting ready. Sorry, I'm running behind. Time got away from me this morning."

"Don't be sorry," he said. "We have plenty of time. Besides, I sort of feel like I owe you considering I messed up your plans at the last minute."

"Oh, by forcing me to go to Thanksgiving dinner at your house?" Anna asked with a wink. She turned and gave her sister a quick hug. "See you, Marie. Let me know what you find out about Frankie."

Joe stepped onto the front porch and waited for Anna to join him. "I invaded your holiday tradition."

"Don't feel bad," Anna said after the door closed behind her. She followed Joe down the sidewalk to his jeep and waited on the passenger side for him to let her in. "Truth be told, I hate spending holidays alone. But there's no way I'm going to ask anyone to change their plans for me."

She climbed inside the jeep and tossed her bag into the back floorboard. Joe climbed in beside her and waited for her to put on her seatbelt.

"Anna," he said, his tone serious. "You need to realize that you are worth changing plans for."

"Thank you," she said with a soft smile. "That means a lot."

"You're welcome," he said before getting the jeep out on the road. "Now let's go have some fun."

Within the hour, Joe had swung by Claire's place, picked up Derrick, and driven them all out to a dirt path leading into the woods behind his house. After shooting a grin in Anna's direction, he threw the jeep down the path, mud flying along behind the tires.

Claire squealed when he slid them around a corner, nearly spinning the vehicle in a complete circle. Mud plunked against the exterior of the jeep and Joe sent another grin in Anna's direction, causing her to laugh.

They bounced along for several more minutes, Claire grumbling and clutching the side of her chair and Anna laughing harder with each clump of mud that flew up on Joe's jeep. Eventually, Joe pulled into a clearing away from the trail and turned off the engine. Claire tumbled out of the jeep and glared at Anna when her shoes sunk in the mud.

"My shoes are dirty," she said.

"I see that." Anna pressed her lips together to keep the chuckle she was holding in from escaping.

"Anybody want a beer?" Derrick yelled while digging in an ice chest in the back of Joe's jeep.

"Yes," Claire said. "You can bring it to me over there."

Anna laughed again when Claire pointed to a log laying across a somewhat dry and mud-free area of the clearing. Joe walked up next to Anna and handed her a beer. Derrick grumbled and walked across the clearing in Claire's direction, holding a pair of beers.

Joe cringed as he looked over at Claire. "I'll take it easy on the way back."

"Don't you dare!" Anna said with a grin. "Don't let her fool you. She's loving every minute. She just has an image to uphold."

"Can't be seen enjoying being thrown around in a jeep and getting all muddy, huh?"

"Absolutely not!"

Joe chuckled and took a drink from the water bottle in his hand before turning to look back at the forest. Anna leaned against the jeep and looked up at the blue sky. The sun was just barely peeking into view over the surrounding trees.

"It's certainly a nice day for this," Joe said. "Thanks for putting up with me and Derrick for the day."

"Thanks for inviting me along," Anna smiled. "And for inviting me to Thanksgiving with your family."

Joe took another sip of the water and said, "I have a confession to make. I haven't been that present at holiday gatherings for a while now. Losing Merida the way I did…it's been hard."

Anna put her hand on his forearm and squeezed it slightly. "I'm so sorry, Joe. I remember how hard those first few years without mom were."

He nodded and met her eyes. "I know eventually I need to be present for things, so I'm trying."

She smiled softly. "I'm glad you are present today."

He returned her smile and said, "Me too."

They held each other's gaze for a few moments until Joe cleared his throat and turned his eyes away from her. Anna pulled away from him and took a drink of her beer.

"Anyway," he said. "Thank you for taking my forced invitation today."

"Seriously, you do not know how old it gets spending holidays alone," Anna said. "Having people around will be so nice for a change."

Joe smiled at her again, but before they could talk more, Claire's voice reached their ears. Anna turned in time to see her friend hurling back toward the jeep.

"I can't believe you just tried to kiss me!"

Derrick followed along behind her, a somewhat amused look on his face. "I'm sorry. I thought we were having a moment."

"Oh, we're having a moment all right," Claire said. "A moment where I shove dirt up your nose."

Joe turned to Anna and raised an eyebrow at her. She chuckled. "Come on. Let's go save our best friends from each other."

"Yeah, we'd better get back," Joe said, looking at his watch. "Mom will expect me there to greet guests as they arrive."

After they'd all climbed back into the jeep, Joe started the engine and maneuvered the vehicle back through the woods and up the road to his parent's house. Anna's eyes widened in surprise when she spotted a familiar car parked along the road.

"What in the world is he doing here?" she mused. "That's Alex's car!"

Chapter 3

"I might have called him," Joe said.

"You? Why did you call him?"

"I figured I could convince him to come to dinner," he said and looked out the window. "Looks like I was right."

Anna shook her head and smiled at Joe before jumping out of the jeep and heading toward Alex's car. He climbed out the moment he realized Anna was back.

"Looks like you guys had fun," Alex said when Anna approached and he spotted a few mud splotches on her clothes.

"What on earth are you doing here?" Anna asked, not able to hide her excited smile.

"I thought it might be nice to surprise you," he said and pulled her into his arms to give her a soft kiss. "I asked my supervisor if I could split up my shift today so I could spend some time with you. I'm going to work a little extra later today."

"You didn't have to do that," Anna said, the excited smile still lingering on her lips. "But I'm glad you did."

"Me, too."

Anna smiled and let him kiss her again. "Good. Now, how about we go inside, and I introduce you to Bryant and Joe's mom and dad? They are going to love you."

Alex took her hand and followed her inside the house, where Anna quickly made introductions to the Malone family. She smiled when Beth gushed over Alex and insisted he have a bite of the dishes she was preparing.

"Hey, while you are busy being spoiled," Anna said. "I'm going to go change out of these muddy clothes."

Anna grabbed her bag and headed off into the bathroom to change. She nearly ran into Joe on her way out of the kitchen.

"Hey," he said, pulling a deck of cards and a box of poker chips out of a drawer by the kitchen door. "Come back to the living room when you get done and I'll see if I can beat you at poker like I do everything else."

"When will you realize you don't beat me at anything?" Anna asked.

Bryant walked into the kitchen behind his brother and laughed at their exchange. "I swear. The two of you are about the most competitive people I've ever met."

Anna laughed and shook her head. "I'd love to beat you at poker, Joe, but I don't want to leave your mom stranded in the kitchen if she needs help."

"Heavens, no!" Beth said from the other side of the kitchen. "I wouldn't dream of it!"

Bryant shook his head and laughed. "I'm going to stick around the kitchen to help finish up dinner."

His mother looked over at him from the stove where she'd been busily stirring pots and moving dishes in and out of the oven. "Well, thank you, honey! I'll put you in charge of cleaning up. Oh, and you can set the tables, too. We'll put the kids in here and all of us can sit in the dining room. Joe, you keep our VIP guests entertained."

"I'm the king of entertainment," Joe said.

"You're the king of something, all right," Bryant said. "Get out of here and let mom and I get to work."

Anna headed off to the bathroom to change. After cleaning up, adjusting her makeup, and making her hair somewhat presentable, she headed back into the living room. Joe and Alex were already deep into a hand of poker when she returned.

"Just in time," Joe said when she sat down in an armchair next to Alex. "Already got you a hand ready."

Anna looked down at the pile of poker chips and the cards laid face down in front of her and frowned. "How do I know you didn't cheat?"

"I always cheat," Joe said with a grin. "But you can make it up when you deal next time."

Anna laughed and picked up her cards. They played through a few hands, Joe occasionally stopping to open the front door and let in another dinner guest. The number of people inside the home grew and while the noise level became overpowering, Anna let the warmth of the family unit invade her senses.

"Ugh," Alex said as they started a new hand. "I fold."

He tossed his cards in the middle of the table and sat back in his chair. Anna looked over at Joe and smiled. "Looks like it's just you and me, then. What's it going to be? Are you going to chicken out, too?"

Joe laughed. "You are a horrible liar."

"What are you talking about?" she asked and brought the cards up to where he could only see her eyes over the top of them. "I have a perfect poker face. Look in my eyes and tell me I don't have a good hand."

This time, Alex laughed and leaned closer to her. "You are a horrible liar, you know."

"Whose side are you on?" she asked and playfully glared at him.

Joe shook his head and picked up his cards again to study them. Before they could continue the hand, the doorbell rang. Joe laid his hand down and got up to answer the door. Claire suddenly plopped down on the couch beside Anna and said, "What did I miss?"

Anna shook her head at her friend before frowning.

"Wait," she whispered. "Where have you been?"

"Well, you know..."

"Claire, you didn't!" Anna looked around and spotted Derrick walking into the kitchen. He disappeared after shooting a wry grin in their direction.

Claire leaned in toward Anna and whispered in her ear, "Joe has this nice garage off the side of the house with a comfy couch."

"Claire!"

"What?" she said before leaning in close again so the others couldn't hear. "It's not like I have many other options today."

Anna shook her head and laughed before glancing at the door as Joe opened it. She smiled when she spotted Marie's fiancé Eddie behind the door, but frowned when she spotted her sister behind him, nearly in tears.

"What in the world is going on?" she asked, hurrying to her sister's side.

"I don't know," Eddie said. He looked at Marie with a look of concern before turning to Anna. "She was on the phone with Frankie and the moment she hung up, she burst into tears. I haven't been able to get a word out of her for five minutes."

Anna pulled Marie to the couch and kneeled in front of her. When Marie covered her hands with her face, Anna pulled them away, and said, "Marie, what is wrong? Talk to me."

"It's Frankie," Marie said through her sobs. "She's gotten wrapped up in something at work and she thinks she's in big trouble."

"What kind of trouble?"

Marie took a tissue from Eddie and wiped a few of the tears from her face. "She discovered some type of money embezzling scheme at work, but whoever is behind it has pointed the finger at Frankie. Now she's being investigated. Frankie has already called an attorney and is expecting a formal arrest and charge any day now."

"Frankie wouldn't do anything like that!"

"I know that, Anna," Marie said. "But the Georgia authorities don't. If they think she's involved with something, they will prosecute in a heartbeat! And if someone is setting her up—she could face some serious time in federal prison."

"We'll figure it out, Marie," Anna said. "We will not leave Frankie stranded down there with no one on her side."

"Is there anything we can do at this moment to help her?" Joe asked from behind the couch where he and the others had been listening to the conversation.

"I don't know," Marie sniffled.

Bryant walked around the couch and stood behind Anna, where Marie could see him. "How about you go catch your breath and then meet the three of us in the kitchen so we can figure out how we can help?"

"Bryant, this isn't work-related," Marie said. "And it's Thanksgiving! I don't want to put a damper on the holiday."

"We're a team, Marie," Joe said, softly. "What affects one of us affects all of us."

Marie looked at Anna and sighed. Anna patted her sister on the arm and gave her a quick nod. "They're right. Let us all help with this."

"Fine," Marie said. "I'm going to go clean up and fix my makeup."

"You want me to come with you?" Anna asked.

"No, I'll see you in a few minutes."

Anna stood up and moved away from Marie so she could leave the couch. She gave her a quick hug before Marie headed off into the bathroom and then turned to the others.

"Well, I guess we've found our next case," Joe said.

Anna looked at Bryant, who seemed lost in thought. "You have a plan?"

"Let's go to the kitchen and start thinking about it," he said. "Joe, can you bring your laptop?"

"On it."

Joe headed off to retrieve his laptop while Anna and Bryant headed into the kitchen. Anna sat down at the table and waited for the others to join her while Bryant explained what was going on to his mother.

Just as he was taking a seat, Joe sped into the room and flipped open his laptop. Anna sighed and rubbed her temples while waiting for the machine to whir to life. When Marie joined them, she looked up and tried to give her a reassuring smile.

"Where do we want to start?" Joe asked, opening a web browser.

"How about you work on figuring out how to get us all down there," Bryant said. "Marie, what more can you tell us about what's going on?"

"There's been some shady accounting going on," Marie said. "Frankie ran across something a few weeks ago and started looking into it. Turns out someone has been embezzling a large sum of money from the company she's interning for."

"How big?" Anna asked.

"At least a million dollars," Marie said. "Whoever has been doing it has taken it in small chunks, so it wasn't immediately noticeable."

"So, Frankie discovered the issue and now she's under suspicion for committing the crime?"

"It sounded like the reason she found the problem was because it was tying back to her."

Joe looked up from his computer at Anna. "If I were to embezzle sizeable sums of money, I'd want to cover it up."

Anna nodded. "Try to pin it on someone else. That would be my plan."

"So maybe they were running it through accounts Frankie handles?"

"That or through her IP address."

"If that's the case," Joe said. "How is Frankie supposed to prove she didn't do it?"

"She can't," Anna said with a shake of her head. "Not without help from someone on her side."

Marie jerked to her feet and started pacing around the kitchen. "What are we going to do, Anna? Frankie is down there all by herself with no one to help her figure this out!"

Anna watched her sister pace around the table twice before getting up to stop her. Marie sighed when Anna gently urged her to a seat. With a frown, Anna sat down next to her.

"Let's walk through it again," she said. "Has she been arrested?"

"Not yet," Marie said, putting her head in her hands.

"What kind of evidence do they have so far?"

"I'm not sure, but Frankie is concerned about it."

"She's only been there six months," Joe said. He leaned back in his chair and peered at them above his computer. "How can she possibly have learned enough in that short time to embezzle all that money?"

"Exactly!" Marie said, throwing her hands up in the air. "There is no way she would be involved in something like that. I know her better than that."

Anna frowned. "You said it all happened over an extended period. If Frankie wasn't there when it started, why are they even looking at her?"

Marie sighed. "They think she's a plant and that she's someone important in the organization."

"That's ridiculous," Anna said.

Marie nodded. "They are saying the internship was all a sham and that the embezzler arranged it to get her inside the company."

Joe frowned and glanced at Bryant, who was silently musing over the conversation, before turning back to his laptop. Anna watched him for a few seconds as he maneuvered the mouse around the screen, only stopping a few moments to type something on the keyboard here and there.

"We know Frankie isn't involved in this, Marie," Anna said, turning her attention back to her sister. "But the authorities will not know her like we do. If all the evidence points to Frankie, they are going to believe it."

"So, what do we do then?" Marie asked, tears brimming in her eyes. "Am I just supposed to let my best friend go to prison? This would end her career before she even gets started. I can't just sit here and let that happen!"

"Sounds like it's time for a road trip," Joe mumbled, his attention still on the computer screen. "There's a flight to Atlanta that we can all fit on leaving at 7 tomorrow morning. We wanna book it?"

"We can't just go down there, Joe," Marie said. "Bryant and I can't practice law in Georgia. We can't represent her!"

"Nothing's stopping us from helping find out the truth," he said with a shrug. "And I'm sure you would love to offer moral support for your friend through all this."

"We can't just go down there and start investigating things," Bryant said. "They don't allow that."

"Maybe they won't let you investigate, but Anna and I can."

"You don't have a Georgia PI license, Joe," Marie said.

"Georgia has a reciprocity agreement. So, Anna and I have 30 days."

"Sounds like it's time for our first Hartman and Malone trip," Bryant said. "Book the flight, Joe."

Marie put her head in her hands and propped her elbows up on the table as Anna put an arm around her.

"Don't worry," Anna whispered while Joe and Bryant were busy getting the flight set up. "We'll get this all figured out."

"I'm just so worried about her, Anna," Marie said. "She's my best friend. I was expecting to have her back here in six months after she finished her internship and everything go back to how it was before. Now I'm worried about whether she's going to come back at all!"

"Hey," Bryant said suddenly. "There's nothing more we can do at this moment to fix Frankie's situation, so how about you relax a bit and try to enjoy the day. Let's worry about all this tomorrow when we get there."

"Yeah," Joe said. "Let's go back into the living room and you can join our card game or something. Take your mind off all this for a bit."

"Ugh," Marie said, looking around the kitchen. "I'm so sorry. I feel like I'm ruining this holiday for you all."

"No reason to feel like that," Bryant said. "What better way to celebrate a family holiday than to help your non-related family members?"

"Come on," Joe said and stood to his feet and reached out to take Marie's hand. "Let's go see if I can continue beating that sister of yours in cards."

"You were not beating me!" Anna replied and followed him back toward the living room.

Chapter 4

The plane's tires touched down on the runway, causing Anna to jerk awake in her seat. Beside her, Joe stretched and pulled the earbuds out of his ears. Anna gazed out the window at the tarmac and the other planes they passed as they taxied to their gate. When the announcer system above them dinged, she glanced up at the ceiling.

"Thank you for flying with us today," the captain said. *"Welcome to Atlanta. The local time is 10:30 AM. If you are traveling on to another destination..."*

"What's our first stop?" Joe whispered, drawing Anna's attention to him. "Are we going to go to Frankie's place first or drop our stuff off at the hotel?"

"I'm sure Marie is itching to get over to Frankie," Anna whispered back. "How about I go with her, and you and Bryant get us checked into the motel?"

"Good idea," he said. "I'll text you when we're done and maybe we can all meet up for lunch."

"You know, we probably should have planned our transportation a little better," Anna said. "We were in such a hurry to get here that we didn't even discuss how we would get around."

"How about we figure all that out after we get settled?" Joe said. "There are plenty of car services around to get us started. If we get in a jam, we can always rent a car."

Anna nodded before turning around and placing her knees in her seat so she could peer over the top of her chair at her sister.

"How's it going back there?" she asked, softly.

Marie looked up at her, and the distress was obvious on her face. "I'm just ready to get to Frankie and see what we can do to help her. I'm so worried."

"I know," Anna said. "We'll work just as hard on Frankie's case as we do on all the other. I promise."

"Harder," Joe said, looking around the side of his chair and smiling at Marie. "We'll figure this out, Marie. Trust us."

"Thank you for the reassurance," Marie said. "That means a lot, but I'd much rather not have to be worrying about my best friend going to jail."

Before they could speak more, the plane clanged to a stop, and everyone waited in silence for the doors to open. When they did, the passengers slowly moved from their seats, reclaimed their overhead bags, and eventually made it off the plane. After they'd walked through the terminal and waited for what seemed like an eternity for their luggage to arrive, they walked outside.

"Um, Anna?" Bryant said when they stepped into the passenger transportation area. "Did you arrange a ride and not tell anyone?"

Anna frowned in confusion and swept her gaze around the area. Joe's eyes found the object that had caught his brother's attention a fraction of a second before Anna did and laughter immediately erupted from him.

"What in the world?" Anna put her hands on her hips and frowned at Derrick, who was casually leaning against a pillar holding a sign that read, *Anna Banana and Crew*.

Joe was still laughing as he walked to his friend, the others following closely behind. "What are you doing here, Derrick?"

"Well, from what I heard, I have an old friend," he paused and grinned around Joe at Anna, "and a new one, who seems to need my help to get around this beautiful city."

"You flew out here just to drive us around?" Anna asked, an amused smile forming on her face. "You must be desperate to have something to do."

"Well, I have a client out this way that needed a little extra schmoozing. Since I was already in the area, I thought I might offer my help. This seems to be an urgent matter, and if I can help, I'd like to."

Anna smiled. "That's awfully kind of you, Derrick. I guess this helps with the transportation issue we'd discovered, Joe."

"So, it seems," Joe said with a smile. He turned to Derrick. "No way are we putting you out, Derrick. If you need to meet with your client or do something for work, don't feel obligated to us."

"Deal," Derrick said with a grin. "Just as long as the lot of you don't start feeling bad about me being your designated chauffeur. I promise it's no trouble at all."

"Thank you," Marie said, joining the conversation for the first time. "I appreciate you jumping in to help us."

"Not a problem," Derrick said. "So, where are we headed first?"

"If you could take Joe and Bryant to the hotel to get us checked in, that would be great," Anna said before turning to her sister. "Marie and I are going to grab a taxi and head over to Frankie's place."

Marie nodded and looked down at the ground. Anna took her suitcase and pulled it over to the car Derrick was driving. She glanced back at her sister as Bryant took their bags and helped Derrick put them all in the trunk.

"We'll get it figured out, Anna," Joe said.

"We'd better," Anna replied. "If this is one that we can't and Frankie winds up in jail, Marie will never let me live it down."

Joe laughed. "We have an excellent track record. Whoever is behind this didn't see us coming."

"Are we ready, Anna?" Marie called as a taxi pulled up for them. "I want to get to Frankie."

"Yep, let's go," Anna said and followed Marie into the taxi.

They rode in silence, Marie fidgeting with things in her purse and Anna watching the traffic outside her window as they drove. Before long, they'd traveled through the city and to an older apartment complex just outside of it.

Marie and Anna hopped out of the taxi, paid the fare, and hurried up to Frankie's apartment. The door opened within thirty seconds of them knocking on it, and Marie immediately wrapped her arms around her best friend.

"I'm so happy you are here!" Frankie said. "I wish it were for better reasons."

"Me too," Marie said, pulling away from her so she could wipe a few tears from her cheeks. "I just hate that you are going through this."

"Thank you for dropping everything and coming to help, Anna," Frankie said after giving her a hug of her own. "I appreciate it."

"That's what friends are for."

They walked further inside the apartment and Frankie busied herself around the small kitchen preparing drinks for them as they chatted.

"This is a nice apartment, Frankie," Marie said after looking around. "I like what you've done with the place."

Anna smiled. "Yes, I think Claire would approve of your decorating tastes. It looks beautiful."

Frankie shrugged. "I was lonely when I first moved here, so I did my best to make things feel like home. Nothing compares to the real thing, though. I'm ready to be back in Virginia with my friends and family."

"After this case is over, I say you cut this venture of yours short and head home," Marie said.

"Trust me. I've already been strategizing a move back as soon as I can."

"How did you get into this mess, Frankie?"

Frankie sighed and brought her drink to the gray upholstered couch in the living room and sat down. The pillow behind her folded awkwardly, but she didn't bother to adjust it. Instead, she leaned forward a bit and took a huge sip from the wineglass in her hand.

"It all started with an invoice," she started. "It wound up on my desk. No big deal. But, when I went to enter it in the system and coded it to the right location, I couldn't find the account it belonged to."

"I take it that was an oddity?" Anna asked. She walked into the living room with her sister and Frankie and claimed an armchair across from the couch. Marie followed her and sat next to Frankie.

"Accounts aren't just supposed to disappear," Frankie explained. "Especially when there's a potential that more charges will need to flow through them. But it got even stranger when I went searching for it."

"What do you mean?"

"I knew I had to put the invoice somewhere, but without an account to tie it to, I had to do some research. Then, I remembered I had posted a similar invoice a few weeks prior for the same project."

"You had a copy of that one?"

Frankie nodded. "I pulled it out of my files and hunted it down. I had the paperwork that went with it, all the information for it, and even the copy of the invoice. Everything. The only problem was nothing matched what was in the system except for the amount."

"How would that be the case?"

"There are two options. Either I put it in incorrectly or it got changed after the fact."

"Assuming someone changed it," Anna said. "How could that have happened?"

"That was the premise I was working with," Frankie replied. "There were so many things different from my records, I don't see how I would have entered it incorrectly.

So, I started digging. I traced the money from account to account and wound up going in a big loop."

"A loop?"

"I never could figure out where the money for that invoice started from or where it wound up since I didn't have access to the actual payment accounts. Plus, it was in an account that shouldn't exist with information attached that wasn't accurate."

"What did you do at that point?"

"The only thing I could do," Frankie said after taking another drink of her wine. "I took it to my supervisor. I printed off everything I could find and took it to him."

"What was his response?"

"He said he would look into it. But before I heard from him, I got wind of the embezzlement thing and it's been a whirlwind ever since."

Marie patted her on the shoulder and said, "We'll figure it out. There has to be something we can do to set things straight."

Before they could continue the conversation, a loud knock sounded at Frankie's door. She frowned and stood to her feet. After setting the wine glass on the coffee table, she walked the few steps to the front door and pulled it open. Three police officers stood just outside.

"Frankie Fritts?" one asked. He continued when she nodded. "We have an order for your arrest."

"Arrest?" Marie said, suddenly shooting to her feet. "Frankie! Ask what the charges are."

"Why am I under arrest?" Frankie muttered.

"We are arresting you for murder," the officer said.

"Murder!" Frankie exclaimed. "Who did I supposedly murder?"

"You are being charged with the murder of Asher Rowley."

"What? Asher's dead? He can't be dead. I just spoke to him yesterday morning!"

"They found his body this morning," the officer said.

"Frankie, who is Asher?" Marie asked, stepping closer to her friend and the officers.

"Asher is my boss," Frankie replied. "I don't know what happened. I don't understand why I'm being arrested."

"We'll discuss everything with you at the precinct," the officer replied.

"She didn't do this," Marie argued with the officers as Frankie shut down and her face went blank. "This is a mistake."

"We're just here to serve an arrest warrant," the officer said. "After she's booked, she'll have to sort everything out in court."

Frankie snapped out of her daze when the officer put his hand on her shoulder and turned her around. As he was securing her hands, she addressed Marie. "Marie! There's a card in my purse for a local attorney. I've already been talking with them and have permitted them to speak with you and whoever else on your team about my case."

"Don't tell them anything, Frankie!" Marie cried after her as the officers pulled her away from the apartment door. "Stay quiet and wait for us!"

Before she could say more, Frankie was out of earshot and silence overwhelmed Anna and Marie. As the door closed softly, Marie buried her face in her hands and burst into tears.

Chapter 5

"Thank you for bringing this to my attention, but I do not require help with my cases. I have my team for that."

Anna frowned and swept her gaze around the attorney's office. Since they'd arrived a little past one, Marie had been busy arguing with Frankie's attorney regarding their ability to help clear her name. So far, she hadn't been successful. About halfway through the conversation, Joe had pulled a laptop out of his bag and started typing.

"With all due respect, Mr. Matthews," Marie said, jerking Anna's attention back to the conversation. "Frankie did request that you give us access to the information related to her case. As an attorney myself, I completely understand your hesitation, but I feel it is important to honor requests made by my clients."

"Right now, I don't even know what we're looking at," Mr. Matthews continued. "As soon as they send over the arrest warrant, I'll be able to—"

"We're dealing with a murder charge," Joe interrupted, looking at his computer screen. "Looks like a strangulation-murder combination that happened yesterday evening. They found the body this morning. Judge Slinsky issued an arrest warrant this morning at 8, along with a search warrant for Frankie's office and her apartment. It looks like they are searching her apartment as we speak. They've already finished up with her office."

The silence in the room was palpable as the attorney took in the information. After a few seconds of mulling it over, he asked, "How do you know that already?"

"They scanned the arrest warrant after they booked Frankie," Joe said with a yawn. "Just had to wait for it to be processed."

"Does it say anything about where they found the victim, Joe?" Marie asked.

Joe looked back at his computer screen and frowned. "Says it was an Asher Rowley. They found him in Lake Clara in Piedmont Park. Park officials found his body when they opened up this morning. He was lying face first in the lake with a scarf tied around his neck. They'll have to do an autopsy to determine the official cause of death and determine if the scarf killed him or the lake."

"Frankie said Asher was her boss," Marie said. "I assume it's the man she was discussing her findings with. The one who said he would look into the situation."

"Tell me about the park, Joe," Anna said, turning to face him.

"It's a park," he shrugged. "It's open until almost one in the morning."

"Even on Thanksgiving?" Anna asked. "Yesterday was a holiday."

He clicked through a few more screens and nodded. "Yep, open on Thanksgiving."

"How far is it from Frankie's place?"

"About ten miles. So, twenty minutes with traffic."

"What evidence do they have?" Bryant asked. "Does the arrest warrant say why they brought her in?"

"They are working off an email that was sent from Frankie's computer to her boss," Joe said. "It explicitly asked Mr. Rowley to meet her at the park at midnight and said she had something to discuss with him regarding the information she had given him."

"It's probably referring to the missing account she found," Anna mused. "Did they find any other evidence in her office?"

"No, but security footage captured a woman matching Frankie's description in the park and a car similar to hers leaving the area."

"This is all very fascinating," Mr. Matthews said. "But I don't have time for all this at the moment. I need to get down to the jail and visit with our client before the police try to interview her."

"If you don't mind, Eugene," Anna said, leaning toward him. "Is it all right if I call you Eugene?"

She continued before he could reply. "If you don't mind, Eugene, my partner and I are in the middle of something here. Now, if you want to get your client out of jail on bond, I suggest you sit there in your comfy chair and let us work for five minutes."

Eugene raised his eyebrows at her but huffed and leaned back in his chair. Anna turned to Joe and said, "Let's continue, shall we?"

With a quick chuckle, Joe said, "All right. Lady and car leaving the park. I also failed to mention there was a witness who saw the woman leaving the park around the time of the murder."

"Did the witness describe the woman?"

"Says she was wearing a blue trench coat and a black hat and heels," he said. "Everything else matched Frankie. Brown hair...dark skin...right height and weight."

"Does it say what type of hat she was wearing?"

"The witness called it a trilby?" Joe said with a frown. "I don't even know what that is."

"It's a felt hat," Anna said, gazing off into the distance for a second. "Has a small brim. Many people wear fedora hats, but those have a bigger brim and the trilby has an angled brim whereas the fedora's brim is flat."

"You certainly know a lot about hats for someone who never seems to wear them," Joe said with a raised eyebrow.

"Claire likes hats," Anna said with a chuckle. "I guess I've learned a thing or two about them. The problem is, Frankie has never been into fashion. She rarely wears hats and heels. That's rather out of character for her."

"Hmm," Joe said, looking back at the paper. "That might not be a good thing, seeing as it could explain the tripping part of the equation."

"Tripping?"

"The witness said Frankie, or whoever left the park, tripped and nearly fell. The hat fell off, and the witness picked it up when it tried to blow away. That's why the witness noticed so much about it."

"Frankie has always been steady on her feet," Marie said with a frown.

Joe shrugged. "The witness said the woman seemed to be in a hurry and that her heel got caught in a crack in the sidewalk."

"Very strange," Marie mumbled.

"Speaking of strange," Anna added. "When we were over at her apartment today, Frankie had a brown coat thrown on the dinner table, not a blue one."

Marie sighed. "She has a blue trench coat. She loves that thing. It's her favorite."

"If it's her favorite coat, why isn't she wearing it?" Joe asked.

"Wait a second," Marie said. She reached down onto the floor and picked up Frankie's purse that she'd brought with her. "When I was getting Mr. Matthews' card out of Frankie's purse, I noticed she had a tag for the cleaners in there."

She grinned when she pulled it out and passed it to her sister. Anna read the tag aloud. "One blue trench coat. Date dropped off–Wednesday. Estimated pickup–Monday. She didn't have the damn coat yesterday!"

"Well, that's a start," Joe said. "Now, why is her boss dead?"

"Let's start at the beginning," Anna said. "Frankie had a weird invoice that didn't have a home, so she started doing research."

Joe nodded. "The account it was supposed to be charged to had disappeared, so she dug a little more."

"She wound up running around in a big circle and only developed more questions than she had answers for, so she ran it up the chain to her boss."

"Boss says he'll look into it, but before Frankie hears back, she's involved in a big embezzlement case with all fingers pointing her direction."

"We know she's innocent, so that means someone is setting her up."

"But why kill the boss? And so sloppily, considering it only took us 15 minutes to shed doubt on the story?"

"Maybe the boss was involved in the crime and was getting nervous."

"Or..."

"Or," Anna said with a smile. "The boss discovered something that would point the finger at someone else."

Joe smiled and nodded his head. "I bet the boss had done some research just like Frankie had done, but his digging brought the attention of the wrong people."

"Pinning the murder on Frankie makes perfect sense considering she was already being investigated for the embezzling."

"But how does the killer expect to get away with it now that Frankie is behind bars?" Joe asked. "It's not like they can keep up their embezzling. It would completely give it away that Frankie wasn't behind it."

"Maybe they don't need to keep it up," Anna said. "What if they are just using the murder and Frankie's investigation as a distraction?"

"You think they are planning something bigger?"

Anna nodded. "Or in the process of executing something bigger."

"But what?"

"I don't know yet. But I know they didn't see us coming. If we didn't know Frankie this well, we wouldn't have been able to figure out about the coat and the strange wardrobe misalignments."

Bryant jumped into the conversation. "They would have eventually figured that out, though. All that information sheds a lot of doubt on the entire theory of Frankie being the killer, so it would surprise me if the courts fell for it."

"That's exactly why I think we should look at this as some sort of distraction tactic," Anna said with a nod. "The actual killer wants to throw off the scent just long enough to complete whatever project they are working on."

"If that's true, we can likely assume the killer is someone who works with Frankie," Joe said. "Or at least close enough to the organization to be involved in regular transactions."

Marie grimaced. "That's a huge organization. It's going to take some time and manpower to weed out whoever is behind all this."

"Not to mention the fact that we no longer have Frankie or her boss inside the organization, which means we currently don't know who we can trust in there," Bryant said.

"It sure sounds like it's going to take a lot of research and legwork to figure this out," Anna said and sent Joe a cocky grin.

He grinned in return. "It certainly appears our attorney friend is going to have his hands full."

Joe and Anna turned to look at Mr. Matthews, who was staring back at them with a shocked look on his face. They waited in silence for him to run through the scenario they'd created. When he cleared his throat, Anna gave him a friendly smile.

"I can't afford to bring on more investigators," he said. "I have my own to pay."

"That's fine," Anna said. "We've been doing just fine on our own, so we can do this one pro-bono."

"Frankie did request for you to allow us to assist with her case," Marie pleaded. "I promise we will all work with you and not against you."

"Fine," Eugene said after thinking it over. "I suppose a little extra free help never hurt anyone. I need the lot of you to remain unbiased throughout the investigation, however. You can't be letting your personal opinions mar the work we do in this office. Remember, I have a practice to continue after you go back home again."

"As do we," Bryant said with a nod.

"All right," Eugene replied. "Where do we want to begin? I need to go see what type of situation we are in regarding bail for Frankie."

"Anna and I will go try to find this trench coat of hers," Joe said. "Then, we will check out the murder site ourselves to see what we are dealing with."

"I probably need to stay close to you, Mr. Matthews," Marie said. "If you wind up getting Frankie bail, I'll need to post it."

Eugene nodded and began gathering up paperwork and compiling it into his briefcase. "You can wait outside. The moment we know more about bail, I'll give you some options."

Marie handed the dry-cleaning claim ticket to Anna. "Here. This will give you the information you need to check on the coat."

"Anything specific we need to ask about?" Anna asked as she peered at the slip of paper in her hand. "Or are Joe and I free to run our investigation at the moment?"

"If they could give us some proof that Frankie's coat didn't leave the premises this weekend, that would be great," Eugene replied. "We may have to subpoena their surveillance footage if they have any, but the earlier we can prove that coat wasn't in Frankie's possession, the better."

Anna slipped the paper into her purse and nodded. While the others gathered up their things and prepared for the new venture, Anna pulled Marie to the side and hugged her.

"We'll figure this out, Marie," she said. "We always do."

"We came down here worried about a five-year sentence and haven't even spent the day and we have already upgraded it to murder," Marie said, tears streaming down her face. "I can't sit here and watch my best friend go to jail for 25 years to life."

"Like I said," Anna repeated. "We'll figure it out. Let me and Joe do our jobs. You hired us for a reason, remember?"

"Thank you for coming with me," Marie said.

Before they could talk more, the others showed they were ready to leave. Anna gave Marie another quick hug before following Joe and the others out of the attorney's office. Marie and Bryant followed Eugene to the parking lot and climbed into a large black sedan. Meanwhile, Joe and Anna walked to the car Derrick was currently waiting in.

Anna turned to throw one last look at her sister. Before opening the door to the car, Joe caught her attention and said, "Hey. We will figure this out."

Anna smiled at him and said, "We'd better."

Chapter 6

"You miss us, buddy?" Joe asked when they climbed into the vehicle.

Derrick grinned and turned off the audio book he was reading. "I could get used to this chauffeur thing. I have a huge list of books I've been meaning to get caught up on."

"Well, if you ever get tired of driving us around, just let us know," Anna said. "We can always rent a car."

"*We* aren't renting anything," Joe said, giving her a sideways glance. "If we rent something, I will do all the driving, thank you very much."

"Why's that?"

"Maybe because the last time I rode with you, you got us into a street race."

Derrick raised his eyebrows and looked at Anna in the rearview mirror. "You are one interesting woman."

Anna laughed. "Not that big of a deal."

"Mmm-hmm," Joe said with a chuckle of his own. "By the way, Derrick, keep that little nugget of information to yourself. Anna isn't exactly open to sharing her driving skills with her sister."

"Mum's the word," Derrick said with a laugh and pretended to zip his lips with his fingers.

"You know you loved every minute of that ride, Joe," Anna said with another laugh. "You drive like a maniac out there in the woods with your jeep, so don't sit there and pretend my driving scares you."

Joe laughed again and shook his head at her. "That doesn't mean I'm going to stop teasing you about it."

Anna sighed and handed Derrick a slip of paper. "As fun as this conversation is, we'd better get to work. Derrick, this is the address we need to go to first."

He nodded and plugged the address into the car's GPS before pulling out of the parking lot. The drive was a short one and soon Anna and Joe stood outside a small dry-cleaning business near Frankie's apartment. Taking a deep breath, Anna led Joe inside and smiled warmly at the desk attendant.

"How may I help you?" the attendant asked after returning Anna's smile.

"Hi, my name is Anna, and this is my friend, Joe," Anna said. "We're hoping you can help us out with something."

"I can certainly try."

"A friend of ours dropped off a jacket a few days ago and said it's supposed to be ready on Monday," Anna continued. "Is there any way you can check that for us? I have her claim ticket."

Anna pulled the slip out of her purse and slid it across the counter to the woman. She glanced down at the claim number and squinted before typing the information into the computer in front of her. When the information came up, she frowned and glanced at Anna before turning her attention back to the screen.

"I'm afraid I need to go get my manager to help you," the woman finally said. "Can you wait a minute for me?"

"Sure!" Anna replied and turned to Joe with a frown.

He shrugged, and they waited in silence for the woman to return with her manager. A slightly older woman soon appeared with the original desk attendant and spent some time looking at the computer screen and comparing the information she found there with Frankie's claim ticket.

After several moments, the woman sighed and turned to Anna. "Would you mind coming into my office to discuss this further?"

"Certainly," Anna said, her stomach dropping.

She and Joe followed the manager through the building and into an office off the side. Joe gave her a reassuring look before they sat down in front of the woman's desk while the manager took a seat in a chair across from them.

"First," the woman said, "my name is Maggie. I'm the manager and owner of this establishment."

"It's nice to meet you, Maggie," Anna replied. "I'm Anna and this is Joe."

"I'm afraid there's a situation with the coat you are asking about," Maggie said, after nodding in greeting. "It's no longer here."

"What do you mean?" Anna asked with a frown.

"Full disclosure," Joe said. "Anna and I are private investigators working with the coat's owner during a legal matter. But Anna is close friends with the owner of the coat."

"I have nothing to hide from anyone," Maggie said. "We had a break-in over the holiday. They took some articles of clothing during it, including this coat."

"You don't say," Joe said. "That's fascinating. Did you relay all this information to the police?"

"Of course," Maggie said. "I told the officer who came to take our report following the robbery."

"You don't have security cameras, do you?" Anna asked. "Anything that could show who took off with the coat?"

"I do," Maggie replied. "I provided copies of those to the police."

"Would it be possible for us to get a copy of them?" Anna asked. "I know we will have access to what the police have, but it would be helpful if we could get a head start on this."

Maggie nodded. "To be honest, normally I would hesitate to provide others with my security footage. But I've grown to like Frankie over the past few months. She stops in here every week to drop off and pick up her dry cleaning. We've talked a lot. I want to help her."

"I'm grateful for your help," Anna said. "She's my sister's best friend. We flew in from Virginia this morning to help her with another matter and now it seems things just became more complicated."

Maggie nodded sadly. "Frankie has talked a lot about her family back home. She's mentioned your sister. I'm glad she has friends to support her during this difficult time. She seemed stressed when she brought the coat in on Wednesday."

Anna smiled softly and sighed. "We're doing what we can to help her."

"Well, let me help how I can by getting you a copy of my security footage," Maggie replied. "Hopefully, you'll be able to find something there that can help Frankie."

Anna nodded, and Maggie turned to the computer on her desk. After spending some time navigating the mouse, she located the file and created a copy. Joe pulled a flash drive out of his pocket and handed it to her.

"You can save it on this if that would be simple enough," he said.

Maggie took the device and moved the file on it before removing it from her computer and handing the drive back to Joe. As Anna and Joe stood to leave, Maggie stood up and handed Anna her card.

"If there is anything else I can do to help Frankie, please let me know," she said.

"Thank you for helping as much as you have already," Anna said. "It's more than we could expect of you."

Joe led Anna out of the building, and they walked back to where Derrick had parked the car. Anna looked down at her phone and sent a quick text to Marie, updating her about their progress before following Joe back into the car.

"We need to go to Piedmont Park, now," Anna told Derrick, as she pulled the address up on her phone. He nodded when she showed him the screen and quickly changed the GPS destination before heading off in the right direction.

They drove in silence for several minutes until Derrick pulled the car into a parking lot near the park. Anna looked out the window and frowned in the lake's direction.

"Was this the closest parking lot to the lake, Joe?"

"Yep," he replied. "I checked it twice to make sure. If the killer parked at the park, it's likely they used this parking lot."

"Let's keep our eyes peeled then," Anna said.

"Well, if you two don't mind the company, I think I'd very much like to see Piedmont Park myself," Derrick said after turning off the car's engine. "It's a nice day for a little hike."

"Suit yourself," Joe said. "I for one would have no desire to sit in the car and wait on us if I were you."

Anna laughed. "Maybe you'll see something that we miss."

Derrick shook his head and laughed. "I highly doubt that."

Chapter 7

The trio walked in silence as they traveled through the park. Anna swept her eyes across the expanse of grass that greeted them when they entered, but nothing caught her eye. She pivoted her attention to the distant trees that surrounded the lake and examined the line of them for clues.

They walked around a sidewalk until they reached a clearing in the trees and a path that led to a bridge crossing the lake. Joe pointed across the bridge and to the south.

"The murder happened on the opposite side of the lake," he said.

Anna nodded and walked across the bridge with Joe and Derrick. Once across, they took a sidewalk to the south and stopped just outside a small grove of trees. Anna surveyed the ground and frowned at the drag marks that still appeared from the day before.

"Let's go look in the trees and see if we can find the meeting spot," Joe said.

Anna nodded and followed him a few steps into the cover of the trees. When they stopped, Anna frowned and looked at the messy ground beneath their feet. Leaves and grass were strewn about, and several smaller sticks and twigs lay discarded and snapped.

"What exactly did the report say happened here, Joe?"

Joe walked around her and pointed out a section of ruffled ground. Anna followed his finger and looked over the ground, where an obvious scuffle had taken place.

"The theory is they got into an argument here," Joe said. "The murderer somehow got the best of the victim and began strangling him with the scarf, which they think belonged to the victim. It matched his coat."

Anna made a circle around the scuffle area while listening, her eyes focused on the ground and the area surrounding where the fight occurred. "Then, what?"

"At some point, the victim must have passed out, and the murderer dragged him over to the lake."

Anna turned her attention to the drag marks leading to the water. She and Joe followed them until they reached the water's edge and the remains of a small puddle of dry blood.

"Well, the evidence seems to line up with the story so far," Anna said. "But what happened here?"

"The police found a bloody rock near the victim," Joe continued. "They think he woke up after the murderer had dragged him to the lake and tried to get up."

Anna nodded. "So, the killer hit him with the rock to knock him out again and then tied the scarf around his neck."

"Exactly," Joe said with a nod of his own. "I suppose pushing his face in the water was overkill at that point. Reports said the scarf was so tight that there wasn't any way he was going to get it off himself."

"That would have taken a lot of strength to get it tied that tight," Anna mused.

"Possibly," Joe said. "But the police could argue that she could have pushed her knee or foot or something into his back to give herself more leverage. That might have been enough to allow her to pull it off."

"True."

Anna frowned and turned away from the water to head back up to where the scuffle took place. She glanced around the area carefully but sighed and put her hands on her hips when she found nothing further to capture her attention.

"Maybe the murder was self-defense?" Derrick said suddenly. "You said there was a scuffle. Maybe the murderer was the victim, assuming it was Frankie who was here last night, of course."

"Not any way to prove that," Anna mused. "Say, Joe, how much do you weigh?"

"What?" he laughed. "Is that relevant?"

"Well, Frankie and I are about the same size," Anna said. "I wonder how you compare to the dead guy."

"You thinking of bumping me off?" he asked with another laugh.

"I was thinking about testing a theory if you are up for it."

"What theory would that be?"

"First, do we know how much the victim weighed and what his height was?"

Joe frowned and pulled out his phone. He flipped through a few screens on the device before quickly reading through a document. "Looks like he was six one and weighed

185 pounds. Same height as me, but he was about ten pounds heavier than I am."

"Perfect," Anna said. "Would you mind lying down?"

"Lying down?" Joe asked. "Like, on the ground?"

"How else does one lie down?"

Derrick laughed. "Do I need to give you two some alone time?"

Anna shook her head and chuckled. "All right. Let me start over. I'm wondering if Frankie could even drag this man to the lake. I want to test it to see how complicated it would have been for her."

"So, you want to drag me into the lake?" Joe asked with a chuckle. "I see where you're going with this."

He quickly got down on the ground and looked up at Anna, who peered down at him. "Now what?"

"Now," Derrick said, jumping next to him, "you wait for me to record this. I so need to document this."

Joe laughed, and Anna rolled her eyes while she waited for him to get his camera ready. When he gave her a thumb's up, she hooked her arms under Joe's and began pulling him toward the lake. Mud and dirt started stirring around beneath them almost immediately.

"Oh, you so owe me for this, Anna," Joe said as he looked down the length of his body at his pants. "My clothes are going to be filthy."

"Not to mention Anna's shoes," Derrick said with rolling laughter. He started laughing harder when Anna lost her footing and sat down hard in the mud herself, Joe falling into her lap as she fell. "It's a good thing Claire isn't here. She'd be a wreck over how dirty your shoes are right now."

"This isn't working out that well, Anna," Joe said with an amused grin. He left his head in her lap and peered up at her.

Anna chuckled and looked down at him. "This is good news for us. Frankie would have had a difficult ti—Wait! Derrick, you're a genius!"

"I am?" Derrick replied. "I mean, of course, I am! Why am I a genius again?"

"The shoes!" Anna said. "The witness said Frankie was wearing black heels. There's no way she would have been able to drag a body while wearing heels. I can barely do it in tennis shoes."

Joe sat up and turned around to look at her. "Not to mention the fact that even if she had pulled it off, her shoes would have been a mess. No way would a witness have gotten close enough to notice what type of hat she was wearing and not noticed a pair of muddy heels!"

"That has to mean someone else was here," Anna said.

Joe stood up and reached down to help Anna up. After she bounced to her feet, Anna began looking around again.

"Yeah, but who?"

"And how do we prove that?"

Anna and Joe began searching the ground just outside the area where the scuffle took place, both hoping to find some signs that a killer had lurked there the night before. When they both came up empty, they met back at their original location to regroup.

"Let's think like a killer," Joe said. "We have just murdered someone."

"If I had just killed someone, I'd want to get away as quickly as possible," Derrick said.

"Me too," Anna said. "But our killer decided the best path was one where obvious security cameras and witnesses were."

Joe frowned. "You know. You're right. They seemed to have planned all this but didn't plan out their exit strategy very well."

Anna nodded. "They went to all the trouble of stealing Frankie's coat and getting someone who looked like her to be at the crime scene."

"If they planned this ahead of time, they would have known about the security cameras," Joe said.

"It's almost as if they were asking to get caught," Derrick added.

Joe and Anna looked at each other and grinned.

"Again, with the genius, Derrick," Anna said.

"What?"

"They were," Joe said, smiling at his friend. "They were asking to get caught."

"I don't understand," Derrick said. "Why would they want to get caught?"

"She was a distraction," Anna said. "They wanted our attention focused on her so we would zero in on Frankie."

"Which is exactly what the police did," Joe said. "The actual killer has had plenty of time to just waltz off into the sunset."

"I don't know about waltzing," Anna said. "But he needs to move a little faster with us after him."

Anna walked back to the water and looked up and down the bank before heading back to where Joe and Derrick waited for her.

"What're you thinking?" Joe asked. "Where'd our guy go?"

"Well, if I were a killer who was trying to distance myself from a murder," Anna said, a slight smile forming on her face, "I'd head off in the opposite direction."

"Back toward where we parked, right?"

"Yep," Anna said. "And I'd probably stay inside these trees as long as humanly possible."

"Let's see what we can find," Joe said before leading them back in the car's direction.

They picked their way through the trees, everyone keeping their eyes peeled for any signs the killer had passed through the area. It wasn't until they'd nearly reached the last section of trees when Anna spotted something small shining in the sunlight.

"What's that?" she asked, pointing to the object that had caught her attention.

Joe crouched near the item and examined it. "Well, well, well. We have some evidence here. It looks like a button from a sports coat or a dress shirt's sleeve or something. And, if I'm not mistaken, it looks like it might have some blood on it."

"We need to get out of this area, Joe," Anna said. "This is a crime scene now."

"Yep," Joe said and pointed to a spot in the grassy field outside the trees. "Let's go just over there and call it in."

Anna pulled out her phone and dialed Marie's number as they walked. After quickly filling her in on the development, she pulled the phone away from her ear.

"Mr. Matthews is calling the detective on the case," she told Joe. "Marie wants us to sit tight for a second."

Joe nodded, and Anna put the phone back to her ear. Marie soon gave her further instructions, and she ended the call. "The detective is on his way. Naturally, they want us to stay where we are. He's going to call me when he gets here so we can direct him to our location."

"Great," Joe said with a chuckle. "Now we get to introduce ourselves to Atlanta's finest. I'm sure we'll get along swimmingly."

"What do we do now?" Derrick asked. "Just wait?"

"Yep," Anna said before sitting down on the grass and folding her legs in a crisscross pattern.

Joe followed suit except instead of sitting, he opted for completely laying down in the grass.

"Is this what the two of you do all day?" Derrick asked with a chuckle. "Poke around in crime scenes, find evidence, then wait."

"Nah," Joe said, his eyes closed. "Sometimes we have to run from bad guys."

"And FBI agents," Anna added with a chuckle.

"What have I gotten myself into?" Derrick asked with a shake of his head.

Chapter 8

"He's taking his sweet time, isn't he?" Joe said from his spot on the grass next to Anna. "Didn't he say he was on his way twenty minutes ago?"

Anna groaned and looked at the clock on her phone. Just as she was about to lay it back down again, it began ringing in her hand. When she didn't recognize the number, she raised her eyebrows at Joe and quickly answered the call.

"Hello, this is Anna Hartman," she said.

"Anna," a voice on the other end of the line said. "This is Detective Morales. I understand you have something I need to check out?"

"Yes, sir," Anna said. "My partner and I found a—"

"Just tell me where you are," Detective Morales said with a sigh. "I'll look at it when I get there."

"We are away from the crime scene, close to the end of the tree line," Anna said. "We are in the grassy area just outside of them."

"You wearing a blue sweater? Got two guys with you?"

"Yes."

"I see you."

Detective Morales hung up before Anna could reply. Anna looked around and spotted a man marching toward them. A young woman with a black case hurried along behind him. Anna turned to Joe and grimaced.

"I'm afraid this might not be pleasant," she said.

Joe laughed. "What else is new?"

Detective Morales finished the march to them just as Anna and Joe were standing to their feet and brushing the grass off their pants.

"Is this how you do things in Virginia, or wherever the hell it is you came from?" Detective Morales fumed. "Just show up, poke around crime scenes, and drag me out here for God knows what?"

"I promise we wouldn't have called you out here if it wasn't important," Anna said.

Detective Morales sighed and pulled a small notebook out of his pocket. He looked up at them expectantly and frowned when Anna and Joe looked at each other in confusion.

"Names?" he said after rolling his eyes.

"Names?" Anna said, sending him a frown. "Oh, our names! I'm Anna Hartman and this is my partner, Joe Malone. We wor—"

"Just need your names right now."

Joe raised his eyebrows at Anna and winked. Anna suppressed a chuckle but quickly grew serious when Detective Morales returned his attention to her after writing their names.

"Why are we here, Anna Hartman and Joe Malone?"

"We were trying to get a feel for what happened here yesterday and came across some evidence that got missed," Joe said.

Detective Morales glared at him. "We don't miss evidence."

"Miss might be a strong word," Anna said. "It isn't with the original crime scene, but we think it's related."

"Where is it?" the young woman standing behind Detective Morales said suddenly. "I'd like to take a look."

"It's just inside these trees," Anna said, pointing back toward the button. "As soon as we saw it and realized it could be connected, we cleared the area so as not to disturb anything."

"How prudent of you," Detective Morales said sarcastically. He walked a few steps toward the tree line and turned back to look at them. "Come on. Let's see it already."

Anna walked around him and led the detective and young woman back to where she and Joe had found the button. She pointed at the ground and the woman sat her case nearby and began taking photos of the scene.

"What do you think, Billie?" Detective Morales asked after a few seconds. "Did they put that here?"

"You think we put that here?" Anna asked, surprised.

Billie ignored her and stepped closer to the button, peering down at it critically. "With what I'm seeing right now, I'd say no. The blood on that button has already started changing colors because of being sat out in the sunlight, and it looks like there's some discoloration forming on the button itself from where it's sat in the dirt."

"Meaning?"

"Meaning," Billie continued after taking a few more pictures of the area. "It's been sitting here for a while. My guess is it got dropped here just after the murder took place."

"Fine," Detective Morales said with a sigh. "I'll let you process the scene. I'm going to take them back out here so we can chat."

Joe gave Anna another look but said nothing as they followed Detective Morales back into the grassy area and away from the newly created crime scene. Once they stopped walking, the detective once again pulled out his notebook and pen.

A little less aggressively, he said, "All right. Let's start at the top."

Anna glanced at Joe before starting the conversation. "Joe and I are serving as consultants to Frankie Fritts's attorney."

"Ahh, yes," Detective Morales said. "Ms. Fritts. I'm well aware of her."

"She's a close friend of mine," Anna said with a frown. "We came down to help her."

Detective Morales huffed. "Help her by trying to poke holes in the case, I suppose. We know how to look at evidence, you know?"

"I've known Frankie my entire life," Anna said. "I know she didn't do this."

"Sometimes we don't know people as well as we think we do."

"And sometimes the evidence is wrong."

"Not in my experience," he said. "But let's talk about what you found here today, shall we?"

Anna frowned and crossed her arms across her chest. "As my partner said, we were just trying to get a feel for what happened. We had no intention of involving ourselves so deeply in this."

Detective Morales sighed. "How did you come to find the evidence?"

"We realized that none of it added up," Joe said. "The victim was much too large for the woman to have done all she did to him."

"What do you mean?"

"The theory is she argued with the man inside the trees up there," Anna said and pointed back toward the original crime scene. "And then somehow strangled him and drag him to the lake. She was too small for that."

"I take it from your appearance that you tested that theory?" Detective Morales asked, looking Anna and Joe up and down. "Continue."

"We did," Anna said with a nod. "Obviously, I wasn't able to pull it off without getting all dirty, and I'm wearing tennis shoes. Your report said the woman who left the park had on heels."

"Which means there was someone else here," Joe said.

Detective Morales jotted a few more notes down in his notebook and looked up at them. "You realize that just because someone else might have been here, that doesn't prove your friend's innocence, right?"

"Of course," Anna said. "But it shows that this case isn't all that it seems. Something else is going on here."

"Maybe so," the detective said. "But the only thing going right now is you two. I have your number, so if I need anything else, I'll be in touch."

"Do you have a card we could have or something?" Joe asked as the detective turned away from them.

"You found me the first time," Detective Morales said. "I'm sure you'll find me again."

Before they could say more, he stalked off toward the fresh crime scene, leaving Joe and Anna behind. After he'd disappeared, Derrick walked slowly back up to them.

"You disappeared on us, buddy," Joe chuckled. "The police scare you off?"

"I didn't want any part of that," Derrick said. "Besides, I knew I had nothing to add to the conversation."

"Well, thanks for not completely ditching us," Anna said with a laugh.

"You're quite welcome, my dear."

Joe shook his head and laughed again. "So, what do we do now? There's nothing left for us to do here."

"I guess we head back to the hotel and regroup with everyone," Anna said with a shrug. "Get some dinner, maybe?"

"That sounds like a splendid plan," Joe said. "I'm starved."

"I suggest the two of you take a shower first," Derrick said and began leading them back toward the car. "I hope you both brought plenty of changes of clothes for this trip."

Anna looked down at herself and then over at Joe and groaned. "We will never hear the end of this, Joe."

"At least this one is completely your fault this time," Joe said with a grin.

Anna rolled her eyes at him, and they walked the rest of the way to their vehicle in silence. While they walked, Anna mulled over the case and thought through everything they had learned. When they reached the car, she sighed and climbed into the backseat, and waited for Derrick to get them on the road.

Before long, they'd pulled up at the hotel and parked. Anna glanced down at her outfit one last time before sighing and following Joe and Derrick into the lobby. After dodging curious glances from the hotel staff, Joe, Derrick, and Anna headed up to their rooms. Bryant raised an eyebrow at them when they entered.

"Well," he said. "I guess a change of location hasn't changed your habit of somehow coming back wearing dirty clothes. What happened this time?"

"Anna tried to drown me in the lake," Joe said in a whiny voice.

Anna rolled her eyes and asked, "Where's Marie?"

"I'm here," her sister called out and emerged from the bathroom. "Good God! What happened to you?"

"Your sister proved that there was no way Frankie could have pulled off the murder," Joe said, sending a smile in Anna's direction. "At least not on her own."

Anna and Joe took turns going through the events of the day, from the missing coat to the meeting with Detective Morales. When they'd finished, Bryant sat down on the bed and sighed.

"This sounds complicated, Marie," he said. "I hate to say it, but I'm not seeing a lot of light being thrown our way. Having another person present at the crime is helpful, but it doesn't prove Frankie's innocence."

"Trust me," Joe said. "We're just getting started."

"We'll figure this out," Anna said, sending a reassuring look in her sister's direction. "I promise we will."

"You'd better," Marie said. "It sounds like the judge wants to hasten this case, and Mr. Matthews doesn't seem too excited to chase a rabbit down a hole."

The room grew silent as the group pondered the situation. After several minutes, Anna could see the strain of the situation on her sister's face. She caught Joe's eye and raised her eyebrows before saying, "Hey, I think we've done all that we can right now. How about we go get some dinner and think about this more after we get a little rest?"

"I think that's a good idea, Anna," Joe said, joining her in her attempt to distract Marie. "We've all had a long day. It was a mad dash down here. We're tired. Let's start fresh in the morning."

"There's a lovely restaurant down in the lobby," Derrick said. "We could get a few drinks, have a nice meal, and all be ready to hit the road running in the morning."

Marie smiled softly. "Don't think I don't see what you are all up to. But thank you. Yes, dinner sounds like a fine idea."

"First, I need to change," Anna said. "Marie, how about you and I meet the guys in the lobby in twenty minutes?"

"Perfect," Joe said. "I need to change myself."

Anna smiled at him and led her sister to their room across the hall. Once inside, she enveloped Marie in a hug. "I'm sorry this is happening, Marie. We'll get through it."

Marie sniffled and hugged her back. "Thank you for being here."

"Of course," Anna said. "After all the times you've had my back, there's no way I'd leave you hanging like that."

"Still," Marie insisted. "Thank you."

Marie sat on the bed, and Anna quickly changed. Within a few minutes, they headed down the elevator to meet the others in the lobby. By the time they had met up with Joe and Bryant, the hostess was gathering menus and preparing to lead them to their table.

"Well, that was quick," Anna said to Joe. "I'm glad we didn't have to wait."

"Ah, yes," Bryant said, looking back at her with a smirk. "The two of you didn't come back with your usual collection of takeout food, so I bet you are both starving!"

"We don't always..." Anna said before trailing off and thinking it over for a second before laughing. "All right. That is an accurate statement."

She smiled when a quick chuckle escaped Marie's lips. They followed the hostess to the table and took their seats. After they'd ordered, Anna leaned back in her chair and sighed.

"I guess we need to talk about what our game plan needs to be," she said. "I'm not sure the information we've found so far gives us anything to work with, so where do we need to go from here?"

"Oh, that reminds me," Marie said. "Mr. Matthews arranged for us to take a tour of Frankie's office tomorrow morning. She has a few belongings left there that we need to pick up for her and he talked them into letting us have a look around. Naturally, they don't want us to disturb the normal flow of their business, so they only agreed for us to be there after hours or on the weekend."

"Well, that's a start, I guess," Anna said. "Hopefully, something will point us in a new direction tomorrow."

"We also have all the computer files, emails, and security footage we need to go through as well," Joe said.

Anna groaned. "More security footage? We need to make sure that Matthews guy has a good coffee pot."

"Now that we have a plan," Bryant said, "how about we put this case to the side and try to enjoy dinner? I'm sure we could all use the mental break."

"Now you're talking," Joe said and grinned when he saw the server head their way with their drinks and appetizers.

Chapter 9

"Who are we meeting with today, Marie?" Anna asked as she took a sip of coffee from the cup in her hand.

Marie had been anxiously tapping her foot on the ground as they waited for Bryant and Joe to join them in the lobby for their morning adventure. When Anna addressed her, she jerked her head in her direction and sighed.

"I'm sorry," she said. "I'm acting anxious again, aren't I?"

Anna smiled and took another slow sip of the coffee. "If there is one thing I know, it's anxiety."

Marie sighed again and rubbed her temples with her fingers. "I feel horrible for Frankie. I want to just fix it so she can come home. I'm terrified that we won't be able to figure this out since we have such little leeway here in Georgia."

"I promise Joe and I won't rest until we get to the bottom of it," Anna said. "But I need you to get out of your head so we can get information from you."

"You're right," Marie said. "I need to quit feeling sorry for myself and Frankie and get to work. I would never forgive myself if we failed Frankie just because I couldn't get a grip on things."

"So, as I was saying," Anna said. "Who are we meeting with today?"

"They were trying to be as discreet as possible," Marie said. "So, we are meeting with the HR director, a member of their IT team, and the head of security will be there too."

"They sound like they are covering all their bases."

"Exactly. They want to make sure the company isn't held liable for employee misconduct while still making sure they are cooperating with the investigation."

"Or at least giving off the perception that they are cooperating."

Marie nodded and looked toward the lobby. Anna smiled when she spotted Bryant and Joe heading their way. Joe returned her smiled and nudged Bryant in the arm when they approached.

"Sorry for the delay, ladies," Joe said and gave his brother a teasing glance. "Someone had to have a chat with that pretty redhead we have hanging around the office."

Bryant laughed. "I didn't realize how much we'd miss each other. It's weird. We haven't been apart that much since we've been together."

"I know what you mean," Anna said, a soft smile spreading across her face. "I plan to have one of those chats of my own tomorrow."

"Me too," Marie said, a smile finally breaking her scowl. "I was expecting to get to spend all weekend with Eddie and his family, so I'm missing him. But for now, let's get this show on the road. We have about thirty minutes before we need to meet the people at Frankie's office."

"We have a taxi that should pick us up any second now," Joe said, glancing at the street outside. "Derrick is off working today, so he can't be our chauffeur this morning."

"Pity," Anna said. "He's had some great ideas."

"Oh, he'll be back," Joe said with a laugh. "He's having way too much fun with this. We might have to hire him when this is all said and done."

Anna chuckled and looked out the door just in time to see a large taxi pull up in front of their hotel. "I'm guessing that's our ride. Let's get going."

Marie's smile quickly faded, and she sighed again as they stood to walk outside. Anna put an arm around her and gave her a quick squeeze before heading outside with the others. Bryant popped in the front seat with the driver and quickly gave him the address of Frankie's office while Anna, Marie, and Joe got settled in the back.

As they drove, Anna watched the large commercial buildings pass her window and enjoyed all the sights she could. Traffic was heavy for a Saturday and plenty of people and cars filled the streets and sidewalks around them.

"You know," Joe said from his side of the vehicle. "This city looks like it would be a fun one to visit. If we weren't working on a case, of course."

Anna laughed and nodded. "I was just thinking the same thing."

"Well, I'll add it to our vacation bucket list," he chuckled.

Soon, they pulled up outside Frankie's office building, and Anna immediately jerked her mind back to the work at hand. Mr. Matthews was already waiting for them by the door of the building. He nodded when they climbed out of the cab and approached him.

"We're supposed to check in with security on our way in," he said. "There's a process."

As they entered the building, Anna looked around the lobby critically. It was a large and comfortable space with plenty of seating, attractive décor, and several potted plants scattered throughout the space.

"I see at least five security cameras," Joe whispered to her after a few moments, causing Anna to avert her eyes to the ceiling.

She nodded as she scanned the ceiling and spotted several cameras herself. "They set the lobby up as though they want to discourage visitors. Keep people waiting for meetings and such out here instead of heading into the office early."

"I agree."

The man sitting behind a desk in the lobby looked up at them when they approached. "Good morning. My name is Thomas Roberts. I assume you are the legal team we have visiting today?"

"Yes, sir," Mr. Matthews said. "I'm Eugene Matthews, and these are my consultants from the Hartman and Malone organization out of Virginia. They are representatives for Ms. Fritts."

"I'll need to see identification from everyone, and I'll need to get everyone to sign in," Thomas said.

He reached across the desk and picked up a spiral notebook. After opening it, he began picking up each of their ID cards and jotting down the information he needed for his log. Once finished, he entered some information onto his computer and printed out badges for them each to wear.

"Is this the normal process for people coming into the building?" Anna asked when he handed her a badge. "Do people working here have to go through this as well?"

"We give permanent badges to wear," he said. "They have to scan their badge every time they leave and enter the building."

"And you keep records of that, I assume?" Joe asked. "We could determine who was in the building at certain times if we needed to."

"Yes," the man replied. "There should be a copy of some of that information in the evidence the police gathered, so you should get a copy if you don't have it already."

"I'm sure we do," Eugene said. "We're still going through all the evidence we have so far. We'll make sure we have a copy and get back to you if not."

"Great," Thomas said. He finished filling out the information in his book and printed off all the badges before stepping out from behind the desk. He pointed toward a set of elevators behind him. "You'll be meeting with our human resources manager, Melissa Fisher, today, as well as a member of our IT team, Daniel Moore. There may also be a few other workers in the building, but we hope to keep this as quiet as possible."

"We understand," Eugene replied. "We appreciate you and your team's accommodations during this trying situation. We hope to understand everything as quickly as possible."

"We appreciate your efforts," Thomas said with a nod. "The quicker we can get this behind us, the better."

The group followed Thomas to the elevators, and he swiped his badge. Before long, the doors opened to reveal a large elevator that was big enough for all of them. Thomas ushered them inside and pushed the button for the 5th floor. They rode in awkward silence, and Anna sighed in relief when the doors swished open, and they stepped back out into open space again.

Thomas led them down a short hallway with glass doors on either side. Anna peered into the open spaces as they went, but most revealed only a collection of computer servers or cubicles. A few workers milled around in the spaces, but mostly the office was empty.

They stopped in front of a closed wooden office door and Thomas knocked gently before entering. After speaking privately to the occupant of the office, Thomas re-entered the hallway and opened the office door a little wider.

"Again, this is Melissa Fisher," he said. "She's our human resources director and will take over your meeting from here."

Eugene gave Thomas a quick nod, then stepped inside the office, followed by Marie and Bryant. Anna raised her eyebrows at Joe and followed the others inside. She took a quick look around the spacious office before turning her attention to the woman who sat behind the desk.

"Ms. Fisher," Eugene said. "I'm Eugene Matthews. Thank you so much for seeing us all today."

The woman behind the desk nodded. "Thank you for coming in. I understand your consultants here are friends of Frankie's?"

"Yes, ma'am," Marie said before turning to look at Anna. "I'm Marie Hartman and this is my sister Anna. We've been friends with Frankie since we were kids."

"I see," she replied. "I'm sure she's happy to have friends to help her through this."

Marie continued making small talk with the woman while Anna let her gaze roam around the room a little slower. She noted the pictures on the wall behind the woman, as well as the trinkets she found on her desk.

She then turned her attention back to the woman herself and used her distraction with Marie's conversation to examine her face and expression a little closer. After a few seconds, the woman noticed Anna's scrutiny and met her eyes with hers. Anna smiled, but the woman didn't return it. Instead, she turned to Eugene.

"Ms. Fritts had some belongings left in the office that I wanted to return to her," she said. "I thought her friends might clear out her desk for her?"

Eugene nodded and said, "I'm sure we can accommodate. I understand you also have some data and information you needed to provide to us that the prosecution already has in their collection?"

"Yes," she replied. "Part of your team will need to meet with my IT director for that information."

"Joe and I can do that," Anna said. "We'll likely be the ones handling that information anyway, and I can take care of Frankie's desk, Marie. That way you can stay with Eugene and Bryant."

"Thank you, Anna," Marie said. "Ms. Fisher, we'll try to keep things short and simple today."

"Please, call me Melissa," she replied. "Yes, it's been hard. Especially now that Ash..."

She stopped when her eyes filled with tears. After pursing her lips together and taking a deep breath, she continued. "Losing Mr. Rowley is hard. We haven't even made an official statement yet, so not everyone on staff knows. Monday will be tough to get through."

"I'm sorry for your loss," Joe said, causing Melissa's eyes to jerk to him. "Losing people we care about is never easy."

Melissa swallowed and jerked a tissue from a box on her desk. She dabbed her eyes with one hand and twisted a pendant that hung from a gold chain around her neck with her fingers. Joe and Anna gave each other a quick frown.

"We can give you a few moments if you'd like," Marie whispered. "I could go get Frankie's things, and Joe and Anna could get started—"

"No, no, no," Melissa said. "The sooner we get this all figured out, the better."

She threw her tissue in the trash and straightened up in her chair a bit before making eye contact with Anna again. "If you and your partner would like to head down the hallway to the server room, Daniel Moore is waiting for you in there. He can also help you find Frankie's desk and make sure you have a box to put her things in."

"Thank you," Anna said. "I believe we passed the server room earlier, so we should have no problem finding it again."

She sent a quick smile in her sister's direction and then led Joe out into the hallway. He closed the office door behind them and gave her a look.

"Was it just me," he whispered, "or did that seem a little more than general office co-worker grieving?"

"Maybe," Anna whispered back. "I say we keep that in the back of our mind while we are running our investigation today."

Joe pulled out his phone. "Just to be on the safe side, I'm going to tell Bryant to see if he can figure out if Melissa is married or not."

"Good idea," Anna said as they approached the server room. After Joe slid his phone back in his pocket, she pulled open the door and stepped inside. She smiled at the man sitting behind a desk in the corner. "Hello, I'm Anna Hartman and this is my partner, Joe. Melissa sent us to see you. I assume you're Daniel?"

The man nodded. "That's right. You're with Frankie's investigative team, correct? I have some files for you. They are already on a flash drive, but I also needed to download some of our security footage and additional log-sheet information that the prosecution team picked up earlier today."

"Great," Joe said. "Melissa said we also needed to go through Frankie's desk. I could wait here for the files and let Anna do that if that would speed things up."

"Oh, that would be great!" Daniel said. "I have a box sitting beside Frankie's desk ready to go. Her cubicle is in the office right across the hall. It's the third one. Right in the middle."

"I'll get right on that," Anna said. "Thank you for all your help so far!"

"Anna," Joe said, "as soon as I get done here, I'll come over to help you finish up. All right?"

"Sounds good," she replied and headed back out the door.

Chapter 10

She hesitated when she walked into the office space across the hall and noticed a man working in the cubicle facing Frankie's. He met her gaze but quickly got back to work after exchanging a quick smile with her.

Anna sighed, walked over to Frankie's cubicle, pulled out the office chair, and sat down. A smile crossed her face when she spotted a picture of herself, Marie, Frankie, and Claire in a frame just beside the computer monitor. She picked it up and examined it, the smile on her face glowing at the memory.

A sigh left her lips, and the smile faded when the thoughts of the predicament made their way back into her headspace. Spotting a box beside the desk, Anna tucked the picture inside and began opening the drawers of the desk. She'd just finished emptying the bottom drawer and started on the middle when the man at the desk facing Frankie's peeked over the divider and smiled at her.

"You a friend of Frankie's?" he asked.

"Yes, I'm Anna," Anna said, returning his smile. "Frankie and I go way back."

"I'm Jason. I see you're here to collect her things."

"That I am," Anna said as she continued. "Are you friends with Frankie, Jason?"

"I've gotten to know her well," he said with a nod.

Anna smiled at him and continued putting items in the box. "Well, I'm happy to learn that she has found at least one friend to keep her company while she was here."

He smiled again. "You know, there's one thing that I never learned about Frankie though."

Anna put a few more items in the box from the last drawer and stood up to start on the items on the desk itself. "Oh, yeah? What's that?"

"She never told me she had such beautiful friends!"

Anna frowned at the sudden change in his voice. "Um, thanks?"

"It would be a shame if you didn't have a good guy to take you out while you are in town!"

"Are you..." Anna said, her frown deepening. "...hitting on me?"

"I'm just saying that there's this elite club we all go to, Club Eclipse," Jason continued. "It's downtown over on Spring Street, and it's a great place to take dates."

"Yeah, I'm going to pass," she replied. "I'm not here for that."

She turned her attention back to Frankie's things and sped up putting them in the box. When Jason continued, she jerked her eyes back in his direction.

"Ahh, come on," he said. "A pretty girl like you should at least get to see Club Eclipse once in her life! They have great drinks, and if you get there right at 8, you can watch the band set up. It's quite the sight."

"I have a boyfriend," Anna replied.

Jason's grin deepened. "Well, I don't see a boyfriend here! I think you should let me take you to Club Eclipse tonight at 8. You could wear a pretty dress. Make me look a heck of a lot better with a pretty girl on my arm."

"Everything all right in here?" Joe's voice suddenly said.

Anna continued to glare at Jason. "Didn't hear you come in, Joe. I'm just about finished in here. You want to carry the box when I'm done?"

"Yep," Joe said, glancing at Jason with a quizzical look. When Anna continued to glare at him, Joe frowned and stuck out his hand. "Hi, I'm Joe. You are?"

"Ahh, you must be the boyfriend," Jason said and shook Joe's hand. "I'm Jason. I apologize for hitting on your girl here, but I just couldn't resist. She's so pretty! I thought she should see Club Eclipse for herself since it's such a great spot downtown. 8 o'clock Saturday is the best time to be there, and I don't have a date tonight, so I thought, what the heck?"

"She's not..." Joe started before raising an eyebrow at Anna. "Wait, what?"

"Ahh, yeah," Jason said. "Club Eclipse! You gotta check it out. It's over on..."

"Spring Street," Anna said, her tone even and annoyed. "8 o'clock is when the band sets up. They have good drinks, and I could wear a pretty dress to make you look better. That about sum it up?"

Jason laughed. "Yeah, sorry for being so forward. I'm bad about that. Frankie gets onto me all the time for that."

Anna shot another glare in his direction. "You don't seem to be the type of person Frankie would be friends with."

"I promise I'm not that bad," Jason said with another sly grin. "If you change your mind, I'll be at Club Eclipse on Spring Street at 8."

Anna gave him one last glare before stepping away from the desk and heading out the door without looking back. Joe joined her a few moments later.

"If you were any madder, your ears would be smoking," he said.

"Unbelievable," she said. "He sat there and had a normal conversation with me for five minutes and all he wanted was a date. I can't stand it when guys do that. It's so annoying."

"Can't blame him for trying," Joe said with a chuckle. "But I hear you."

Still grumbling, Anna led Joe back to Melissa Fisher's office. When they reached the door, she blew a quick puff of air out of her lips to release some of her anger. Before knocking, she turned to Joe and whispered, "Did you get everything we needed from the IT guy?"

"He gave me a flash drive with all the information and videos he gave to the prosecution team earlier in the day," Joe said with a nod. "I think we should be all set."

Anna tapped on the door softly and pushed it open once she heard Melissa's voice calling them inside. Marie looked up at her from a chair by Melissa's desk when they walked in.

"Melissa was just finishing up telling us about Frankie's work and the type of employee she is," Marie said. "Did you two get everything you needed?"

Anna nodded. "I believe so. Daniel gave all the files and videos to Joe, and I cleaned out Frankie's desk."

"Great!" Melissa said. "I'm happy to do all we can to help."

"Did you two have questions for Melissa before we leave?" Bryant asked and raised his eyebrows at Joe. "She is hoping to get home soon as her husband is arriving home from a business trip tonight."

"My goodness!" Melissa said. "I've just been chatting away in here. I didn't even think about whether you might have questions for me."

"What type of relationship did Frankie have with her boss?" Anna asked. "Asher, wasn't it?"

Anna didn't miss the pang of sadness that floated through Melissa's eyes like a wave. Melissa swallowed and tugged at the pendant on her necklace again before answering.

"Yes, it was Asher," she said. "I honestly don't believe they had a super close relationship."

"Oh?" Marie said with a frown. "Frankie always spoke favorably of him."

"Well, yes," Melissa said. "They got along just fine, but I don't think he saw himself as her mentor or whatnot. She was just his temporary employee, so he didn't spend a significant amount of time trying to get to know her or build her career."

"I see," Anna said. "I suppose that makes sense. Did he ever mention anything about things she'd told him or any concerns he may have had?"

"Never," Melissa said. "She was always an outstanding employee, and I never needed to intervene on a human resource basis. They kept any type of work situation they discussed between them."

"Were there any others Asher was close to in the office?" Joe asked. "Anyone who he might have confided in regarding sensitive information."

"Asher kept to himself mostly," Melissa said. "He did his job, and that's what he cared about here. If he was investigating something, the higher management team wasn't aware of it."

"What about Frankie?" Anna asked. "Was there someone she might have been confiding in around the office?"

"I'm afraid I wasn't familiar with Frankie's comings and goings around the office," Melissa said. "Unless HR has to get involved, I honestly have little to do with the employees. We have to keep a buffer between ourselves and the workforce because of sensitive information."

"You probably have to worry about not developing a bias against certain employees," Joe said. "That's understandable."

"Exactly," Melissa said. When they all fell silent, she sighed and said, "I hate to say it because I know how close you all are with Frankie, but I honestly don't know who else could have been involved in this but her. Everything leads directly back to her."

"We appreciate your honesty," Marie said, "but naturally we want to look into things a little closer to see if there's something everyone is missing. I've known Frankie my whole life, and never would have thought she'd be capable of something like this."

"Sometimes people surprise you," Melissa said.

"Thank you for taking the time to see us around today," Anna said. "We appreciate your help."

"Here, let me get you my card," Melissa said and pulled a handful of cards from a holder on her desk. "That way, if you have any more questions, you can reach me directly. That will make things much easier for everyone."

"Thank you so much," Marie said and took the cards from her. "I think we have everything we need at the moment, right guys?"

Anna nodded. "We'll get out of your hair. Do we need to do anything to get back out of the building again?"

"Just stop by the security desk to let Thomas check you back out again," she replied with a smile. "Call me anytime."

Joe picked up the box of Frankie's belongings and they all filed out of the office. When they were in the elevator, Bryant pulled out his phone and pushed a few buttons on it.

"I'm calling our cab back," he said. "It says there is one available to pick us up in five minutes."

"I'm sure that will be perfect timing," Joe said. "We still need to check back out again."

The group walked back to the security desk and Thomas smiled at them as they approached. Before addressing them, he pulled open his logbook and flipped it to the current date.

"I do hope we were all helpful today," he said. "I'll need to have each of your badges back, please."

"Thank you for your help today," Marie said as he began making marks in his book. "We certainly appreciate the accommodations everyone is making for us."

"We just want to make sure we do everything correctly," Thomas said. "Would hate for anyone to think our company was doing something that wasn't on the up and up."

"We understand."

Just as he finished, a taxi pulled up outside the building. "Looks like I finished checking you out just in time. Your ride is here."

"So, it is," Bryant said, looking out the front door. "Thank you again for everything."

They waved goodbye to Thomas before heading outside to the waiting taxi. After Joe stowed Frankie's box in the trunk, they climbed inside, and Bryant gave the driver the address for the hotel.

"I figured we could go back to the hotel to regroup after that meeting," he said.

"Shoot," Joe said, sending a grin in Anna's direction. "Anna has to get ready. She has plans later."

Anna groaned. "Jason was bad enough. Don't you get started too!"

"Oh, you met Jason?" Marie said. "I wish I had met him. Frankie always talks about how great he is!"

"Yeah, well, Anna would disagree," Joe said with a laugh.

"Really?" Marie frowned. "Frankie loves him. She was one of the few at his wedding the month before last."

Anna and Joe frowned at each other and said in unison, "Wedding?"

"Yeah," Marie said. "He likes to keep his personal life private, so many people at work didn't realize he was getting married."

"So, you're telling me that Jason, the guy that sits across from Frankie, that is great friends with her, just got married?" Anna asked. "How is that possible?"

"That's what Frankie said," Marie said with a shrug. "She seems to like him a lot. Why? What did he say to you?"

"Oh, he hit on me. Hard," Anna said. "It was awful."

"I came into that office and her cheeks were so red I thought she was sick," Joe said with another laugh. "He's lucky she didn't punch him."

"But why would he hit on me if he's married?" Anna asked.

"That doesn't make sense," Joe said.

"What did he say?" Bryant asked from the front seat.

Anna's frown deepened. "He just kept going on and on and on about a specific nightclub and making sure he took me there at 8. He said..."

Her eyes widened, and she looked at Joe. He shook his head at her. "You thinking what I'm thinking?"

"I think I am?"

"One of you want to fill us in on the secret?" Marie asked. "I'm a little lost."

"You said Jason was good friends with Frankie and few people would have known he is married beside her, right?" Anna said.

"Yeah?"

"Then, what better way to get a message across than to do something so out of character that your good friend would notice," Joe added.

"I'm sorry," Marie said with a frown. "I'm still not following."

"He was giving us a clue," Anna said. "He was hoping Frankie would have told us about his wedding, and we would have clued in on what he was telling us."

"Which was?"

"Which was that we need to make an appearance at Club Eclipse tonight at 8," Joe said. "Anna, did you bring a dress?"

Chapter 11

"Marie, are you sure you want to do this?" Anna asked as she watched her sister adjust her shoe. "You and Bryant could stay here and let me and Joe take care of this."

"Anna," Marie said, straightening up and glaring at her sister. "You and Joe are not the only members of this team who can leave the office and investigate things."

"I'm just saying that these things sometimes get intense," Anna replied. "It would be nice if we didn't have to worry about the two of you."

"Exactly why we are going, Anna. We don't even know what we are walking into. No way am I letting the two of you walk into a nightclub blind. There are too many ways that can go wrong."

"It would be easier to handle the things that go wrong if we all didn't have each other there to worry about."

"Ah, so you just want it to be me alone who has to worry. I get it," Marie said. "Not gonna happen. We're all going. Now be quiet and zip up my dress."

Anna sighed and zipped Marie's dress before checking her reflection in the mirror. Marie headed into the bathroom to touch up her makeup and hair. Soon there was a knock at their door, and Anna took one last look in the mirror before heading to answer it.

"Hey, you're back!" she said with a smile when she spotted Derrick standing behind Joe and Bryant. "I thought you had work to do."

"I was not about to miss a night out on the town," Derrick said. "And, wow, am I glad I didn't! You ladies look fantastic!"

Anna rolled her eyes and turned back to look at Marie. "Are you ready? The sooner we get done with this, the better."

Derrick laughed. "I'm just playing." He hesitated when Anna glared at him. "Not that you both don't look great or anything. I just meant...Joe? Help?"

Anna laughed. "How about we just go? We need to make sure we get there in plenty of time to check out the place before 8. We don't even know what we are looking for."

"We're taking separate cars," Bryant said. "Anna, you and Joe can ride with Derrick, and Marie can ride with me in a cab. That way it won't be obvious that we all arrived together."

"Good idea," Anna said as they all headed toward the elevator. "We probably need to have an exit plan or code or something. Some way to know that we all need to get out."

Joe nodded and pushed the button to signal the elevator. As they waited, he reached into his pocket. "Got that covered. I didn't know what we'd be up against when we got here, so I brought along some communication devices just in case. Got one for each of us. Even you, Derrick."

"Well, thanks, buddy!" Derrick said as the elevator arrived and they all stepped inside. "It's nice to know you were thinking of me!"

"Whatever," Joe said with a laugh. He pulled a small bag out of his pocket and gave each of them a tiny device that they could clip to their clothing. "Just clip them anywhere. They have a pretty decent listening range, so they should be able to pick up our voices wherever we put them."

"How do we hear?" Bryant asked.

Joe smiled and pulled a second bag out of his pocket. "With these." He fished through the bag and handed each of them a device similar to a hearing aid. "We'll all be able to hear each other as though we were standing just next to one another."

"If any of us get into trouble, we all get out," Bryant said. "We aren't putting ourselves at risk tonight. That won't do Frankie any good."

"I wish we knew what we were looking for," Anna said. "I feel like we're looking for a needle in a haystack."

"Let's just hope that whatever it is Jason wanted us to see that it will be obvious when we see it," Joe said.

Anna sighed when the elevator doors opened to the lobby, and they began heading outside. She followed Joe and Derrick to Derrick's car and Marie headed toward the cab that was waiting for her and Bryant.

Before they all climbed into the vehicles, Bryant called out, "Remember. If we get into trouble, we get out."

"Let's just make sure that doesn't happen," Joe called back.

Anna slid into the backseat and Joe climbed in beside her. Derrick took his place behind the wheel and looked back at them. "I feel like a chauffeur for a rich and famous couple."

Joe laughed. "You volunteered for this job, buddy."

Derrick shook his head and grinned before turning back to face the front of the car. He put the address to the club into the GPS and pulled out into traffic. Before long, the bright downtown lights caught Anna's attention, and she stared out the window again.

"Definitely a vacation destination," Joe said.

"I agree," she replied with a smile, although she kept her eyes on the surrounding buildings.

When she spotted a few parking spots close to the club, she pointed out the window. "Hey, it might be a good idea to park close if we can. That way, if we need to leave suddenly, we don't have to run a mile to the car."

"Good idea," Derrick said and found one just a few spots away from the front door.

Anna climbed out of the car after Joe and looked up and down the sidewalk in front of the club. A few others headed into the building ahead of them, and she studied them closely before turning her attention to the building itself. A member of the security team stood outside the door, checking IDs and handing out wristbands to those who entered.

"So far, it looks like just a regular club," Joe said. "I don't see anything amiss."

"Me neither," Anna agreed. "Let's go inside."

She, Derrick, and Joe headed to the door, and each showed the security guard their IDs before heading inside.

Soft music floated around them when they entered, and groups of people milled about with drinks in their hands. The bartenders appeared relaxed and happy while preparing drinks for customers who approached the bar.

"Well, this is a pretty mellow place right now," Anna said.

"I agree," Joe said, looking around. "Doesn't seem like a hardcore dance club. More of a quiet place to have adult conversations."

"You sound like a tour guide," Derrick snickered. "What now?"

Joe chuckled. "Now, we probably should spread out a bit. Why don't you go hang by the bar? Get water or something since you're driving. Anna and I will head to the other end, so we aren't all together."

"Cool," Derrick said. "What am I supposed to be looking for?"

"Anything that might seem suspicious," Anna said. "Not sure what that might be, but hopefully we know it when we see it."

Derrick nodded and slunk away to the bar. Anna and Joe followed suit but headed to the other end. As the bartender approached, Joe said, "It would be best if we had a drink in our hand. Just so we don't stand out. But let's keep it pretty mellow."

"What can I get for you two?" the bartender asked.

"Could I get some sort of spritzer?" Anna asked with a smile. "I'm not picky."

"Sure thing!" he said, returning her smile. He turned to Joe and asked, "And for you?"

"Ah, I'll take a bottle of beer. I'm also not picky, so just a cheap bottle is fine."

"Easiest customers I've had all day," the bartender said when he brought back their drinks and took their money. Anna gave him another smile and took a sip. She spotted Marie and Bryant at a table nearby and made eye contact with them.

When Joe also spotted them, he said, "Bryant. Marie. Can you hear me?"

"Loud and clear," Bryant returned.

"Good," Joe said. "How about you Derrick? Can you hear me?"

"Yep," he replied. "Still not sure what I'm supposed to be watching for, but I can hear you."

"Good," Joe said. He looked down at the watch on his arm and then looked over the small club again. "It's almost 8. Wonder how long we should wait for something to happen."

Anna shook her head and looked at the small stage in the corner. As Jason had said, a small band started setting up right at 8. She raised her eyebrows at Joe. "Well, there's the band. Now, where's the—"

Joe cut her sentence short when he jerked her into his arms and spun her away from the bar in a semi-embrace. She floated with him and put her arms around his waist instinctively. She looked up at him, her eyes widening in surprise. His gaze traveled across the club toward the booth where their siblings sat and then back to her. When their eyes met, his arms tightened slightly around her and he hesitated for a moment.

After clearing his throat, he whispered, "Sorry. Melissa Fisher just walked in. I was worried she would recognize us."

"She sat next to some guy at the bar," Bryant said. "You two can't go near her, though. She'll recognize you in a heartbeat."

"Derrick," Joe said. "Any way you can get close to her and see if you can overhear her conversation? She's wearing a blue dress. Has long brown hair that's a little wavy."

"The guy she met with is wearing a gray suit," Bryant added. "There's a stool open right next to her."

Anna peeked around Joe's arm at Melissa and the man she'd met and watched as Derrick casually approached them and took the stool next to her.

"Go ahead and order a beer, Derrick," she said. "You look weird sitting there with a glass of water."

"But just sip on it," Joe added.

They all grew quiet so they could make out what Melissa was saying to the man. Luckily, Derrick's mike could pick up most of their conversation.

"Chris," Melissa hissed quietly. "You told me everything was going to be all right."

"It is all right, my dear," the man named Chris replied. "Everything is going exactly as we planned. This will all get cleared up in a week or two when all the evidence points to that girl, and they have to accept a deal."

"No, it's not all right," Melissa said and pulled on the pendant of her necklace. "Asher is dead! I...I..."

"You, what?" Chris asked. "Loved him? Please, Melissa. You run around clutching on that stupid necklace he gave you, but truth be told, you're sleeping around with me, him, your husband, and God knows who else. You don't love any of us."

"He was different," Melissa said, quietly. "He loved me, and I loved him."

Chris laughed and took a drink of the brown liquid in the glass in front of him. "You think he would have continued loving you when he figured out you kept climbing in my bed just to make sure you got good raises?"

Melissa ducked her head and took a long drink from her wine glass. "All I wanted was to protect the company. I never wanted Asher to get hurt."

"And that's exactly what you did," Chris said. "That entire issue would have been detrimental to the company. Would have opened up a whole slew of investigations into our practices. Investigations we don't need right now."

"I know that," Melissa said. "That's why I brought it to your attention as soon as Asher told me about it."

"And I certainly appreciate that," Chris continued. "Unfortunately, Asher's untimely death helped to get us out of the situation. We can now completely sweep the unfortunate financial issue under the table."

"Did you have something to do with his death?" Melissa asked.

"Of course not, my dear," Chris replied. "The young lady was the sole perpetrator of that. All the evidence truly points to her. She went off the deep end and gave us the biggest distraction of them all, and now we don't even have to worry about figuring out how to keep the feds off our case about that embezzling issue. Now we just have to sit back and wait for justice to be served for our devoted employee."

"I don't plan to sit back and wait," Melissa said. "I plan to make sure they have all the evidence they need to put her behind bars."

"You do that if you must," Chris said. "Just make sure whatever evidence you share with them points back to the girl and doesn't include even a whisper of that messy financial mistake. We have controls in place to keep that from happening again now, so we won't ever have to worry about it or speak of it again after this case is closed. We just need to make sure that everything about it dies when she goes to jail. None of us can afford to let word get out to our investors about the embezzling."

Melissa finished the wine in her glass and set it back down. When the bartender arrived to offer another glass, Chris held up his hand. "Thank you, sir, but my lady friend and I are taking our leave this evening." The bartender swept their glasses away and Chris took Melissa's hand. "Come, my dear. I have the limo out back. I want to have my time with you before you must return home."

Melissa picked up her phone and gazed at it. "We'll have to make it quick. Mike's plane lands at 9, and I don't want him to get home before me."

Chris chuckled. "You know that's not part of our arrangement. You will leave when I'm ready for you too."

Melissa sighed and rose from her stool to follow him. As they passed, Joe swept Anna into an even tighter embrace and pulled her face closer to his. Melissa and Chris walked straight past them and out the backdoor without a second glance.

When they passed, Joe pulled away from her slightly but held her gaze for a second. Anna covered the device that allowed the others to hear her with her hand and whispered, "I imagine you would be an excellent dancer."

He smiled at her and whispered, "With the right partner, yes."

She returned his smile but didn't reply. He pulled one hand away from her and covered his speaker.

"Derrick was right, by the way," he said. "You look beautiful tonight."

She chuckled. "I'm pretty sure he said fantastic."

"Hmm," he said, his eyes twinkling.

"Guys," Bryant said suddenly in their ears. "What now?"

"I suppose that's what Jason wanted us to see," Anna said quietly after pulling her hand away from the speaker on her dress. "Melissa isn't trying to help us at all."

"I to agree," Marie said through the microphone. "We're going to have to question every piece of information she gave us today. Including everything she said about Frankie and Asher's relationship."

"Should we stick around?" Bryant asked. "You think there's more?"

"I think we've probably seen all we need to see at this point," Joe said. "Why else would Jason have wanted us here right at 8. Any other time, she obviously wouldn't have been here."

"We need to get in touch with Jason," Bryant said. "He's got to know more about what's going on here than we think he does."

"I agree," Marie said. "I'm pretty sure Frankie has his information at her place, or at least in her phone. Let's call him in the morning and see if we can meet."

Joe untangled himself from Anna and took her hand. "Let's get out of here before we stick around long enough for someone to recognize us."

"Right behind you."

They met Derrick and the others outside and hurriedly climbed inside Derrick's car. As they were pulling away, Anna spotted a dark limo in a back parking lot with a driver standing outside awkwardly.

"This certainly just got a lot more interesting," Anna said.

Joe gazed at the limo with her and nodded. "I have to say I didn't see that one coming."

Chapter 12

"Where's my purse?" Marie rushed around the hotel room in a frenzy. The moment it was in her hands, she jerked back around and said, "Oh, shoot. I need Frankie's paperwork."

"Right here," Anna said, handing her sister a stack of papers. "Marie, you need to calm down."

"I can't believe that judge waited until the last minute to let us know we could come to get her," Marie complained. "And here we are meeting Jason at noon."

"It will be alright, Marie," Anna said. "You and Bryant can go get Frankie, and Joe and I will go talk to Jason. It will all be fine."

"Are you sure you and Joe can handle Jason on your own? What if something goes wrong?"

Anna laughed. "When has something going wrong ever stopped me and Joe?"

Marie narrowed her eyes at her. "We can't afford for something to go wrong with Frankie's case."

"Marie, relax," Anna said. "You know we wouldn't jeopardize Frankie's case. Besides, picking Frankie up from jail should be easy. You've bailed me out enough times that you're an old pro!"

Marie laughed. "Oh, is that what you're going with? That's a heck of a silver lining stretch there, Anna. But you're right. I've bailed you out enough times that bailing out Frankie is going to be a breeze."

"Yeah, well, at least it's been a while?" Anna shrugged, causing Marie to laugh again.

"Come on," Marie said. "I'm sure the guys are waiting on us downstairs, and I want to get Frankie home and settled, so I have plenty of time to talk to Eddie later."

"Ah, that's right. I'm supposed to talk to Alex tonight, too," Anna said with a smile. "See, now that is a silver lining."

Anna grabbed her bag and followed her sister out of the hotel room and to the elevator. As Marie had predicted, Bryant and Joe were already waiting for them in the lobby. Anna smiled when she spotted Derrick sitting in a chair as well.

"You just can't get enough of us, can you?" she laughed when they approached.

"I have to admit," Derrick said, "this has all been fascinating. Maybe I should come back and join the team."

Joe chuckled. "You know we couldn't afford you, Derrick, and I promise you'd tire of this, eventually."

"Well, for now, how about I just put my chauffeur hat on and get the two of you to your next destination?"

"Sounds like a plan," Anna said before turning to Marie. "Marie, if you and Bryant run into any trouble getting Frankie out of there, Joe and I are just a phone call away."

Marie hugged Anna. "Thank you, Anna."

Anna smiled and returned the embrace. "Send Frankie my love. Tell her we will see her soon."

They all separated and stepped outside the hotel. Marie and Bryant headed off in one direction to catch a taxi, and Anna followed Joe and Derrick to Derrick's car. Once they were inside, Derrick put Jason's address into the GPS, and they were once again speeding across the city.

When they arrived at the apartment complex where Jason lived, Anna looked up at it. The building was well-kept and the sidewalk clean. Several people walked up and down the sidewalk outside the building on their way to other destinations. Derrick found parking nearby, and Joe and Anna popped out of the car.

"You sure you'll be all right in here, Derrick?" Joe asked before closing the door. "I don't know how long we will be."

"No worries," Derrick replied, waving them off.

"Thanks, buddy," Joe said. "We'll call if we get into any trouble."

Derrick leaned across the car and raised an eyebrow at Anna. "You two must get into an awful lot of trouble if you keep warning everyone about the potential trouble you might get into."

Anna chuckled. "You have no idea."

Derrick laughed and shook his head while Joe shut the door. Anna and Joe then took off across the parking lot, hastened up the sidewalk, and pressed the buzzer for Jason's apartment. Before long, they had ridden up in the elevator and were gently tapping on his apartment door. Jason opened the door with a smile and welcomed them inside.

"Thank you so much for coming today," Jason said. "I'm so sorry I had to treat you that way, Anna. I was afraid to come out and tell you what I needed you to know."

"I understand," Anna said with a smile. "I imagine you are in a precarious situation."

"Exactly," he replied. "And I knew that if you were friends with Frankie, you would figure out what I was telling you."

"We did," Anna said. "Thank you for being brave enough to give us that tip."

"I just wish there was something else I could do for Frankie," Jason said with a frown. "I feel it's my fault she's in this predicament."

"How so?" Joe asked.

"I originally came across the issue and got her input on it because everything was running through accounts she handled personally," Jason said. "She wound up looking at it herself since she'd dealt with that earlier invoice. She completely took ownership of the whole thing once she realized the danger she was in."

"That sounds just like Frankie," Anna said with a smile. "Don't feel too bad about it. If we are reading the situation correctly, she would have ended up in the same spot regardless of anything you did or didn't do."

"I suppose."

"What else can you tell us?" Joe asked. "We're still just getting our bearings with all this, and a lot of the information seems misleading."

"Well, hopefully, you came away with some insights into Melissa last night," Jason said. "I'm hoping she kept with her typical schedule?"

"Yep," Anna said. "We ran into her at your Club Eclipse. She was there with some guy named Chris."

"Chris...er, Mr. Shepard is the company's CEO," Jason said.

"He and Melissa are having an affair?"

"Not exactly," Jason said. "She was having an affair with Asher. She only spends time with Mr. Shepard so she can get the things she wants. Raises and things for the office...stuff like that."

"I see," Joe said, raising his eyebrows at Anna. "She seemed pretty upset that Asher was dead."

"She is," Jason said. "And that's really what I wanted you to see. I wanted you to know that you can't trust her. Whatever she told you about Frankie and the entire situation revolving around the account and embezzling is probably not accurate."

"A lot of the things she told us during our meeting with her made little sense."

"I suspected it wouldn't."

"She said she didn't know Asher well at all and that she wasn't aware of the situation he and Frankie were dealing with," Anna said. "The Asher part is a lie. What about everything else?"

"Everything about that is a lie," Jason said. "She was well aware of the entire situation. She, Frankie, and Asher had multiple meetings about the invoice. She was up to her ears in information about that."

"So, she's trying to hide her involvement then," Joe said to Anna. He turned back to Jason. "What else can you tell us about Melissa?"

"Um, not a lot," he replied, thinking for a second. "She gets around. It's well known around the office that she is sleeping with Mr. Shepard. She tried to keep the affair with Asher a secret, but plenty of us knew about that as well."

"How did she keep all that from her husband?" Anna asked. "You'd think he would clue into that, eventually."

"He travels a lot, so he's constantly out of town," Jason said. "She also lied to him about her work schedule."

"How so?"

"She tells him she gets off two hours after she gets off," Jason said. "That way, when he is home, she can meet Asher or Mr. Shepard at Club Eclipse for drinks before going home to her husband."

"That gives her time for the rendezvous in Shepard's limo, too," Joe said with a shake of his head. "What does she do now that Asher is gone? And how do you know all this stuff about her? You can't tell me she just went around blabbing everything about her affairs and private life to half the office."

"Asher talked," Jason said. "He was pretty proud of the fact that she wanted him so badly. He bragged about it a lot around the office. She liked him a lot more than he liked her."

Anna frowned. "I would almost feel sorry for her if I didn't know how crappy she is to her husband."

Jason shrugged. "She's just with him for his money. He keeps her supplied with all the nice things. She uses her inflated paycheck to pay for personal vacations and weekend trips with her girlfriends."

"Melissa sounds like a piece of work," Anna said. "I think with everything you've told us, we need to take what she tells us with a grain of salt."

"Or even throw it out completely," Joe said. "If she's angry about Asher, she may try to sabotage Frankie and get her thrown in jail simply for revenge."

"Sadly," Jason said. "I think you are right."

Anna sighed and thought through everything Jason had told them. After a few moments, she sighed and looked at Jason. "Having someone on the inside working against us isn't making this any easier, Joe."

"I'll do my best to find out any information I can and pass it along," Jason said. "I just wanted to make sure you knew the truth about Melissa."

"We appreciate your help," Joe said. "Unless you have anything else to share, we'll get out of your hair."

"I wish I did," Jason said.

Anna stood to her feet and reached out to shake Jason's hand. "Thank you again for your help, Jason. You'll be happy to know that the judge awarded Frankie bail. My sister is getting her out as we speak."

"That's such great news," Jason said with a smile. "Please tell her to call me if she needs anything at all."

"I'm sure she will appreciate that," Anna said.

She and Joe headed toward the door, stopping long enough to say their goodbyes to Jason. They walked back to Derrick's car in silence as they each solemnly pondered everything they had learned. Derrick smiled at them when they opened their doors and slid into the vehicle.

"Well, I see you returned in one piece," he said. "Learn anything."

Anna sighed. "We probably learned a little too much about ole Melissa, to be honest. We're going to have to regroup with the others to determine our next step."

"Great!" Derrick said. "I hear the lobby bar is great. I could use a few cocktails tonight after being deprived of the fun last night."

Joe laughed. "Always one for a good time, aren't you, Derrick?"

"Naturally," Derrick said with a big grin.

Chapter 13

Marie heard Frankie sigh when they walked in the front door of her apartment complex. When she also ducked her head when they passed one of the other occupants, Marie patted her arm. After a brisk walk to the elevator, Marie pressed the button and put her arm around Frankie while they waited.

She gave Frankie a little smile when they entered the empty elevator, but she didn't receive one in return. Frankie watched the doors slide close, and Marie could see the relief that no one else was joining them all over her.

When they reached the third floor, Frankie began shuffling through her purse. The frown on her face deepened when she pulled her keys out, only to drop them on the floor of the elevator. She sighed again and looked down at them, her eyes resting briefly on the monitoring device that was snuggly attached to her ankle.

"Let me get those," Marie said, immediately stooping to pick up the keys. She held them out in Frankie's direction. "Which one is it, and I'll open the door for you?"

Frankie pointed out her apartment key. "It's that one."

Marie nodded and looked up when the doors to the elevator opened. She gave Frankie another pat on the arm and led her down the hallway to the apartment. After putting the key in the lock and swinging open the door, Marie sucked in a deep breath at the sight that stood before her. Frankie peered around her at the mess left behind after the executed search warrant and sighed again.

"It'll be all right," Marie said, trying to put a reassuring smile on her face. "We'll get everything cleaned up in no time. You go get settled and I'll get started."

Frankie sighed again and followed Marie into her apartment. She sat her purse on the kitchen table and looked around, her eyes filling with tears. Marie wrapped her arms around her friend and squeezed her.

"How did I get here, Marie?" Frankie asked through her sniffles. "I don't understand how things went so bad so quickly."

"I know, honey," Marie said. "We'll figure it out."

Frankie shook her head and pulled away, her gaze sweeping across the messy apartment again. Marie looked over the same space and furrowed her brow.

"Hey, why don't you go take a shower and relax for a minute," Marie said. "I'll get started with this mess. At least I can get that one thing off your mind. Then we can chat about what's going on."

"Great," Frankie said, sighing again. "Yes, let's talk about the pending demise of my entire future."

Marie hugged her again and said, "I'm sure you will feel much better after the shower. Trust me."

Frankie nodded and headed off toward her bathroom. Marie got started cleaning up and soon heard the shower turn on in Frankie's bathroom. By the time she heard it turn off, she'd cleaned up most of the living room and all of the kitchen. She finished that portion of the cleaning while Frankie was getting dressed.

Frankie gave her a small smile when she emerged from her bedroom wearing a t-shirt and shorts.

"I think I've gotten just about everything cleaned up in here," Marie said. "How's the rest of your place look?"

"Not too bad," Frankie said, turning back to look at the bedroom door. "I cleaned up the bathroom while I was in there and I had little in my bedroom for them to mess up."

"You want to get a drink and sit down while I clean it up a bit?" Marie asked. "I can at least make sure you have a comfy place to sleep tonight. You need some good rest."

Frankie nodded and headed toward a cabinet in her kitchen. "I'll have you a glass of wine waiting when you get done."

"Sounds good," Marie said over her shoulder as she headed into Frankie's bedroom.

She sighed in relief to see that Frankie's bedroom was mostly unscathed from the search warrant. It took her less than ten minutes to straighten Frankie's closet and dresser. After she finished, she turned her attention to the bed, where she pulled the sheet and comforter in place and fluffed the pillow. After a final quick look around, she headed back out to meet Frankie in the kitchen.

"See, good as new," she said with a smile as she joined Frankie at the dining room table. A glass of wine waited for her, and she took a grateful sip of the liquid.

"So, what now?" Frankie asked. "What do we do?"

"How about I start by getting you up to speed on everything we've learned this weekend?" Marie said. After Frankie nodded, Marie spent a few minutes summarizing everything they had done over the weekend. When she told Frankie about her missing blue coat, Frankie gasped.

"So, my coat is missing?" she asked. "And some woman posed as me in it?"

"That certainly appears to be the case," Marie said. "We're going to work on figuring out who she is, but we can prove that you dropped your coat off at the cleaners and didn't have possession of it during the murder, so that is helpful."

"Still doesn't prove I didn't murder Asher though."

"I know," Marie said. "But it's a start. And as long as we have a start, there will be more avenues to follow."

Frankie grimaced. "What else have you found out?"

"Lot of things about Melissa," Marie said. "She's trying to sabotage you. Gave us a lot of information that was completely untrue. I'm sure she led the police astray as well."

"You don't say," Frankie said. "I thought Melissa and I were friends!"

"She seems to have been having an affair with Asher and is furious at you for his murder," Marie continued. "Your friend Jason helped us figure that out."

"Good ole Jason," Frankie said. "I didn't want him to get involved in this."

"Anna and Joe are at his place right now talking to him," Marie said. "He's already given us a lot to work with. He sent us to a club Melissa likes to go to, and she met up with your company's CEO, Chris. They had a lot to say about things."

"Like what?"

"Like how Chris was trying to make the issue you found to go away and how Melissa hadn't expected Asher to get murdered," Marie said. "They both seem to be trying to throw you under the bus on both issues."

"Well, that's reassuring."

"Now that we know about it, we can work against them."

Frankie sighed and closed her eyes. After a few moments of silence, both she and Marie took a sip of wine before continuing their conversation.

"What do I need to do?" Frankie asked. "How can I help with this?"

"Other than rest and try to keep yourself from going crazy?" Marie asked with a humorless chuckle.

Frankie laughed with her and said, "I'm pretty sure I'm going to go crazy here in this apartment if I can't help."

"I know," Marie said. "I promise I'll be here with you as much as possible. I wish I could stay with you, but your attorney thinks it might be a bad idea. Plus, I want to make sure I'm close to the others in case there is some sort of break that requires my attention."

Frankie nodded. "I just feel like there has to be something I can do to contribute."

"How about we start at the top?" Marie said. "Anna and Joe like to do that sometimes. I'll get a pen and a notebook, and we'll go through everything that happened. That way, we can identify anything we might be missing. Anything we might need to look into further."

Frankie nodded. "That sounds like a good plan. That would at least make me feel as though everything was out on the table."

Marie pulled a notebook and pen from her bag and opened the notebook in front of her. After opening to a blank page and taking another sip of her wine, she looked up at Frankie and said, "All right. Where would you like to begin, Frankie?"

"I suppose, let's start at the beginning," Frankie said with a shrug. "Maybe there was something in the early days of my internship that I missed."

Marie made a few marks in the notebook. "How about we start with a timeline? You've been in the internship about six months, right?"

"Yep, six months," Frankie said with a nod. "Remember, I moved right around the time you guys opened your law firm."

"And they intended the internship to be for an entire year," Marie continued, jotting down a few notes. "Let's start with the obvious. How did you learn about the internship and what was it like when you started working there?"

"I found out about the internship at school. The company was quite active at all our career days and job fair events. I'd become familiar with them during my last couple of years in college."

"Hmm, so that seems to imply that they are regularly hiring interns," Marie said. "Why do you think that is?"

Frankie shrugged. "When we talked about the internship programs, they told me they enjoyed investing in the future of the financial industry. They had a new internship program starting every month of the year."

"And they all ran for a year?" Marie asked. "That means they have at least twelve interns working for them at all times."

"I'd say that's accurate," Frankie said. "It always seemed like a new intern was coming on board, and just as you were getting to know one intern, they would leave."

"What was it like working there?"

"It was great, at first. I got to know my little team well, really fast, and we just all clicked with each other."

"Jason is on this team?"

"Yes, he's on it. We became good friends quickly. He's a good guy."

"What about the rest of the team?" Marie asked while writing a few more notes in her notebook. "What were your initial impressions of the team?"

"Everyone was great," Frankie continued. "Everyone seemed interested in making sure the interns could be successful. Seemed invested in our careers. Wanted to make sure we learned a lot of real-world experience while we were there. They were great."

"What about Asher and Melissa?"

"Asher was a great boss," Frankie said. "Supportive of his team. Willing to get in there with us and do the work. An outstanding leader. All the things you could want in a good boss. That's the reason I took the invoice issue straight to him after we'd discovered it. I trusted his judgment and knew that it would get handled."

"What about Melissa? Did you have much to do with her?"

"She was always involved in the things we did. Of course, she got all the interns started and trained. We would have weekly team meetings with her or her department. About once a month, she'd plan an after-hours networking event either at the office or somewhere in town."

"Did Asher and Melissa seem close?" Marie asked. "From what we've learned, they were having an affair."

Frankie nodded. "I think Asher talked about it with the guys on our team, but he never really mentioned it to us women. Still, word got around, and we all knew about it, mostly. I don't think anyone was brave enough to bring it up to Melissa, however."

"What about Melissa's affair with the company's CEO?"

"We'd all heard whispers of that one as well."

"Jason implied Melissa went to that club he sent us to pretty regularly."

"Yep, that was another known thing. She goes there pretty much every night, so she has a reason to stay away from her house."

"So she can have affairs without getting caught?"

"Exactly," Frankie said.

"Anything else you can think of that we should know about her or Asher or anyone else in your office?"

Marie and Frankie sat in silence for several moments while Frankie thought through the rest of her coworkers.

She shook her head and frowned when she couldn't provide any more information.

"I'm sorry," she said. "That's all I can think of right now."

"That's fine," Marie said. "We can circle back if you think of something else. How about we move onto the invoice that started all this?"

"Jason initially brought it to me because he couldn't find the account and it was something I had worked on recently," Frankie said. "As I told you the other day, I looked into it and kept running in circles with it."

"And that's when you took it to Asher?" Marie asked.

"Yes, I took it to Asher, who seemed genuinely confused about the ordeal. He told me he would look into it."

"Was that the last you heard on the matter?"

"Everything snowballed from there," Frankie said. "Before I knew it, Melissa was involved, and I was being investigated for embezzling."

"When you say Melissa was involved, what do you mean?"

"She was originally the one who brought up the embezzling issue with me," Frankie said. "She called me in for a one-on-one meeting and began questioning me about the invoice I'd brought to Asher and accused me of stealing money."

"How did you react to that news?"

"Naturally, I was appalled by the allegation," Frankie said. "I knew there was no truth behind any of her claims, so I was at a loss how she could have concluded that."

"She claimed there was proof?"

"She said IT was looking into it, but unauthorized transactions were flowing from my work computer's IP address," Frankie continued. "It had been going on the entire time I'd been part of the company."

"If there was proof, why didn't they fire you right away?"

"That was exactly what I asked her," Frankie said. "She seemed to take my side in the matter, honestly. Said how great an employee I was, and how she was shocked that this type of thing would come up."

"So, she didn't believe the allegations either?"

"I left the meeting believing that she was just as confused as I was," Frankie said. "That's why I could keep my job while the investigation continued. Melissa seemed to believe that it was all a misunderstanding."

"All right," Marie said with a frown. "So, assuming she was in on the embezzling situation, what's our theory about why they kept you onboard?"

Frankie shrugged again. "Maybe they wanted to keep me around so they could pin the entire thing on me."

"Or maybe they were hoping they could scare you off."

"Maybe so," Frankie said. "If Melissa had come back to me a week after that meeting and told me that everything had been a mistake, I would have believed her and been relieved. I honestly probably wouldn't have thought about the invoice or any of that part of the situation again after they'd cleared my name."

"But, of course, Asher was murdered just a few days later and now everything is out in the open," Marie said.

"Maybe Asher wouldn't drop it," Frankie said. "If he kept digging, maybe he uncovered something too dangerous for him to know."

"And since they couldn't make it go away, they needed a scapegoat."

"Yeah, me."

Marie sighed and tapped the notebook with the end of her pen while she mulled over everything they knew. Frankie rubbed her temples with her fingers and closed her eyes.

"Well, I think we can safely say that Melissa is not on our side, and we can't trust anything she tells us," Marie said with a frown.

"That's not that reassuring, considering she's the one that's been supplying both our side and the prosecution with information about me," Frankie said. "She's in the perfect position to completely screw me over."

"We'll just have to figure out a way to stop her," Marie said. "There has to be some way we can prove she's playing both sides of this."

"How would we get that proof?"

"I don't know at the moment," Marie said. "I'm going to get back to the team, and we'll go over all this. Surely one of us will come up with a good plan."

"In the meantime," Frankie said. "I'll just sit here and wait to spend the rest of my life in jail."

Chapter 14

Joe adjusted the collar of his shirt and ran a hand through his hair before turning to look at his brother, who was reading through some documents at the table in their hotel room.

"You sure you don't want to go get some dinner with Derrick and me tonight?" he asked. "Might be fun to take a break on this case before we hit it hard in the morning."

Bryant shook his head but didn't lookup. "Nah, I plan to give Allie a call when you leave, then spend the evening looking through this stuff the IT guy gave us today. I've been through it once and found nothing. I'm going to look again and see if I can find something that would give us an in with Melissa."

Joe sent a mischievous smile in Bryant's direction. "Well, you certainly have an in with Allie. She's got you wanting to stay home at night, huh?"

Bryant chuckled and looked up at him. "Yeah, I'd say my wild nights of chasing women are officially over for the foreseeable future."

Joe laughed harder. "When have you ever 'chased women?' You know, we did just sign an apartment lease together. Should I be concerned that you're going to ditch me soon?"

"Nah, we're a way off from that still," Bryant said. "Not that I don't want to get there with Allie. Just, not yet."

Joe laughed again. "Good, cause I'm leaving you to deal with getting out of our lease if you kick me out."

Bryant shook his head at him and rolled his eyes. When a knock sounded on the door, they both turned to look at it.

"Must be your date," Bryant said with a snicker. "You and Derrick better behave yourselves tonight. We need to be firing on all cylinders if we want to help Frankie."

Joe took a few steps toward the door and swung it open. Derrick grinned at him from the hallway. Before stepping out of the room himself, Joe turned to Bryant. "Don't worry. I told Derrick that it is just dinner tonight. No shenanigans."

"Shenanigans?" Derrick asked with a laugh. "I don't know what you're talking about."

Bryant laughed and shook his head. "As I said. Be good, Joe."

Joe smiled at Bryant before letting the door to their hotel room close behind him. Derrick took off down the hallway and stopped at the elevator to push the button. While they waited, Derrick looked Joe over and raised his eyebrows at him.

"What?" Joe asked with a laugh. "You don't approve of my outfit tonight?"

"No," Derrick said. "I'm just wondering if you are ever going to ask me why I'm really here in Atlanta with you."

Joe frowned. "You said you decided to take a holiday or whatever."

"Yeah, well, that's just what I wanted the others to believe."

Joe laughed. "Why are you here, then?"

Derrick grew serious. "Honestly, I'm worried about you."

Now it was Joe's turn to raise his eyebrows at his friend. "Worried about me? Why?"

Derrick gave him another once over before replying. "Joe, when's the last time you dated someone?"

Joe laughed. "Trust me. I date plenty."

"Your style of dating or mine?"

"I didn't realize there was a difference," Joe said with a playful smile.

The elevator doors opened, and Joe stepped inside. After Derrick followed him through the doors, Joe pushed the button for the elevator and watched the doors swish closed.

"You know there is," Derrick continued when the elevator began its descent. "And I can't help but worry about my friend who is suddenly super invested in the life of a woman who is completely off the table as far as dating goes."

"Ah," Joe said with a raise of an eyebrow. "This is about Anna then, is it?"

"Don't get me wrong," Derrick said, raising his hands in front of him. "I like Anna. She's great."

"But?"

"But nothing. That's just it. She's great...and unavailable, which means she's safe. You don't have to put yourself out there for her. You can keep all those walls you've built nicely intact. As long as you have a few women to date here and there, nobody will be none the wiser."

"I'm fine, Derrick," Joe said. "You seriously don't have to worry about me. You're right that I don't want to be in a serious relationship right now. It's only been a little over a year and a half since Merida died. I'm just not ready for that."

"Yeah, but how are you ever going to get in a place to be ready for serious dating if you spend all your time completely focused on a woman you can't have?"

"Look, Anna, Marie, Bryant, and I own a business together," Joe said. "I'll admit that I care about Anna. Just as I care about Marie. But me being vested in their lives has nothing to do with me not being ready to date."

"Forgive me for being hesitant to believe you," Derrick said.

"I guess it doesn't matter if you believe me or not," Joe said. "Anna and I are a team. She's got my back, and I've got hers. That doesn't mean my personal life is suffering because of her."

Derrick shook his head and sighed when the door opened. "I know you can take care of yourself, but you are my oldest friend, Joe. I worry about you."

"I appreciate you more than you know," Joe said. "You're more like my brother than my friend, Derrick. But you don't have to worry about me."

"I wouldn't be a good friend if I didn't," he replied.

Joe shook his head again and stepped out of the elevator with Derrick on his heels. The two walked through the hotel lobby and past the lobby bar. Joe stopped in his tracks when he spotted Anna sitting at the bar. He watched her for a second, Derrick waiting for him a few steps ahead.

When Joe lingered, Derrick glanced at Anna and stepped back in Joe's direction. Turning his attention back to Joe, Derrick whispered, "Keep walking, Joe. Let her be."

Joe frowned. "Something's wrong. She looks upset."

"See, this is exactly what I mean," Derrick said. "She's sitting at the bar having a drink like any normal person. Why in the world would you think something's wrong? She's not your responsibility to fix, Joe."

"Derrick, besides you, she's my best friend," Joe said. "If something's wrong, I want to help her."

"What if helping her is bad for you, Joe?" Derrick asked. "What if you're giving her more than she's giving you?"

"I don't care," Joe said and walked away from him. Behind him, he heard Derrick sigh as he walked into the bar area and took a seat at a small table just inside.

Anna looked up at Joe when he approached and gave him a small smile. "Hey, what are you doing down here?"

"Derrick and I were just about to head out to dinner," Joe said. "I didn't expect to find you down here, though."

Anna sighed and picked up the drink she'd been absent-mindedly sipping on. "I was trying to give Marie some privacy. She and Eddie are checking in with each other."

"I see," Joe said. He looked up at the bartender when he approached and offered him a drink. "Yeah, I'll just have whatever it is she has. Bring her a fresh one, too."

"Thank you," Anna said with a smile. She moved her straw into the fresh drink when the bartender returned and took a sip.

Joe took a drink and wrinkled his nose. "Ugh, what is that?"

Anna laughed. "Strawberry vodka."

"It's so sweet!" Joe said. Anna chuckled when he took another drink. "I guess it's all right."

"Well, if you don't like it," she said, her tone a little sour. "I can drink it for you."

Joe took another drink and studied her. "I think I'd better drink it, so I don't have to carry you back upstairs later."

Anna laughed and stirred her drink with her straw. "Suit yourself. I can always order another."

"So, Marie's talking to Eddie, huh?" Joe asked. "What about you? You talk to Alex yet?"

Anna sighed and took another drink before answering. "Yeah. I called him just after we got back to the room after lunch. We talked for a minute."

"Just a minute?" Joe asked softly.

Anna sighed again. "It was supposed to be for longer than a minute. He was...busy."

"Busy?"

"I don't know," Anna said, a frown crossing her face. "He was supposed to be off today. We should have had more time. He just...he was distracted. I don't know. It was a quick call."

"I'm sorry," Joe said. "I'm sure the next time you chat it will be different."

Anna didn't reply. Joe watched her face as she took another drink and frowned. "What's wrong, Anna?"

"I don't know," she whispered, her voice cracking slightly. "I...Do you think Alex is seeing someone else?"

"Why would he do that, Anna?" Joe said. "He would be crazy."

"I know it sounds crazy," Anna replied and wiped a tear from her cheek. "He just seems distant right now, and I don't know what's going on."

"It doesn't take a scientist to see that he loves you, Anna," Joe said with a frown. "Why would he throw that away?"

"I don't know," Anna said. "I just have an unsettled feeling. Something's off. What do you think I should do?"

Joe shook his head. "Oh, no. Don't you bring me into this. I can't even keep my relationships afloat for longer than a week or two. No way I'm going to take a stroll through yours."

Anna gave him a small smile. "I think you're better at relationships than you think, Joe. You just have to find the right person and be willing to put yourself out there."

"So, what makes you think something's off with Alex right now?"

"Ah, there's Mr. Deflection," Anna said, her smile growing. "I was wondering when he'd show up."

"I have no clue what you are talking about," he replied.

"Mmm-hmm," Anna said. "You just keep on building that wall, Joe. Just don't think some of us can't see through it."

Joe gave her a sideways glance. "Have you been talking to Derrick?"

Anna laughed. "Why would I be talking to Derrick?"

"Just making sure my two best friends aren't conspiring against me."

"Well, I definitely wouldn't be doing that," Anna said. "I promise."

Joe took another drink and watched her pick up her glass, only to set it back down with a sigh. She closed her eyes and rested her forehead against her fingers.

Joe sighed and said, "Anna. Listen. I don't want to get in the middle of your relationship with Alex."

"I know," Anna said. "I'm sorry I tried to drag you into the middle of it."

Joe held up his hand to stop her. "I wasn't finished. I don't want to get into the middle of it. However, if you were Merida and felt how you do right now, I would want just one thing from you."

"And, what's that, Joe?"

"I would want you to talk to me," Joe said softly. "I would want you to tell me how you feel about our relationship."

Anna sighed and looked at the straw between her fingers.

"You know I'm right on this, Anna," Joe said. "Talk to him."

"See," she said, looking at him with a teary smile. "Told you, you weren't bad at keeping relationships alive."

Joe smiled and squeezed her hand. "Trust me on this, Anna. You need to talk to him."

"I will," she replied and nodded toward Derrick at the back of the bar. "You need to go to dinner. Derrick's waiting for you."

"You'll be alright?"

She smiled. "I'll be fine. Thank you."

"You're welcome," Joe said with another smile. "Go get some rest, so we can start figuring out our Melissa problem."

Anna froze and stared off into the distance for a second.

"What?" Joe asked with a confused look.

Anna met his eyes with a big grin. "I think I know how to get our angle on Melissa."

Chapter 15

Joe glared at Anna as she circled the hotel room while gathering her jacket and shoes. She stuck her arms through the sleeves of the jacket and pulled one shoe onto her foot before hopping toward the bathroom as she attempted to attach the other shoe.

"Marie, can I borrow your earrings?" she asked, completely ignoring the answer. She whirled around the room. "Where's my purse?"

Marie shot Joe an annoyed look but picked up the earrings Anna was looking for and handed them to her. Anna put them in while speeding around the room, still gathering things.

"All right," she said. "I have my purse and my phone, of course. If something goes wrong, I'll call."

"You'll call?" Joe asked, his tone sounding angry even to himself. "What do you mean 'you'll call'?"

"Exactly what I said," she replied evenly and stopped to look at him. When he met her gaze with a glare, she put her hands on her hips. "What?"

"You've got to be kidding me," he replied. "You expect us to be all right with you gallivanting out into the night on some solo witch hunt?"

"Why not?" she asked with a frown. "This is the best opportunity we have to get an ear inside Melissa's office."

"We can find another way than you sacrificing yourself," Joe said.

"Joe, we've been trying to figure out another way all day," Anna argued. She threw her hands in the air. "And, if I don't leave right now, we're going to mess around and miss our shot."

"We are rushing into this, Anna," Marie said. "We are going into this blind, and you are going to get hurt!"

Anna rolled her eyes and turned away from them to check her image in the mirror. "I will not get hurt. I'm just going to talk to her at the bar."

"And then what?" Joe asked. "Where does it go from there? Because if you think you're just going to roll around with her and that Chris guy in that limo of his, you have another thing coming."

"You are all overreacting," Anna said. "What harm does it do to go chat with this woman in a bar?"

"The woman is trying to throw Frankie under the bus, Anna," Marie said. "Someone killed Frankie's boss over this. I will not sit here and wait for you not to come back and have to hunt down your body in the morning."

"Marie, that will not happen," Anna replied.

"Damn right, it won't," Joe said. "Cause I'm going with you."

"Uh, no you aren't," Anna argued. "How is that going to work? Remember, I'm supposed to be trying to get her to feel sorry for me. How am I going to do that if I have you there? She will not talk to me."

"We'll do like we did the other night," Joe said, handing her a set of the listening devices they'd used the last time they'd gone to the bar. "I'll be nearby where I can at least hear what's going on."

"You're not coming," Anna said, glaring at him. "That's the last thing I need. You rush in the moment you think something's going south."

Joe laughed. "You think I'm a liability? Are you kidding me?"

"I didn't say that."

"You didn't have to," Joe said. "It was pretty obvious what you meant."

"All right, guys," Bryant interjected. "This isn't helping."

"Yeah," Marie added. "We can't be fighting amongst ourselves if we want to help Frankie."

Anna sighed. "You're right. I'm sorry, Joe."

"Yeah, me too," Joe mumbled. "We just always do everything as a team. I don't feel comfortable with this. It seems reckless."

"So, what do we do, then?" Anna asked. "Nobody has come up with a better plan."

"I still think I should go with you," Joe said. "At least that way someone would have your back if you get into trouble."

"Fine," Anna said. "But I don't want you barging in. You could blow the whole thing out of the water if you appear out of nowhere and then nothing is wrong."

"Well, I'll be listening. How about we come up with a code word? Something you can say that will let me know you need my help."

"All right," Anna nodded. "What do you want that word to be?"

"How about a place?" Marie asked. "Somewhere you haven't been that would make it obvious you weren't using the word on accident."

"I haven't been to Colorado," Anna said with a shrug. "I'm sure I could work that into a conversation on the fly."

"Colorado it is," Joe said. "If you get into trouble and I don't realize it, that's your word."

"Fine," Anna said. "Can we go now? Frankie and Jason said that Melissa gets to the bar right at 5:30 on Mondays. I want to get there before her."

Joe put a pair of the listening devices in his ears and checked to make sure he and Anna could both hear each other before he turned to the others. "Bryant, why don't you come with me? It'll be kind of weird if I'm drinking in a booth by myself. Might be a little conspicuous."

"Wouldn't be the first time you've done that," Bryant said with a smirk.

Joe rolled his eyes. "Yeah, but that wasn't while I was trying to keep a friend from going to jail for murder, either."

"Yeah, yeah, yeah," Bryant said, standing to his feet. "Let me get my coat. Marie, are you going to hang out here?"

"I think I'll go over to Frankie's and keep her company," Marie said. "That way, I can fill her in on any details that pop up. I'll have my phone on me."

"Great," Anna replied. "Can we go now? Or are we going to keep discussing this until the end of time?"

Joe pivoted her direction and returned the frown she was sending him. "The word patience is not in your dictionary, is it?"

"Every second we waste is one second closer to missing this opportunity," she said, her frown deepening. "If we don't walk out that door in about 10 seconds, I'm going by myself."

Bryant chuckled. "Why don't you go, Anna? It probably would be better if we didn't all arrive at the same time."

Anna was gone before Bryant could even finish his sentence. Joe shook his head as he watched her leave.

"Well, Bryant," he said when the door shut. "Are we ready to go too?"

"Right behind you."

Joe called a car for him and Bryant as they rode in the elevator to the lobby. To his relief, it pulled up in front of the hotel just as they were walking out the front door. The brothers said little on the ride to the club and soon found themselves inside.

Joe spotted Anna at the bar but ignored her as they walked past. He and Bryant secured a table nearby where they could somewhat stay hidden while still monitoring Anna. When a server approached, they both ordered drinks and quickly set about watching the door for Melissa.

"How long are we going to wait?" Bryant asked when they'd been waiting for about twenty minutes.

"As long as it takes," Anna whispered into her communication device.

"Eventually, we have to call it a day, Anna," Joe mumbled. "We can't just stay here all night."

Anna ignored him and took another sip of her drink. Joe shook his head at Bryant, who gave him a grin and said, "She's pretty stubborn, Joe. Reminds me of someone else I know."

"I can still hear you, you know," Anna grumbled.

Joe chuckled but grew serious when the door to the club opened and Melissa walked in.

"Showtime," he whispered.

Anna kept her attention on her drink and did a good job looking gloomy when Melissa walked by. Joe sighed in relief when Melissa immediately swept her gaze over Anna and frowned. She sat a few seats away from her and quickly ordered a glass of wine. Anna continued to ignore Melissa, who hadn't taken her eyes off Anna since she first noticed her.

"Come on," Joe whispered after a few minutes. "Do something, Melissa."

As if on cue, Melissa picked up her wine glass and slid down the bar to sit next to Anna. Anna glanced up at her when she approached.

"Hi," Melissa said. "I think I know you. Aren't you Frankie's friend? Anna, wasn't it?"

Anna studied her for a few moments, as if trying to jog her memory. "Oh! You're her HR manager, right? Was it Melissa?"

"That's right," Melissa said. "What are you doing here?"

Anna sighed. "I just needed to get away for a bit."

"Everything all right?"

"Yeah, I'm just having some issues with my boyfriend back home," Anna said with another sigh. "I'm worried something's going on, but I'm stuck here and can't go straighten it out."

"I see," Melissa said. "Men cause trouble, don't they?"

"And sisters," Anna mumbled, a frown crossing her face.

Melissa leaned in closer, her interest piqued. "You're having issues with your sister? Boy-related?"

"No," Anna said with a sigh. "She has a fiancé. I just have this obligation to help her with this case, so I can't go home right now to fix things with my boyfriend."

"Do you want to help your sister with this case?"

Anna sighed again. "I don't know. Frankie is her friend, not mine. I honestly don't know if I believe her story or not."

"You think she's guilty?"

"I don't know what I think," Anna said. "The evidence certainly isn't doing her any favors."

"Asher was such a great guy," Melissa said. "He didn't deserve this."

"You were close with him, weren't you?" Anna asked.

Melissa nodded. "I was. I hate to say it, but I feel that Frankie is responsible for his death."

"You, too, huh?" Anna asked with another sigh. "The longer I look at things, the more convinced I become."

Melissa glanced at her phone and toward the back door before turning her full attention in Anna's direction. She studied her for a few moments before continuing the conversation.

"I think I can help both of us get what we want," Melissa said.

"How's that?"

"Well, you want to get home to your boyfriend, and I want to get justice for Asher."

Anna nodded.

"Easy, Anna," Joe whispered into his microphone.

Anna ran a hand through her hair and tucked a strand behind her ear in response to him. "Sounds like we both want the same thing."

"Good," Melissa said and leaned closer to her. "I have some things that can speed up this case and make it easier to get closure for your sister."

"You mean you have evidence that shows Frankie is guilty?"

"I have something that could sway opinions."

"Where?"

"It's something a partner of mine has," Melissa said, and looked toward the back door. "He's out back if you want to come with me to get it. I'll explain everything about it when we get out there."

"Don't you dare," Joe hissed. "Anna..."

"You want me to go out back with you?" Anna asked, a look of suspicion passing across her face. "That doesn't seem like a good idea."

"It's the only way," Melissa said. "I promise it won't take but a few minutes."

Joe turned his face into his shoulder so he could protest a little more aggressively. "Anna, if you go out that door with her, I swear—"

"Five minutes," Anna said in Melissa's direction, but more to Joe. "I'll give you five minutes. And just know that

I've already sent my location to my partners, so they know where I'm at if something happens to me."

"Oh, heavens, no!" Melissa said. "I promise you we are on the same team here. Five minutes is more than enough time."

Anna and Melissa stood from the bar and began walking toward the back door. Joe glared at Anna when she glanced in his direction, but she ignored him.

When they were out of sight, Joe said into the microphone, "If you don't come back through that door in five minutes, I'm coming to get you."

"Joe, I don't like this," Bryant said, turning in his seat to look at the back door. "This is not good."

Joe ignored him and clicked a few buttons on his phone so he could track Anna's phone location. "I swear, she's going to give me an ulcer."

"Is her phone still back there?" Bryant asked. "I can't hear her anymore."

"Me neither," Joe said. "We probably lost range once she went outside. Her phone is still out there, though."

"What do we do?"

"I started a timer the moment she walked out the door," Joe said, his eyes focused on his phone's screen. "If she's not back in five minutes, we're going out there."

Bryant and Joe sat in tense silence for a few minutes, Joe completely focused on his phone. Finally, he sighed in relief and looked up at Bryant. "Her phone's moving. She's coming back in."

"Finally."

Joe stood to his feet so he could see the back door. When Anna walked around the corner with a handful of papers, a wave of relief flooded over him. She nodded toward the front door, and both he and Bryant followed her. Once they were all outside, she led them to a darkened spot near the side of the building.

"I have a car coming," she said. "We need to get out of here while they are busy."

"That was stupid, Anna," Joe said to her. "What were you thinking?"

"Everything was perfectly fine," Anna whispered. "No way they were going to risk hurting me before they knew if I was on their side or not."

"What did they want?"

"They want me to switch out some documents that were given to Frankie's attorney."

"What type of documents?" Bryant asked.

"A log sheet," Anna said. "An email came from Frankie's computer and the log sheet we have says she wasn't in the office."

"It's a test," Joe said. "They are testing you to see if you are telling the truth."

"I agree," Anna said. "The email they mentioned wasn't that important. But, if they can get me to switch this document, who's to say they won't try something a bit more in the future."

"We certainly can't go about sabotaging our case," Bryant said. "We'll have to discuss this as a team."

"Well, one thing is for certain," Anna said. "We know that Melissa and her buddy Chris will frame Frankie if given the opportunity."

"Just what we needed," Joe said with a groan. "The police and Frankie's employers working against us."

Anna shook her head and pointed at the car that just pulled up at the curb. "That's us. Let's get back to the hotel and get some rest. We can break the news to Marie in the morning. She's going to spend the night with Frankie. Sounded like she could use the company."

Joe followed Anna and Bryant into the car and glanced at the back parking lot and the limo that was parked there. He shook his head. "Let's just hope this doesn't get any more complicated."

Anna followed his gaze and shook her head at the limo, too. "I'm almost starting to think that Frankie was lucky to have gotten away from these people. They are all quick to throw each other under the bus."

Joe shrugged. "Maybe we can use that in our favor."

"That's a good idea," Anna laughed. "Let's just drag everyone into separate rooms and make them rat each other out."

"Wouldn't be the first time that's happened," Joe said with a chuckle.

"Something tells me this won't be that simple," Bryant said.

"Party pooper," Anna said, causing Joe to laugh.

"Don't worry, Anna," Joe replied. "He's just jealous he didn't think of the idea first."

Bryant shook his head at them as they laughed. "You two are ridiculous."

"Maybe so," Joe said with a snicker. "But we've saved your tail before."

"You're never going to let me live that down, are you?"

"Nope!" Anna replied, causing all three of them to break out into laughter.

Chapter 16

Marie took a sip of wine from the glass in her hand and flipped through her phone with her other. When Frankie sighed, she glanced up at her with a frown.

"Are you all right?"

"Yeah," Frankie said with a frown. "I'm just wondering if I'll ever get to go on vacation again."

Marie looked over at the television screen and the vacation show Frankie was watching. They watched the host showcase the beautiful beach resort for a few moments together until Frankie grumbled to herself and changed the channel.

"We'll figure it out, Frankie," Marie said. "And, when it's all over, we'll take a nice vacation together."

"I'm glad you're so optimistic about it," Frankie replied as she mashed the buttons on the remote. After flipping through a few more channels, she sighed and sat the remote on the coffee table. "I'm sorry. You're just trying to help, and I'm making things difficult for you."

"No, you're not," Marie said. "You're frustrated. I get it. I was frustrated too when I was being investigated for that crime earlier this year. It comes with the territory."

"Still, I should at least try to not make things difficult for the one person in my corner."

"Seriously, don't worry about it! How about we do something else? Take your mind off your case?"

"Like what?"

Marie shrugged. "How about we talk about what you've been up to since you moved out here? Outside of work, I mean. Who have you met? What have you been doing?"

Frankie laughed. "There's not much to tell, honestly. It's been all work."

"What about the weekends? What have you been doing? Seen any good movies recently?"

"I went to the aquarium when I first got here."

"There you go!" Marie smiled. "How was that?"

"It's huge," Frankie said. "Tons of people. Lots of fish. I had fun, though."

"Aquarium, check," Marie laughed. "What about the nightlife? Have you been doing anything fun there?"

"Well, let's see," Frankie said. "I have gone out a few times. There are certainly a lot of clubs and bars around. I went with Jason and his wife before the wedding once. I went on a double date with them once as well."

"What did I tell you about dating?" Marie laughed. "You're going to find you a guy down here and never move back!"

"No way," Frankie laughed. "After this, I'm never coming back again! I may never leave the state of Virginia again after I get home."

"Sounds good to me," Marie said. "Hey, do you have any pictures of you at the wedding? That would be fun to look at."

Frankie stood and walked to a bookshelf next to the television. "Yeah, I think I have a pile of pictures here somewhere. Jason got a good deal on them and printed me off a bunch of them." She paused and laughed a bit. "I'm pretty sure he just gave me a full set of their pictures."

"He sounds like he was excited," Marie said with a smile.

"He was," Frankie said as she returned with the pictures. "They had been together since high school, so it was a long time coming."

Frankie handed Marie the pictures, and she began flipping through them. Marie stopped and smiled when she spotted one of Frankie.

"That is a beautiful dress," she said, holding the picture in Frankie's direction. "It looks great on you."

Frankie laughed. "You know, you'd think after all these years of being friends, you would know a picture of me when you saw it."

"What are you talking about?"

"That's not me!"

"What?" Marie frowned and looked at the picture a second time and gasped. "Frankie! This girl could be your sister. She looks just like you."

"I know," Frankie said. "If you don't pay close attention, she does."

"Who is this?"

"That is Eliana Warren," Frankie said. "She's dating a guy Jason and I work with."

Marie looked at the picture again and frowned. "How close are you to this Eliana person, Frankie?"

"Not very," Frankie shrugged. "We've run into each other a few times at work events and such. Why?"

"Any way she might have, I don't know, pretended to be you at some point?"

Frankie froze. "Wait. Are you suggesting that she was the person at the park?"

"That would certainly explain why someone who looked just like you was seen leaving the park that night."

"How would we prove something like that?"

"I don't know?" Marie said, studying the picture a little closer. "Do you have any more of them with her in it?"

"I'm not sure."

"Let's start by going through all these pictures and pulling out the ones that she's in," Marie said. "That's a start at least."

"Give me part of those."

They spent the next several minutes sorting through the pictures, pulling out ones with Eliana. Once they had looked through all the pictures, Marie pulled the stack with Eliana in them closer to her. She started looking through them, only to sigh a few brief moments later.

"I don't know what good this is doing us," she said. "The only thing we can prove is that she looks a lot like you."

"Which doesn't help us that much."

Marie stared at one picture for a few more moments in silence. "We're going to have to talk to her."

"Seriously?" Frankie asked with a frown. "You want to just go ask her if she pretended to be me? Like she's going to admit that!"

"Maybe she will if we can find some proof," Marie said, picking up her phone. "Are you friends with her on any of your social media pages? Let's start there. Maybe there's something we can use."

Frankie jerked her phone into her hand and began thumbing through her pages. When she found the woman's page, she showed the screen to Marie. "This is her."

Marie duplicated the information on her phone and said, "All right. Let's see what we can find."

They spent several more moments thumbing through Eliana's social media pages. After spotting nothing noticeable, Marie sighed and said, "I'm going to check her boyfriend's page. You keep looking at hers."

"Good luck," Frankie said. "I'm certainly not seeing anything in what I've found so far."

"Me neith—" Marie froze, her eyes glued to her screen.

"What?" Frankie asked, leaning toward Marie. "Did you find something?"

Marie took a screenshot of her phone before replying. "Is this your coat, Frankie? Eliana is wearing it in this picture her boyfriend posted on Thanksgiving."

Frankie gasped when Marie turned the screen in her direction. Tears formed in her eyes, and she covered her mouth while nodding. Marie frowned and turned the phone back around.

"We need to document this," she said. She quickly saved the picture on her phone and took multiple screenshots.

"Do you have a pen and paper? We need to write all this information down."

Frankie leaped from the couch and ran to the kitchen for a pen and notepad. Marie spent several minutes documenting the photo and ensuring she had all the information saved on her phone and written down. After she'd finished, she sat back and took a sip of her wine.

"Now what?" Frankie asked. "What do we do now? Should we call the police?"

"We need to go over all this with the team before we involve the authorities," Marie said. "The last thing I want to do is alert Eliana and cause her to delete this photo. We need it to stay online for now."

"What if she deletes it between now and tomorrow?"

Marie shook her head. "I have it saved just in case, and I've taken screenshots that show the timestamp and where the picture was posted. We should be good. Besides, that was posted the same day as the murder, so it's been up for a few days now. It's likely she's completely forgotten about taking it."

"Or doesn't realize her boyfriend posted it."

"Exactly."

"Is this enough, Marie?" Frankie asked quietly. "Is this enough to get the charges dropped?"

"I don't know, Frankie. But it's definitely enough to give Anna and Joe something to work with."

Frankie sighed. "I guess that's a start."

"I told you we'd find something," Marie said with a small smile. "This is just the start. There will be more."

"Until then, I guess we just sit here and drink a bunch of wine and wait for all the right pieces to fall into place?"

Marie smiled, picked up her glass, and held it in Frankie's direction. "At the moment, I say we toast and celebrate the fact that Anna and Joe aren't the only ones on this team who can do a little investigative work."

Chapter 17

Anna peered around Joe's arm at the images he'd pulled up on his laptop when they'd all arrived at Eugene Matthew's office.

"This is huge, Marie," Anna said. She smiled at Frankie when she shifted anxiously in her chair.

"Now, we need to figure out what to do with it," Joe said with a frown. He continued filtering through the pictures and other tabs on his laptop while the others continued the conversation.

"We'll have to get the police involved," Bryant said. "They need to find that coat."

"It would be great if we could chat with her before the police get to her," Anna said. "We need more to go off than just this, and she might have information we could work with."

Eugene had been busily jotting down information on a form but looked up at Anna's comment. "I could request the DA notify us when the police execute the warrant. Not sure if they will honor that request, but I can at least ask."

Joe closed his laptop and leaned back in his chair. "How about Anna and I just go talk to her now?"

"What do you mean, Joe?" Anna asked.

"From what I just saw on her social media page," he said, "she checks in every morning at the same coffee shop after hitting the gym."

"Let me guess," Anna said. "She also checks in at the gym?"

He grinned. "Yep. She just did."

Anna was already on her feet. "Let's go, then."

"We'll get this info to the police and DA right now," Eugene said. "With any luck, they'll exercise a warrant within the hour."

Joe nodded. "We'll make sure we watch her until we hear from you, so she doesn't have time to go get rid of the coat if she still has it."

"Can we go now?" Anna asked.

Joe laughed when she headed to the door without him. "I don't know where you are going. You don't even know where she's at."

"I figured you'd catch up with me eventually," she said with a chuckle.

When they reached the car, Anna climbed in the backseat and Joe flopped down beside Derrick in the front seat. He held his phone in Derrick's direction and grinned.

"Mr. Chauffeur, we need to go to this address now, please."

Derrick looked at the phone in surprise and said, "That didn't take long. You two weren't inside for fifteen minutes."

Anna leaned up between the seats and said, "We decided we needed a coffee break."

Joe grinned back at her. "Anna here spent too much time partying last night and needs a little boost."

Anna rolled her eyes at Joe and said, "Can we get a move on?" To Derrick, she smiled and said, "We're chasing a lead, Derrick. And it appears we are on a bit of a time crunch."

"Ooh, you mean I get to speed?"

"I don't care what you do," Anna said, leaning back in her seat when he put the car in drive. "Just don't get pulled over."

Derrick laughed and sped out of the parking lot in the coffee shop's direction. Joe explained the situation to Derrick as they drove, and Anna anxiously watched the minutes tick by on the car's clock as they drove. Sensing her anxiety, Joe turned around to look at her.

"Stop worrying. We'll get there in time."

Derrick glanced up at her in the rearview mirror. "Yep, GPS says we'll be there in three minutes."

"I just hope we find something when we get there," Anna said. "What's our plan, Joe?"

Joe frowned. "I say we all go in and split up. Derrick, you can sit by the door and block her exit path if she tries to leave."

"That's a good idea," Anna said. "She's probably more likely to talk to you, Joe, so how about you approach her. I'll wait nearby and we can corner her if she tries to get away from you."

Joe raised an eyebrow at her. "Why would she be more likely to talk to me than to you?"

Anna shrugged. "Just act like you're interested in her and she'll stop. Trust me."

Derrick chuckled and leaned in Joe's direction. "She's saying you're attractive if you didn't catch that."

Joe looked in his direction and grinned. "I think she is."

"Stop it," Anna said. "You're being ridiculous. You know what I mean."

Joe laughed. "Yes, I know what you mean. That is probably a good idea."

"Well, I'm glad you both have it all figured out," Derrick said as he pulled into a parking spot. "Because we are here."

Anna and Joe both grew serious as they scoped out the coffee shop. Anna swept her eyes across the street to the gym and watched the door for a few minutes as they got out of the car. Joe flipped through his phone as they walked.

"She hasn't checked in here yet," he whispered as they approached the door. "So, hopefully, that means we are in time."

Anna sighed in relief when they walked inside and found very few other patrons. After a quick look around, she gave Joe a relieved look and whispered, "I don't see her."

"Me either," he whispered back. "Let's get a coffee and split up."

Anna nodded and made an order at the counter after Derrick. After he'd paid for and retrieved his coffee, Derrick headed toward the front door to claim a chair. Just as Anna was picking up her coffee, she heard the bell above the door ring. When she looked up, she spotted Eliana making her way toward the cashier.

Anna glanced at Joe before heading off to the sugar and creamer station near the cashier. Meanwhile, Joe lingered at the counter and put a friendly smile on his face. Eliana smiled at him when he caught her eye.

After Eliana ordered, she stepped closer to Joe to wait for her coffee. He again turned in her direction and smiled.

"I think I know you from somewhere," he said when she smiled back.

"Oh, yeah?" she asked. "Where would that be?"

"You remind me of a friend of mine," he said, his smile widening. "She has a pretty smile, just like yours."

"Really? Who?"

"Her name is Frankie," he said, his smile never wavering. "Frankie Fritts. Do you know her?"

Eliana immediately turned to dart around him, but Anna was there to stop her.

"We just want to talk," she whispered.

Eliana glanced at the door, but when her eyes met Derrick's, who had stood to block the door, she sighed. "Fine. Can I at least get my coffee first?"

Joe picked up her coffee and his and handed her the cup. She glared at him but walked to a table and sat down, Joe and Anna following her.

"What do you want?" Eliana grumbled after taking a sip of her coffee. "I have nothing to tell you."

Anna opened the screen of her phone and pulled up the picture of Eliana in Frankie's coat. She slid it across the table silently and waited for all the pieces to fall into place in Eliana's mind.

"Where did you get this picture?" Eliana asked.

"Your boyfriend posted it," Joe replied.

"God, he's an idiot," she grumbled as she gazed at the picture.

"Please talk to us, Eliana," Anna said. "Frankie is a good person. She doesn't deserve to go to jail for a murder she didn't commit."

"And, I do?" Eliana asked. "If this gets out, they'll think I did it instead of her."

"It's already out," Anna said. "The lawyers have this photo and know when it was taken. They know this is her coat."

"If you help us, you will only help yourself," Joe added.

Eliana sighed and took a sip of her coffee. When she sat it back down, she looked up at them with tears in her eyes. "He's my ex."

"You broke up?" Anna asked. "When?"

"Just this weekend," Eliana replied. "He has a gambling problem. Couldn't ever seem to climb his way out of it."

"Did that have to do with the picture?" Joe asked.

Eliana nodded. "I was just trying to help him. I thought if I could just get him out of the hole he had dug, things would get better."

"I'm guessing they didn't?" Anna asked.

Eliana shook her head. "It was just supposed to be a simple job. Nobody was supposed to get hurt. At least that's what Rob told me when he got me involved."

"What happened, Eliana?"

"That's just it," she said. "Nothing. Nothing at all happened. I was told to go to that bridge in the park that night and pretend like I was Frankie. Rob wanted me to tell the guy I had found something about that account we had talked about and pass a manilla envelope off to him. He said to tell him I was scared to bring it into the office, which was why I wanted to meet him at the park."

"And, you did that?"

"No! He never showed up. I swear!"

Anna and Joe exchanged a look.

"What did you do with the envelope, Eliana?" Joe asked, leaning forward in his chair a bit.

She hesitated.

"Eliana, I promise you we are the ones to trust in all this," Anna said. "Sorting this out mess will be the best option for everyone, including you."

Eliana sighed and reached for a bag she had sat on the floor beside her when she sat down. "After hearing that someone had killed the guy, it terrified me to do anything with it or let it out of my sight, so I've been carrying it around with me."

She slid the envelope across the table to them. Anna picked it up but didn't open it. "Do you know what's in here?"

"No," Eliana said. "He instructed me not to look at it. Just to hand it over to the guy that was killed. I never opened it."

"What about Frankie's coat? Do you still have that too?"

"It's at my apartment," Eliana sighed. "I was terrified after I heard the news. I didn't know what to do, and once I'd broken it off with Rob, I didn't have any communication with anyone anymore. I didn't know what to do!"

"Did you break it off with Rob because of this?" Anna asked.

Eliana nodded. "I just couldn't believe that he had gotten me in the middle of a murder investigation. And, to top it all off, I caught him at the casino the night after the murder. I just couldn't take it anymore."

"I'm so sorry, Eliana," Anna said.

"Love makes us do some crazy things sometimes," Eliana said and wiped a tear from her cheek. "I just wish I'd seen how stupid I was being before it went this far."

Joe gave her a comforting look. "I'm afraid the police are going to want to know all this information, Eliana. They might want you to testify even."

Eliana sighed and nodded. "I have to do what's right. I can't keep protecting Rob. I'll tell them what I know."

"Thank you for your help, Eliana," Anna said. "We'll get out of here and let you enjoy the rest of your day."

Joe glanced at his phone and then at Anna. "Just so you know, Eliana. It looks like the police are searching your apartment right now."

Anna picked up her phone and read the text Marie had sent her. "Yeah, looks like they are looking for the coat at your place."

Eliana closed her eyes and sighed again. "It's in the front closet. I put it in a black trash bag and stuffed it in the corner."

"Thank you," Anna said softly before sending a text back to Marie. "Hopefully, with this, they won't tear your apartment apart. I'm sorry about that."

"It is what it is," she said. "Is there anything else I need to do right now? Just wait for the police to want to talk?"

"It would benefit you to go to the station to make a statement," Joe said. "Get everything out on the table so they know about it all."

"I can do that," Eliana said. "I don't have to work today."

Anna looked over at Joe and stood to her feet. "Again, we can't thank you enough for helping us today."

"I didn't have a choice, did I?"

"Still, it takes a lot of bravery to admit to being involved in something like this," Anna said.

Joe stood to his feet and stepped away from the table. "Yes, thank you, Eliana. We'll leave you in peace now."

Eliana picked up her coffee and took another sip. Joe and Anna walked away from her, the manila envelope in their possession. Derrick followed them out the door, but they all waited until they were back in the car before speaking.

"Man, that was intense!" Derrick said. "I thought my heart was going to beat out of my chest there for a minute."

"All in a day's work for us," Joe said with a grin. "Anna, you got that envelope."

"Yep, I'm going to figure out what's in it right now," she replied, already pulling out the documents inside.

"What's the verdict?" Derrick asked after she spent too long looking at the document. "Or are you just going to keep us waiting?"

"It looks like it might be evidence that implies Melissa was behind the embezzling," Anna said. "They also implicated Asher in these documents. I'm not sure what to make of it."

She handed it to Joe in the front seat and he frowned as he looked it over. "If I didn't know better, I'd say this is a threat. They were trying to scare Asher enough to get him to quit digging into the account and the embezzling."

"That's what I was thinking as well," Anna said. "I'm sure it's fabricated."

"I agree," he said, looking at it again. "Whoever was involved in this embezzling must have created this to get Frankie's boss off their trail so they could sweep the misconduct under the rug and not receive any penalties or discipline from the board of directors."

"Then why murder him?"

"That's the million-dollar question."

Chapter 18

Anna was out of the car and heading back inside the attorney's office before Derrick could even turn off the engine. Joe chuckled a bit when he had to jog to catch up with her.

"You in a hurry all of a sudden?"

She slowed down and said, "We need to get in here and get copies of these documents before the police come and take them away."

"You know they have to give us a copy, right?"

"Yeah, but I'd much prefer to have a copy now so we can start working on it and not have to wait for them to give us a copy."

Joe laughed. "Well, if we get in here and someone tries to take those papers away from you, I promise to hold them off until you can get a copy."

"I'm going to hold you to that," Anna said with a laugh of her own.

Joe pulled open the door to the office and Anna sped through. She stopped the moment she found a copy machine, ignoring the quizzical look of the employee sitting at the desk next to it. Tapping her foot, she frowned at the machine when it pulled the pages through the system and only relaxed when the last page shot out into the bin.

"Feel better?" Joe asked with another chuckle.

"Yes. Yes, I do."

"Let's get this on back to Frankie and Eugene so she can tell us what we're dealing with."

They walked through the office and found the others in the conference room where they'd left them. Anna handed the original papers to Eugene and laid the other copies on the table in front of Frankie. Frankie immediately picked them up and frowned at them as she read through the information.

"I'll go get these over to the DA," Eugene said and stood to leave the room.

Anna let Frankie look through the copies for a few moments before speaking.

"What is all this, Frankie?" Anna asked. "Eliana said her boyfriend instructed her to pretend like she was you and give these pages to Asher. What's on them?"

"I agree with your assessment of it implicating Melissa," Frankie said. "It wouldn't be a stretch to include Asher in it as well. This also attempts to explain where my missing account went."

Bryant leaned forward in his chair. "What do you mean?"

"So, the initial problem was I had invoices that were being paid to an account that suddenly disappeared," Frankie replied. "That isn't supposed to happen. We're supposed to keep track of everything we spend. There are rules in place for a reason."

"Since the account disappeared, you worried that someone in the company was sending money where it shouldn't go?" Anna asked.

Frankie nodded. "It was too early for me to say there was embezzling going on, but I had my suspicions."

"Was it possible that someone simply made a mistake?" Joe asked.

Frankie looked up at him. "I hoped that was the case, but we needed to make sure. That's why I took the problem to Asher, so he could dig into it."

"If someone got Eliana to play the role of Frankie," Anna said to Joe. "I would assume that he dug into the issue, and someone noticed him poking around."

Joe nodded. "I agree. It appears they wanted to send him off course or something. Get him to quit looking, maybe."

"I would quit looking too if the information I was being given started implying that I had done something illegal," Frankie muttered.

"You know," Anna said. "This explains why they went to all the trouble of making it easy to get caught."

"How's that?" Joe asked.

"Let's look at it from the beginning," Anna continued. "Frankie runs into this invoice issue that uncovers a situation they had been trying to keep under wraps from the feds and the board of directors."

Joe nodded. "The embezzling. It probably terrified Chris to think the board of directors would throw him under the bus for that. Fire him. Get charges thrown at him. Something."

"Exactly," Anna said. "So, he puts in place strategies for keeping it from happening again."

"I would agree with that," Bryant said. "Eugene's team has been going over and over everything the company gave us, and there is no evidence that the embezzling is still going on. It's almost like finding this invoice was the trigger to make it stop."

"See, so Chris gets the embezzling to stop," Anna said. "Maybe he is secretly trying to figure out who did it so he can eliminate them. But, whatever the case, he got it to stop."

"At least for now," Joe said. "And that is assuming it isn't him behind it."

"Let's assume he isn't involved for now," Anna said. "He's trying to cover it up, but this intern comes along and blows the whole thing out of the water. Finds this invoice and starts an internal investigation."

"Well, he can't have that," Joe said with a nod. "So, he needs to get them to stop."

"And what better way to get someone to stop investigating than to throw shade at the woman he's sleeping with," Anna said. "Of course, you would also want to make the person investigating think *they* might get in trouble themselves."

"Bingo," Joe said. "Investigation is over."

"But not without some assurances," Anna said.

"Ah, I see," Joe said. "He wanted a fallback. Someone to blame in case it all went south, and it still got found out."

Anna nodded. "So, he got a Frankie look-alike and had her deliver the threat. Also made sure they saw her on security cameras. Just in case."

"Great," Frankie groaned. "So, I was the scapegoat after all."

"And we are sure this report is implicating Melissa?" Bryant asked. "I just want to make sure we aren't reading too much into this."

"I don't believe there is any other way to look at it," Frankie said. "This report includes a lot of invoices, including the one that got me started on this journey, that don't belong in here. This is Melissa's travel and corporate spending account. None of these things should be in there."

"Wait," Marie said. "Where does the money go that goes into this account?"

"It's a reimbursement account," Frankie said. "HR sets up all those accounts for the employees. We reimburse the money in this account back to the employee."

"But none of those invoices should be items they reimburse Melissa for?" Anna asked with a frown. "How in the world would she expect to get away with that?"

"I don't know if it's real," Frankie said. "There are some inconsistencies with some data and coding information. This report is probably fabricated."

"But some of the information is real?" Joe asked. "Enough to where Asher might have believed that his girlfriend was in danger?"

"Possibly," Frankie continued.

Anna sat down in a chair next to Frankie and looked at the document over her arm. Joe sat on the other side of Frankie and did the same. After several minutes of silence, they looked across the table at each other.

"I'd be willing to bet that Eliana's boyfriend isn't involved in all this," Anna said.

Joe nodded. "We can't rule him out, but I'd agree with that. He just had a girlfriend who looked a lot like Frankie."

"And a gambling problem, which made him buyable."

"Everyone has a price," Marie mumbled with a sigh.

"Exactly," Anna said, looking across the table at her sister. "So, they pay the guy's gambling debt, and he sends his girlfriend off to deliver this to Asher."

Anna turned to Frankie. "Frankie, do you think this would be enough to scare off Asher?"

"He seemed to care about Melissa," Frankie said, looking over the papers again. "Rumor was she had even tried to get him to let her leave her husband for him, but he wouldn't let her. Didn't want her to go through a messy divorce. Plus, her husband is loaded, so she is in a great financial situation."

"Getting arrested for embezzling would certainly put a damper on your financial situation," Joe said. "Probably wouldn't make the husband thrilled either."

"He would have been super angry," Frankie said. "I only met the guy a few times, but he seemed like a no-nonsense kind of guy. Didn't seem to have a humorous bone in his body."

"This is all a fascinating theory," Bryant said. "But I think we are completely disregarding something. If they sat all this up to scare off Asher, why go through the trouble of killing the guy?"

"Yeah," Marie said, folding her arms across her chest. "Didn't you say that Eliana never even saw Asher that night?

Why would they kill him before they even attempted to let their plan work itself out?"

"Maybe someone got impatient?" Frankie asked. "Or worried that it wouldn't be enough to throw Asher or me off the trail."

Anna frowned. "I suppose that would explain things, but that still seems a little strange. They paid Eliana's boyfriend to do a job and then didn't give him the chance to make it happen."

"Besides, that is putting even more people on the playing board," Joe said. "Now, you have Eliana and her boyfriend, as well as Frankie, Jason, and whoever else knew about this situation. Asher probably talked to someone about this when he was looking around. No way these guys are going to risk that much exposure just to commit murder."

"Not to mention the fact that killing Asher has now brought about a whole other type of investigation into the company," Anna said. "Now, not only are the authorities clued in to the possibility of some shady accounting work, but they are investigating a murder of an employee that was potentially committed by another employee."

"That is so much attention being thrown at the company," Bryant said. "It's hard to believe they would have done that on purpose."

"What about this theory?" Anna said after they sat quietly for a few moments. "They put all this into play just like we said. But, somehow, something changed. Maybe Asher did something or asked someone else to be at the meeting with him."

"That person could have snapped," Joe mused. "Or maybe someone was watching over the proceedings of the meeting, but Asher spotted him."

"Many things could have happened if that were the case," Anna said. "He could have spotted the person's car in the parking lot and went on a hunt for them. Or come in a direction the killer wasn't expecting."

"Hell, a mugger in the park may have killed him, for all we know," Joe said.

Anna sighed and sat back in her chair. "I'd say we still have more questions than we have answers."

"We know one thing," Joe said. "Melissa and whoever created these documents...I'm assuming it's Chris, by the way...will go the extra mile to make sure Frankie looks guilty."

"That's right," Anna said. "What are we doing with those logs she wanted me to switch out?"

Marie looked at Bryant. "We talked it over with Mr. Matthews and decided that we should roll the dice with it."

"We aren't using it as factual evidence, but we are logging everything that she gives us and keeping detailed reports about the things she told you," Bryant said. "Mr. Matthews has tentatively reached out requesting specific information from the company that would imply that you did your job, Anna."

"I see," Anna said. "So, Melissa is going to get notified of that request and know that it means that I switched out the logs."

Bryant nodded. "Which hopefully will spur her to trust you even further."

"You just need to be careful with her, Anna," Marie said. "We can't jeopardize Frankie's case or make evidence get thrown out because they think you are meddling with things."

Anna nodded. "I will run everything through the team beforehand. I promise I won't do anything that we don't agree on first."

"And I'll be right there with you to make sure you stay safe," Joe said. "No running off on your own with her, you understand me?"

Anna laughed and pretended to salute him with her hand. "Yes, sir!"

"I'm serious, Anna," he replied with a frown.

"I know," Anna said. Her phone made a sound, and she looked down at the screen. "Speaking of which, Melissa wants me to meet her again tonight at the bar."

"Probably wants to continue her mission to ruin my life," Frankie said.

"I won't let her, Frankie," Anna said. "I promise."

Before they could talk more, Eugene walked back into the conference room and sat down. They all turned his direction in anticipation of whatever he'd learned.

"Well, I got those over to the DA," he said. "Sounds like they already picked up Ms. Warren and her boyfriend. She's being a lot more cooperative than he is."

"Did he tell them anything?" Anna asked.

Mr. Matthews shook his head. "From what they are gathering so far, he knew very little. They conducted everything over email. He thought he was corresponding with his direct supervisor, but the email is a burner one and the IP address doesn't match up."

"So, they know the supervisor wasn't in on it?" Joe asked.

"The supervisor had to have surgery a couple of weeks ago and one email supposedly from him came while he was in the middle of it."

"Can't very well send an email when you are in surgery," Anna said. "I guess that rules him out."

"So, back to square one, then?" Frankie asked with a sigh.

"Not exactly," Eugene said. "This is enough to throw doubt on your involvement in this murder. I'm going to meet with the DA and see about getting the charges dropped. I also have a bit of other news to go along with this."

"Oh, what would that be?" Bryant asked.

"Ms. Eliana's boyfriend admitted to being the one who stole the coat from the cleaners," he said. "I had my team go through the security footage, and based on the pictures I saw of the guy, he matches the general description of the thief."

"That's great news," Anna said. "I'm also quite pleased that Joe and I don't have to go through all that footage now."

"You and me both," Joe said. "So, Rob broke into the cleaners, stole the coat, and sent his girlfriend off to pretend like she was Frankie on the night of the murder. I think that throws a big wrench in the believability factor of Frankie being the murderer."

"I would say so," Eugene said. "Which is why I'm hoping we can get them to drop these charges."

"That would be such a relief!" Frankie said. "What can I do to help?"

"You can go home and write up a timeline for your evening on the night of the murder," Eugene replied. "We may not get you a verifiable alibi, but we can at least have something solid to show the DA."

"I can do that," Frankie nodded.

"I need to get back to the hotel so I can prepare for my meeting with Melissa," Anna said. "Joe, do you want to come with me? We can get some food and go over the plan for tonight?"

"Sounds like a good plan to me," Joe said.

Marie turned to Bryant. "Do you want to come with Frankie and me to get a timeline together?"

"Are you sure I don't need to go keep our siblings out of trouble?" he asked with a chuckle before turning to look at Joe. "Can the two of you promise to come back in one piece tonight?"

"And preferably in clean clothing?" Marie asked with a chuckle of her own.

"You know," Anna said, turning to Joe. "Maybe we should start invoicing the office for all the clothes we ruin on our outings together."

"You're right, Anna!" he replied. "Since I started this job, I've ruined more pairs of jeans than I have in my entire life."

"Not gonna happen," Marie said. "You two are on your own when it comes to clothing."

"Yeah, your inability to stay out of messes is not our problem," Bryant said with another laugh.

Joe looked at Anna and grinned. "Well, it was worth a try, at least."

Chapter 19

Her apartment's front lock had barely clicked open before Frankie was slinging the door open and whirling into her apartment. She tossed her coat and bag on the floor near the front closet and nearly sprinted to a small desk in the living room.

After grabbing a handful of pens and notepads, she trotted to the kitchen table and pulled a chair out so hard it fell over. With a frown, she righted the chair and sat down, the pens spilling onto the floor.

When she sighed, Marie chuckled softly and said, "Let me help you there, Frankie."

Marie followed her friend to the table and picked up the pens. Bryant took a chair across from them and pulled a notepad in front of him. Once she'd picked up all the loose pens, Marie laid them down on the table and sat in the chair next to Frankie.

"You know you can relax a bit, right?"

"I know," Frankie said with a frown. "But I'm so worked up right now that I just want to get all this down on paper."

"I just don't want you to rush through anything," Marie said. "We want to have the timeline as detailed as possible."

Frankie picked up a pen and situated a notepad in front of her. "I understand. Where do we start?"

"How about starting at the beginning of the day you realized you were in trouble. The Wednesday before Thanksgiving, right?" Marie said. "What happened when you went into the office that morning?"

"Well, that's when I first got official confirmation that there was an investigation going on," Frankie said. "Melissa pulled me into her office with a member from the legal department. They questioned me about my involvement in the embezzling and implied there was some type of investigation starting up."

"Did you get much information from them during that meeting?"

"Not really. I was more surprised and confused by the allegations," Frankie said. "They gave me very little information, and I defended myself the entire time."

"The police probably think that interview prompted you to send Asher the email you supposedly sent," Bryant said. He pulled some papers out of a bag he had laid on the table. He looked them over for a few moments before continuing. "It looks like it was sent later that day from your computer and email address."

"When does it say I sent it?"

"It says you sent it at 1:02 on Wednesday," Bryant said after peering down at the report in his hand.

"I was at lunch around that time," Frankie said. "I remember because I left later than normal that day. I was so stressed out from the meeting and had been gathering all my evidence into one location that I lost track of time."

"What time did you leave and where did you go?" Marie asked, jotting down a note on her notepad.

"I think I left around 12:45," Frankie said. "It was nice out, so I walked down to the sandwich shop on the corner. It was probably a ten-minute walk, and I had to have waited for at least five minutes before I got to order."

"Do you have a receipt?" Bryant asked. "That would be super helpful in narrowing down the time."

"I have a habit of keeping all my receipts," Frankie said. "I clean them out of my purse every week."

She got up to retrieve her purse and quickly brought it back with her. After a few minutes of sorting out her receipts, she smiled and handed the slip of paper across the table to Bryant.

"I checked out at 1:05 PM," she said. "No way I could have made it from the office to the sandwich shop in three minutes."

"That's a great start," Marie said, writing down more information. "Hopefully, the restaurant will have security cameras where we can verify that you were there during that time."

"All right, so we've determined that I wasn't at the office to send the email. Now what?"

Marie frowned at Bryant. "Something's been bugging me about that email. Why would you or whoever sent that email want Asher to meet at some obscure time of night in the middle of a deserted park?"

"The email says that 'Frankie' had found something she needed to share with Asher but was nervous about bringing it into work," Bryant said. "It says that she wants to meet him the following evening and would text him to let him know a time."

"And he received a text from my phone number?"

Bryant nodded. "There was a text that supposedly came from your number that asked him to meet you in the park. It said that it was life or death and involved Melissa."

"I didn't send that text!" Frankie jerked up her phone and looked through her sent messages. "There's nothing on my phone like that at all!"

"How in the world would they have pulled that off?" Marie asked.

"I suppose they could have hacked her number or something, but I'm not sure," Bryant said with a shrug.

"I guess. Let's go back to our timeline for now," Marie said. "We'll catch back up to the text. So, after lunch on Wednesday, what happened, Frankie?"

"Nothing remarkable. I went back to work and finished out my day," she said. "I didn't see Melissa again, nor did anyone further mention the investigation. I was a ball of nerves when I finally got out of there for the day."

"Security shows that you left sometime around 5:30 that day," Bryant said after shuffling through the papers and looking at a time log. "Does that sound about right?"

Frankie thought for a second and then nodded. "I'm sure that was probably accurate. I tried to visit Mr. Matthews after work that day, but he was already gone. His receptionist said he normally leaves around 5:30. She gave me one of his cards. The one I had in my purse that I gave you, Marie, remember?"

Marie nodded. "I remember. After you left his office, what did you do?"

"I picked up some dinner after that and headed home."

"What time did you eat and where?" Marie said as she wrote several more notes on her timeline.

Frankie fished through her pile of receipts again and handed Marie the dinner receipt. Marie glanced at it and jotted down the information she found there.

"I ate dinner, took a bath, and tried to distract myself by watching a movie before going to bed," Frankie said.

"Did you make any phone calls or send any texts that night?"

"Not that I know of."

"Great," Marie said. "So now we're up to the morning of the murder. What time did you wake up?"

"Well, if you remember, I had plans to head your direction for the day," Frankie said. "But with the investigation and how stressed I was, I called you to cancel. Do you remember what time that was?"

Marie pulled out her phone and frowned. "Let me check." She spent a few minutes searching back through her call logs. When she found the right date, she looked up and said, "You called me a little before 7. I remember you were distracted and upset but didn't tell me much then. I remember telling Anna that I was worried and would call to check in on you later."

"Which you did," Bryant said. "Just before you got to our house."

"She called me about half an hour after I spoke with the FBI agent," Frankie said. "He showed up at my apartment and wanted to question me. It was then that I got worried. He accused me of being involved in the embezzling. Told me they would find evidence to prove I was involved."

"I'm so sorry they blindsided you with that," Marie said. "They were probably trying to put you on edge."

"Well, he did! I could barely function after he left," Frankie said.

"What did you do the rest of the day?" Bryant said. "Let's walk through it and see if we can figure out an alibi."

Frankie shrugged. "I'm afraid there isn't that much to walk through, honestly. I spent the day trying to distract myself from my pending jail sentence."

"Humor me."

"All right, I ate lunch here and caught up on some housework," Frankie said. "I finished up cleaning in the early evening and sat down to watch a movie."

"Nothing too exciting there," Marie said. "You didn't leave at all during that time?"

"Nope," Frankie said, watching Bryant jot down notes. She waited for him to catch up to her before continuing. When he looked up, she frowned and said, "Let's see. After the movie, I realized I needed to run some laundry."

"Did you do that in the apartment?" Marie asked. "I haven't seen a washer and dryer in here."

"I have to do that in the basement," Frankie said. "It's included in the rent."

"Wow, that's a nice perk," Marie said. "Anna and I had to buy our machine for our apartment. Cost a fortune."

"Yeah, I'm certainly glad I didn't have to mess with that, considering I'm just going to be here a year," Frankie said.

"My work sets up this place for the interns. We are just responsible for the rent. I guess the apartment managers want to stay on their good side, so they throw in the laundry usage since they don't have washers and dryers in the apartments."

"So, you just go down there and use them whenever you want?" Marie asked. "That sounds risky for the apartment complex. How do they control who uses it?"

"Yeah, how do they stop people who don't live here from using the machines?" Bryant asked.

Frankie laughed. "I have a key. It works like a hotel room key. When I go in, it tracks..."

Her eyes widened as her words trailed off.

Marie gasped. "Frankie!"

Sensing their excitement, Bryant stopped them from continuing. "Slow down, ladies. Let's not rush into this. First, how does it track you?"

Frankie cleared her throat and took a deep breath. "I was told that there is a database that our key swipes go into when we use the laundry. Plus, they have cameras in there so they can verify we aren't letting others use the facility."

"All right," Marie said. "So, what time did you start your laundry?"

"I would say around 4," Frankie said.

"That's entirely too early to give you a solid alibi," Marie said. "You would have finished in plenty of time to get to the park."

"I didn't stay in the laundry room to wait," Frankie said. "I had a few loads to run. Three, I think. While one was washing, I came back to the apartment and paid some bills and such."

"All right, so what time did you head back to the laundry room?"

"Around 5," Frankie continued. "I started the second load of laundry and put the first in the dryer."

Bryant added to their timeline and looked up at Frankie. "Then what happened?"

"I did a few more errands around the apartment and headed back down to the laundry room around 6:30 to pick up the first dried load and start the final one."

"Did you take the load back to your apartment, then?"

"Yep. I watched about an hour's worth of TV while I folded the load and put it away. Then, I headed down to move the last load and pick up the second."

"You fold that one too?" Bryant asked. "What time did you get done with it?"

"I decided I was hungry, so I dropped that load off at the apartment and went to dinner."

"Receipt?"

Frankie fished around in her pile of receipts and handed it to Bryant. He looked down at it before writing on the paper.

"Did you eat at the restaurant, Frankie?" Marie asked. "What time did you get back home?"

"Yep, I ate there and finished up around 8," she replied. "I was home by 8:30."

"Shoot," Marie groaned. "That's still time for you to have gotten to the park."

"What about that third load of laundry, Frankie?" Bryant asked after he had caught up with the timeline. "It was still in the dryer, wasn't it?"

"As soon as I got home from dinner, I turned on a new movie and folded the second load," Frankie said. "I wound up falling asleep and forgot about that load of laundry."

"Did you ever go get it?" Marie asked.

"I woke up just as the movie was ending," Frankie said. "I was just going to go to bed, but I tripped over the laundry basket, and it reminded me about the load I had left in the dryer."

"Please tell me you went to get it?" Marie pleaded.

"Sure did," Frankie said with a grin. "I remember glancing at the clock just as I was leaving the apartment, and it was about five before 11."

"What time was it when you got back home?" Bryant asked.

"By the time I got all the way downstairs, loaded up my laundry, and made it back to my apartment, it was 11:20."

"Well, that does it then," Bryant said, sitting back with a grin. "The coroner put Asher's death around 11:30 that night. No way you could have gotten to the park from your laundry room in ten minutes."

"We need those records," Marie said. "How do we get them?"

"They told me to talk to the security manager on the first floor whenever I have a problem," Frankie said. "I would assume he could get them."

"You think he's there now?" Marie asked. "Looks like it's about 3."

"I don't think he leaves until 5," Frankie said. "You want me to go see?"

"Marie, why don't you go with her?" Bryant said. "I would say we could all go, but I'd hate to overwhelm the guy and make him not want to help us."

"I see," Marie said with a smirk. "Play the female card, right?"

Bryant shrugged. "I'm just saying he will probably feel more intimidated if I show up too."

"Yeah, that is three to one," Frankie said. "Well, let's get going, Marie. I'd hate for him to leave early, and we miss him."

Marie nodded and followed Frankie into the hallway outside the apartment. Together, they walked to the elevator and waited in silence for it to arrive. Frankie took a deep breath before stepping inside when the doors opened.

Marie spent the time in the elevator staring at the floor and counting the tiny dings the elevator made as they passed a floor. As much as she tried to avoid it, they only worked up her heart rate that much more. Finally, the elevator reached the right floor, and the doors opened.

Frankie pointed down a hallway and lead Marie toward the security manager's office, which held a small desk behind a wall and a clear divider with a hole separating them. Frankie sighed when she saw the empty office, but quickly pressed a button on the wall. Marie sighed in relief when the manager sped into the room a few moments later.

"What can I do for you, ladies?" he asked with a smile.

"I need your help," Frankie began. "I live in apartment—"

"14 A, right?" he interrupted. "I remember you. Frankie, isn't it?"

"That's right," Frankie said with a smile. "I'm afraid I'm in a bit of a jam."

"You're telling me," the manager said with a frown. "Caused quite a ruckus here in the past few days."

"I'm sorry about that," Frankie said. "It's all a big misunderstanding. I promise. And actually, you can help me get rid of the problem."

"How's that?"

"The night I was supposedly doing what they've accused me of doing, I was here."

"I'm not following how I can help."

"I was doing my laundry," Frankie said, sounding exasperated because of his constant interruptions. "I couldn't have been there, because I was doing my laundry."

"Ah, and you want me to look at the laundry room swipes."

"Exactly."

"What day was it?"

"It was on Thursday. Thanksgiving."

The man turned away from her and walked to a computer on the desk behind him. After clicking through the screens for a few minutes, he frowned. "This is odd. The entire record for Thanksgiving isn't here."

"What do you mean?" Frankie said, her eyes filling with tears. "How can that be?"

"I don't know," he said. "I'm going to have to look into it. It should be right here."

"What about the security footage?" Marie said. "Didn't you say there were cameras in the laundry room, Frankie?"

"Ah, that's right!" the security manager said. "Let me check those out."

Marie squeezed Frankie's hand while they waited for him to click through a few more screens on his computer. She grimaced when she spotted the frown returning to his face.

"So strange..."

"What's strange?"

"That entire day is missing, too!"

"Where could it have gone?"

"I have no idea," he said, his attention on the computer screen. "I'll have to look into that too."

Frankie sighed and stepped away from the window. Marie gave her a small smile before reaching into her pocket.

"Here," she said to the manager. "If you don't mind, I want to leave my card with you. That way you can call me the moment you find out something about either the key swipes or the surveillance footage."

The manager walked to the window and picked up her card. "Trust me. I will sort this out. I don't tolerate my security measures failing or being altered. If I can't figure out what happened to those files, I will figure out why they are missing."

"Thank you," Marie said and smiled at him before turning to walk away. She caught up with Frankie at the elevators and quietly pushed the button to head back upstairs. When they stepped inside and the doors closed them in, Frankie sank to the floor of the elevator in tears.

Marie sat down beside her and put her arms around her. "It's ok, Frankie."

"How are we going to deal with this, Marie?" Frankie said between her tears. "Someone is trying to set me up. How are we going to fight it?"

"We'll figure it out," Marie said, trying to convince herself as much as Frankie. "We won't stop until we figure this out. I promise."

Chapter 20

Anna sighed and flipped through a few screens on her phone before dropping it in her lap and staring out the window. Within a mile, she'd picked it back up and was flipping through it again. She ignored Derrick's quizzical look in the rearview mirror, but couldn't avoid Joe.

"You tried calling him again, didn't you?" he asked when she put the phone down again.

"Yeah. He didn't answer." She went back to staring moodily out the window.

"Maybe he's busy?" Derrick suggested.

"He's supposed to be off work today," she replied and picked up her phone again.

"Hmm," Joe said.

"Hmm, what?" Anna asked, a frown floating across her face. "You think something's going on? Should I be worried?"

Joe chuckled. "You are reading way too much into my 'hmm.' I was just acknowledging that I was listening."

Anna sighed again and laid her phone down. "I don't know what it is. I don't usually worry like this, but something feels off."

Derrick winked at Joe in the mirror. "Maybe he's—"

"Don't you dare," Joe said with a frown. "Don't start putting ideas in Anna's head. I'm sure it's nothing, Anna. He's probably just busy."

"Maybe," Anna said with another frown. "It just feels like we aren't spending that much ti—"

She sighed before starting again. "I'm sorry. You two don't want to hear all this. This is not your problem."

"Seriously, Anna," Joe said. "I'm sure it's nothing. But you're worried enough about it that I think you should talk to him when you get home."

"I agree," Derrick said. "I'm sure talking it out will fix everything."

"I hope so," Anna said and looked at her phone again.

"How about you put all that in the back of your mind now, though, Anna?" Joe said softly. "You need to be in the right headspace for this mission we're on. Remember?"

Anna tucked her phone away in her purse and nodded. "You're right. I can't be messing up this case for Frankie because I'm too busy thinking about my stuff to help her."

"Good thing," Derrick said. "Because we are here."

He parked in a lot near the bar and the three of them got out of the car. Anna looked around the parking lot and at the building before turning to Joe. "Why don't you two get settled somewhere, and I'll wait a couple of minutes before I come in?"

"Sounds like a plan."

Joe and Derrick quickly made their way into the bar, and Anna waited a couple more minutes before following them. Once inside, she made eye contact with them before claiming a pair of stools at the bar. When the bartender approached, she ordered two glasses of wine and turned toward the door to watch for Melissa.

Within ten minutes, Melissa was speeding through the door. She caught Anna's eye the moment she entered but did not return her smile. With a few furious steps, Melissa made her way to the stool beside Anna and sat down. Before addressing her, Melissa took a big drink from the wine glass Anna had ordered her and signaled the bartender to bring her another one.

"Did you know all this when we talked the other day?" Melissa demanded. "About all that money that supposedly moved through my reimbursement account?"

"Of course not," Anna said. "That was something the others ran across while they were investigating. I had no way of knowing any of that was going to come to light."

Melissa sighed and took another drink from her wineglass. "I'm sorry. I'm just stressed out. They searched everything. My office. My home. I'm just overwhelmed."

"I'm sorry, Melissa," Anna said. "If it makes you feel any better, I don't believe that you killed Asher."

Melissa's eyes filled with tears. "Of course, I didn't."

"I know you cared about him, Melissa," Anna said. "I'm so sorry for your loss."

Melissa nodded and took the last drink of the wine. She pushed it toward the bartender and pulled her second glass in front of her.

"I just don't know what to do," she complained. "Those documents were obvious forgeries. I didn't move that money around!"

"I'm so sorry, Melissa."

"This is all Frankie's fault," Melissa continued. "If she hadn't started digging around, Asher would still be here and I..."

"Do you know anyone who would want to set you up for this?"

"No," Melissa said with a shake of her head. "I mean, I'm sure there are plenty of people around work that don't like me and who can pull this off, but I wouldn't be able to narrow it down on the spot."

"Did the police find anything other than that account information when they conducted their search?"

"They seemed disappointed when they left," she replied. "I assumed that meant they found nothing. Of course, there isn't anything for them to find."

"I'm assuming there is a way to verify if those documents are genuine?"

"They already had the IT team check our system for those transactions."

"Were they there?"

"No, and there wasn't a record of them ever existing either."

"I would say you are probably in the clear unless they find something else about you."

Melissa seemed to relax a bit. "I promise there isn't anything to find. I had nothing to do with Asher's death, and I certainly had nothing to do with any funds that were misplaced."

"That's good," Anna replied. "If I were you, I would just make sure I have all my records in place. Do you have an alibi for the night of Asher's murder?"

"I was at my mother-in-law's house two hours away," she replied. "I couldn't have gotten back in time to commit murder. We stayed the night and drove back Friday morning."

"See, your alibi is already taken care of, then."

Melissa sighed again and took a smaller sip of her wine. "That's a relief."

They sat in silence for a few moments before Melissa turned to Anna. "So, you still think Frankie did it, right?"

Anna shrugged. "They have a lot of evidence."

"I think we have more we can provide," Melissa said. "If that would be helpful."

"What do you have?"

"Let's talk about it outside," Melissa said. "Chris should be here soon. He has it."

Anna made eye contact with Joe again from across the bar, and his eyes narrowed at her. She quickly jerked her attention back to Melissa. "My friends are waiting for me to come back. I don't have long."

"It won't take but a second," Melissa said, and picked her phone out of her purse. "Let's go. He just texted to say he was out back."

"Five minutes," Anna said. Joe frowned at her again when she got up from the bar to follow Melissa outside, but she ignored him.

A dark limo was waiting for them in the alley behind the bar. A driver opened the back door for them when they approached, and Anna followed Melissa inside. Chris looked them both over when they sat down, but pivoted his attention to Melissa.

"What did you do?"

"Nothing, I swear!"

"The police have been asking all sorts of questions about you."

"I don't know what's going on," Melissa said. "I have nothing to do with that."

"They didn't find any evidence," Anna interjected, causing Chris's attention to shift to her. "Melissa said they left without taking anything with them."

"I swear, there is nothing for them to find," Melissa pleaded. "I'm not involved in any of this."

"If I find you are lying to me," Chris warned.

"I'm not."

Chris sighed. "Well, now that we have that taken care of, let's get down to the other matter, shall we?"

"What do you have for me?" Anna asked.

"Well, now I need to throw attention away from Melissa, so I have some documents that show Ms. Fritts' involvement in some of the shady activity that was going on before Asher's death?"

Anna took the papers out of his hand and looked at them. "Are these real?"

"You just do what you need to do and don't worry about how real they are."

"I don't want to get into trouble myself by falsifying documents," Anna said with a frown. "I will not jeopardize myself."

"All right, all right," Chris said. "Don't get too hasty there. These aren't falsified."

"Then Frankie is involved?"

"After Asher's death, I started looking into the financial situation at the business," Chris explained. "This is all information I've run across during that time. They moved some of it. Some was hidden. And someone had tried to wipe a good deal of it."

"They were trying to make it disappear?" Anna asked, looking at the documents again. "Why would they do that?"

"I don't know," Chris said. "Perhaps they knew the police would start looking into things and wanted to get rid of it."

"How does this tie to Frankie?"

"It doesn't tie to Frankie," Chris said. "But it does tie to her department."

"What do you mean?"

"The department Frankie worked in is mostly interns," Melissa said. "It is an entry-level department and has a significant amount of data entry involved. It was a learning department."

"Which meant people came and went regularly," Chris added. "Tying back illegal activity to this group of workers was a great way to hide something. Since they were all new workers and didn't stay for an extended period, it was less likely they would have identified something like this."

"That still doesn't explain why Frankie would be involved," Anna said.

"The bulk of the problems started when she got here," Melissa said.

"That proves nothing."

"Of course not," Chris said. "However, I've traced these accounts. They trace back to the company that hired her into our intern program. The one that's based out of her college. It seems the trouble all started about the time Frankie would have been taking advanced classes."

"Wait, are you saying you think Frankie's been scamming you for years?"

"I don't know what to think," Chris said. "I'm just following evidence."

"Evidence that you found that the police somehow missed."

"Think what you want about the evidence," he shrugged. "I am simply doing my duty and turning it over to the people investigating Asher's death. Is that wrong?"

Anna looked through the papers again. "I'm going to have to look through all this and do my investigation before I submit them to any type of case. I'm not submitting something I don't know is factual."

"That is understandable," Chris said.

"Thank you," Anna said and looked at the clock on her phone. "Our time is up. I must get going. Melissa, do you want to walk back in with me?"

Melissa gave Chris a look and then shook her head at Anna. "No. I'll be all right. We'll be in touch, Anna."

Anna opened the door to the limo and stepped out without looking back. The driver shut the door behind her, but before she could walk away, he grabbed her arm. Anna looked up at him in surprise when she couldn't jerk her arm away from him.

"You need to stay away from these people," he whispered. "They are nothing but trouble."

He let go of her arm and went back to pretending he wasn't paying attention to her. Anna gave him a frown and walked back into the bar. She caught Joe's eye and nodded to the door. Joe and Derrick caught up with her just as she was reaching the car.

"So, how did it go?" Derrick asked. "Did you have a fun play date?"

"We need to talk," Anna said and sent a grim look back toward the bar. "And I don't think we should leave just yet."

Chapter 21

"What do you think he meant by that, Anna?" Joe asked with a frown. He rifled through the papers Chris and Melissa had provided her and his frown deepened. "This is a lot, Anna. I don't know what to think about it."

"I know."

"Back to the guy," Derrick interrupted. "Why do you think he was warning you?"

Anna shrugged. "Maybe he has seen some stuff and didn't want another person caught up in it all."

"I suppose he could just have been being nice," Joe said. "But if he knows something..."

"We need to know it, too," Anna said with a nod. "Which is why I think we should stick around. See if we can figure out where Chris goes next."

"And see if we can't figure out what the driver knows," Joe agreed. He looked back towards the bar. "Derrick, I think we need to move the car. If we could hide somewhere where we can see the limo but them not see us—"

"On it," Derrick said, already popping the car into gear. He pulled around the back of the bar and found a crowded parking lot. He parked in a space near the limo and cut the lights. Anna and Joe peered out the back window at the limo behind them.

After about ten minutes, the limo door opened, and Melissa stepped out. The driver frowned at her, but she ignored him and straightened her skirt before heading back inside the bar. This time, instead of closing the door behind Melissa, the driver poked his head inside.

"He must be getting directions from Chris," Anna said. When the driver stepped away from the door and climbed into the driver's seat, Anna turned back around and put on her seatbelt. "Looks like we're moving."

Derrick watched the limo pull away and waited until they were almost out of sight before popping the headlights back on and backing out to follow it. Anna watched out the window as they drove and monitored the limo. Each mile made her stomach sink a little further.

"This is quite the familiar route," Joe said, the tone of his voice matching Anna's feeling of concern.

"It's almost like I didn't need to follow him," Derrick said.

Anna groaned when the limo stopped, and she looked up at Frankie's apartment complex. "What is he doing here?"

They didn't have to wait long to find out. Soon a man was speeding out a side door of the building and climbing into the limo.

"Who is that guy?" Anna and Joe asked in unison.

"Him?" Derrick asked. "Oh, he's the night security guard."

"How do you know that?"

"I saw him at the security desk the other night," he said. "I had brought you back over here for something and went downstairs to find a vending machine. I had to walk right by his desk. I'm sure it's him."

"What would the night security guard at Frankie's building be doing with Chris?" Joe asked.

"I have no idea," Anna said. "But we need to find out. I'm calling Marie."

Joe kept his eye on the limo while Anna connected with her sister. When Marie answered, Anna quickly gave her a rundown of their evening. When she got to the part about the security guard, Marie gasped.

"That explains everything!" she said.

"What do you mean 'that explains everything,' Marie? I don't understand."

Anna flipped the phone on speaker so Joe could hear the conversation, too.

"We found an alibi for Frankie," Marie explained. "She couldn't have murdered Asher because she was downstairs in the laundry room that night. She has a key that lets her into the laundry facility. It tracks who goes in and out, and there are security cameras down there."

"That's great!"

"Except that when we went to check on the security footage earlier today, it wasn't there."

"Someone deleted it?"

"It was at least missing," Marie said. "The security manager was going to look into it. He seemed mad about the whole thing."

"Well, I'm guessing we know who was behind its disappearance now," Joe said.

"Do you think that means Chris is behind the framing of Frankie?" Anna asked.

"Possibly," Joe replied. "And, Melissa too, I imagine."

"Guys?" Derrick said, alerting them to the opening of the limo door.

"Marie, we'll have to talk about this later. We have some action going on right now."

"You guys be careful," Marie said. "Don't do anything risky."

"We won't," Anna said. "Just trying to get a bearing on what's going on around here."

"Good," Marie said. "Call me when you head back to the hotel, so I know you are all right."

Anna hung the phone up with Marie just as Derrick was pulling away from Frankie's apartment complex to follow the limo again. This time, the route wasn't a familiar one, and they soon found themselves in a suburban area. The limo stopped in front of a large house on the corner, and Derrick pulled to the side of the road behind a big van.

"Looks like Chris is getting out," Joe said. "I bet this is his house."

Anna picked up her phone and opened the map app. "I'm going to save this address in case we need it again."

"Good idea."

Chris walked to the house and went inside. The moment the door closed behind him, the limo pulled away from the curb.

"Now what?" Derrick asked.

"I say we follow the limo," Anna said. "I'm sure Chris isn't going anywhere else tonight. Now we need to see what the limo driver is up to."

"Away we go," Derrick said and pulled away from the curb.

The limo sped away from Chris's home and made a left. Derrick stayed far enough away from the vehicle to avoid detection. Before long, they had followed the limo onto the highway and driven several miles.

"Where is this guy going?" Joe asked after they passed three exits.

Anna shrugged and continued monitoring the limo out the front window. After a while, she pointed. "Hey, Derrick, looks like he's getting off."

Derrick nodded and maneuvered their car into the exit lane a few cars back from the limo. The limo turned right and continued down the street for a few miles before stopping on the side of the road. Derrick kept driving and pulled around a corner where they could still see the limo, but would be mostly out of sight.

"What is he doing?" Anna asked. "There's nothing here."

They didn't have to wait long to find out, for soon a dark car pulled up behind the limo.

"Anna, if I didn't know better, I would say that looks just like the vehicle our FBI friends back home drive," Joe said.

"Uh oh," Anna said when two men got out of the door and walked to the limo. "If I didn't know better, I'd say those guys are dressed just like them too."

"The fact the two of you can identify potential FBI agents from an entire parking lot away scares me just a bit," Derrick said with a shake of his head.

"Trust me," Anna said, her attention still on the limo and the pair of men standing outside it. "I wish we weren't so aware of what the FBI looked like."

Joe chuckled and suddenly grew serious when he noticed the limo door open and the driver step out. The FBI agents walked back to their car and pulled away. The driver turned away from his car and looked at Derrick's car.

"Oh, crap!" Derrick said. "I think he sees us. Should we go?"

The driver started walking in their direction, and Derrick put the car in gear.

"Hold on," Anna said. "I have a feeling we might want to know what he has to say."

"One sign of danger and I'm getting us out of here," Derrick replied, not putting the car back in park.

The driver walked around their car and tapped on Anna's window. She lowered it just enough where she could hear what he had to say.

"I told you to stay away from these people," the driver said as he glared down at her. "Not follow them all over town."

"I have no intention of spending any more time with them than I need to," Anna said. "But I need to know the truth."

"Just let it go," he said. "This doesn't concern you."

"It concerns one of my best friends, though," Anna argued. "And I plan to make sure she doesn't go to jail for something I know she didn't do."

"You're playing them?" he asked with a shake of his head. "You must be crazy. You are in way over your head."

"I know what I'm doing."

Joe leaned across her and looked out the window. "Who are you concerning this case? Is there more to this story that we should know?"

"There is nothing I can tell you," the driver said. "Other than you need to stay out of it. You dig much deeper, and you are going to be in lots of danger."

"Again, I'm not abandoning my friend," Anna said. "We do this for a living, anyway."

"Yeah, we're pretty used to being in danger," Joe added.

"It's your funeral, I suppose," the driver said. "Don't say I didn't warn you, though."

He went to walk away from their car but turned back after a few steps. "Oh, and quit following me. I will not give you any information that will help your case."

Anna and Joe turned in their seats to watch him walk back to the limo. They frowned at each other when he'd driven away.

"That was intense!" Derrick said. "I can't believe he just came over here like that."

"What do you think that means?" Joe asked. "The FBI is investigating at least Chris."

"With all the shady stuff we've dug up, it wouldn't surprise me if they weren't investigating the entire company."

"Good point," Joe said. "I guess at the moment we can't worry about what they are up to until it collides with our case."

Before Anna could reply, her phone started ringing. She looked down at it and frowned. "It's Melissa."

"How does she have your number?"

"I gave it to her in case she needed to give me more info," she said before holding a finger to her lips to silence them. She took a deep breath and answered the line. Before she could get a greeting out of her mouth, however, she jerked the phone away from her ear as Melissa's screams were deafening.

Chapter 22

Shocked, Anna pulled the phone back into the range of her voice and tried to calm Melissa down. "Melissa! Melissa, calm down. What is going on?"

"You've got to help me!" Melissa cried. She grew silent and Anna could hear a lot of shuffling on the other end of the line.

"Melissa?" she whispered. "Mellissa, are you alright?"

When Melissa came back on the line, she was whispering. "I need help. Please help me."

"What can I do?"

"Please send help," she replied. "I'll send you my address."

The line went dead while Anna was asking for more information from Melissa. Within seconds, a text came through with Melissa's address.

"She sounded like she was in trouble," Anna said. "In danger even."

"We need to get the police out there to her," Joe said. "I'm calling 911."

Anna waited in silence while staring at her phone, only to look up at Joe in shock when he lowered the phone.

"No answer," he said and began dialing again.

"How can there be no answer at 911?" Anna asked. "They have to answer."

"Not when the entire system is down," Derrick said, glancing up at her from his phone. "I just looked it up. The 911 system is down for the entire state right now."

"Derrick," Anna said. "Move."

She got out of the backseat and jerked open his door. He looked up at her in surprise.

"I can still drive, you know," he protested. "I'm a great driver. Really fast."

"Joe, get up here in this passenger seat," Anna ordered. "I need you to navigate."

Joe sighed and got out of the car. When he'd sat down in the passenger seat, he looked at Derrick. "I promise you, man, she needs to be behind the wheel right now."

Derrick silently slipped out of the driver's seat and around Anna. He had just shut his door when Joe turned to look at him. "You're going to want to buckle up."

Anna ignored them and quickly adjusted the seat and mirrors to fit her size and driving style. The moment Derrick clicked the buckle closed, she was speeding away from the street where they had met the limo driver.

Following Joe's careful directions, she whipped the car back onto the highway and through a steady stream of cars. Eventually, they took an exit and found themselves in the middle of the suburbs.

"Two streets up and then a right turn," Joe said as Anna sped through an intersection.

She nodded and pulled the e-brake as she propelled the car around the corner. "Now what?"

"Three streets and a left."

She repeated the process to the left and again requested information.

"Second house on the right."

Anna pushed the car to its limits before slamming to a stop in front of Melissa's house. She threw it in park.

Derrick leaned forward between Anna and Joe and said, "I don't know if I'm turned on or if I just peed my pants." He turned Joe's direction. "Does she drive like that all the time?"

"She has every time I've ridden with her," Joe said. "Which is why I prefer to drive most of the time."

"Good choice," Derrick said and turned back to Anna. "How do you still have a license?"

"We don't have time for this," Anna said and was out the door before Joe could stop her.

"Anna, wait," he called out his window. "You can't just barge in there!"

"The hell I can't," she replied. "She needs help!"

"Good God, woman," Derrick called to her from the back seat. "You are going to get yourself killed!"

"I'm fine," she argued. "I can defend myself. You two need to go get help. I have my listening device in."

Joe went to get out of the car. "I'm not letting you go in there alone, Anna."

Anna stopped and walked back to him. "We don't have time for this, Joe. She could be testing me again. I need to go in there and check things out by myself."

"I'm not leaving this property," he said.

"Fine, Derrick, you go get some help," Anna said. "Joe, you stay outside. I have my listening device in, so you can hear what's going on."

"Same as before," Joe said. "If you get into trouble, just say 'Colorado.'"

"Got it," Anna said and turned away from him. Derrick pulled away from the house, and Joe hid behind a tree near the front door. Before she knocked on the door, Anna straightened her hair and tried to wipe the concern from her face.

Within a minute of her knocking on it, a man walked to the front door. He opened it and looked at her with a disheveled and distracted look.

"Um, hi," Anna said. "I'm a friend of Melissa's. Is she home? She said she wanted me to stop by."

"Yes, do come in," the man muttered. "Melissa is in the living room."

Anna followed him and mentally documented all the signs of a struggle she saw throughout the house. A glass vase had fallen over in the front hallway and several dishes were shattered on the floor by the kitchen. When they reached the living room, a table was overturned, and a rug had completely flopped in half. Melissa was lying on the couch.

"I'm afraid Melissa..." the man said, "...had too much to drink."

"Is she alright?" Anna asked, her feeling of worry and fear growing in the pit of her stomach. "Should we call an ambulance?"

"No," the man replied and revealed the knife that he was holding behind his back. "We shouldn't. How about you just go over there and sit by her for a bit?"

Anna gulped and headed to the couch, her eyes never leaving the man.

"Anna, what is going on?" Joe whispered through her earpiece.

Anna ignored him and continued talking to the man. "I don't believe we've met. I assume you are Melissa's husband. I'm afraid I don't remember your name."

"Michael," he muttered. "Yes, I'm her husband. Not that it mattered to her much."

He circled behind Anna and looked out the living room window. When she shifted on the couch, he jerked back in her direction and brought the knife closer to her. Anna tried to remain calm.

"How long have you and Melissa been married?" she asked. "She always speaks so fondly of you."

He snorted. "I'm sure she does. We've been married for seven blissful years. I spent every second of that time with her trying to bleed me dry while she fu—"

"I'm so sorry," Anna said. "I don't like to get in the middle of my friends' relationships."

"Whatever," Michael said. "I don't care if you do or don't."

"Anna!" Joe whispered again. "Talk to me!"

"Are you sure we don't need to call an ambulance for Melissa?" Anna said, turning her attention to the woman beside her on the couch again. "She doesn't look well at all."

"I said no," Michael yelled, causing Anna to shrink away from him.

"I'm sorry."

Michael rolled his eyes. "I have something I need to do. You stay there. If I find out you've moved while I'm gone, I swear..."

Anna nodded and sighed in relief when he walked out of the room.

"Anna, you need to get out of there," Joe said.

"I don't think I can make it," she whispered. "Besides, I can't leave Melissa."

"What did he do to her?" Joe asked.

"I can't tell," Anna said. "I'm going to see if she's breathing."

Anna touched Melissa's leg and said her name, but got no response. She watched her chest for a few moments but sighed when she didn't see any movement.

"I don't think she's breathing," she whispered. "I'm going to see if I can check for a pulse."

Anna reached across Melissa's body and gently lifted the hair out of her face. When she found Melissa's eyes open and her face frozen in fear, she quickly dropped the hair and pulled away from her.

"She's dead, Joe," Anna whispered.

"I'm coming in there," Joe said.

Just as he was finishing his sentence, Michael walked back into the living room holding a large shotgun.

Chapter 23

"I'm sure you've discovered by now that my wife is no longer with us," Michael said and opened the shotgun. "Now you are going with her."

"Why are you doing this?" Anna asked, trying to keep Michael's attention. He ignored her and walked to a desk to the side of the couch. Anna gulped when he pulled out two shotgun shells and began loading his gun. "Have you and Melissa ever been to Colorado?"

Michael stopped loading the gun and looked up at her in surprise. "What?"

"Colorado is nice. Maybe you could just go out the front door and head there. Plenty of areas to hide and start over there."

"Colorado, huh," he said. "You think they would accept me up there?"

He flipped the shotgun shells in his hand and walked back in front of her. Anna sighed in relief when she caught the image of the front door opening out of the corner of her eye. She glanced behind Michael and was relieved to see that the entrance to the living room was behind him.

"Yeah," she said, trying to keep his attention. "I'm sure they would."

"I guess I'll find out after I get rid of you now that you know where I'm going," Michael said with an evil grin.

"Where did it all go wrong?" Anna asked, causing Michael to stop and look at her again. "With Melissa? What happened?"

"She couldn't stay out of other men's beds," Michael said. "I already took care of that Asher idiot she was seeing. But that wasn't enough."

He turned his attention to Melissa's body and yelled. "Was I not enough for you? It wasn't enough to have a husband to come home to? You had to go sleeping around with every man you knew?"

Michael stomped over to Melissa's body and jerked off the necklace she was wearing. "You just had to keep this stupid thing, didn't you?" He threw it at Melissa, and it bounced onto the floor. Anna realized it was the same necklace she'd seen Melissa tugging on when they'd had their initial meeting.

Anna noticed Joe walk into the room but quickly realized he was still too far away from Michael to help with the situation. When Michael started turning in Joe's direction, Anna stopped him.

"Was that a necklace you bought Melissa?" she asked. "She seemed fond of it."

Michael laughed and went back to loading the shotgun. "That man she was seeing bought it. She dared to wear it all the time, even in front of me. I think she thought she loved him. Idiot. We could have had a glorious life together, but she had to ruin everything!"

Before Michael could say more, Joe walked up behind him and grabbed his neck. Michael struggled with him and tried to finish loading his gun, but Anna quickly kicked the device out of his hand.

"Who the hell are you people?" Michael asked in a choked voice. "How did you get in here?"

Joe grunted and pulled Michael to the ground in a headlock. "I tell you what. The next time you decide to try to kill one of my friends, how about you lock your front door?"

Before he could fight back any further, Michael's eyes fluttered closed, and he went limp. Joe pulled away from him and pushed Michael's body onto his stomach. He looked back at Anna.

"You can defend yourself, huh?"

"Well, how were you planning to help me if you were stuck in here with me?"

"Oh, I see," Joe replied as he looked around for something to secure Michael. He settled for a blanket that was lying across a nearby chair. "Make me worry myself half to death about you and then figure out a way to come save you?"

"It worked, didn't it?"

As Joe finished tying Michael's arms together, Anna looked out the window to see several police cars heading toward them. She sighed in relief when she saw Derrick's car pull up outside as well.

Joe took a deep breath and leaned back against the couch where Anna sat. Before they could say more, the police had invaded the living room and ordered them to the ground.

"They aren't the ones who did it," Derrick argued as Anna and Joe were pulled outside. "They are the ones that were trying to help."

"We'll get all of it settled in a minute," an officer called back to Derrick. "Just stay back."

The officers pulled Anna and Joe away from each other so they could give their statements. Anna quickly filled the officer they assigned her in on the evening and what she was doing at the home. He wrote everything she said and added her contact information to his notebook.

"It sounds like you survived a pretty major crime here, honey," he said. "You need to be more careful."

"We tried to call the police, but the lines were down," she said. "We didn't know the emergency line to call instead."

The officer sighed. "That's caused all sorts of headaches this evening, I'm afraid."

Anna looked back at the house. "There's one more thing I didn't tell you."

"What's that?" the officer asked, pulling out his notebook again.

"You're going to want to call Detective Morales," she replied, looking at the officer again. "He's with homicide. He's investigating a murder that involved these people."

"Involved how?"

"Well, for starters, the victim in there," she said and pointed back toward the house, "was having an affair with

Detective Morales's murder victim. Michael implied to me that her affairs are the reason behind this murder."

"I see," the detective said. "I'll pass that along. Anything else."

"You're going to want to take the jacket Michael is wearing into evidence."

"Why?"

"It's missing a button."

"Lots of people have coats that are missing buttons."

"That may be, but the buttons on that coat match the one that my partner and I found at the crime scene Detective Morales is investigating. The crime lab picked it up a couple of days ago and is processing it."

Chapter 24

"Oh, my God," Marie said the moment Anna walked into the conference room at Frankie's attorney's office. "Are you alright?"

"I'm fine," Anna said, brushing off the hug her sister tried to give her. "What's the update? This has to change everything."

Marie sat down at the table next to Frankie and Anna sat next to her.

"Mr. Matthews is on the line with the DA now," Marie said. "I can't imagine they will continue this case at this point."

"Melissa's husband murdering her and admitting to Asher's murder at the same time kind of blows their case out of the water," Bryant added. "If they don't automatically drop the charges, Frankie's attorney will certainly file a motion himself."

Eugene walked into the conference room and sat down at the head of the table. Anna leaned forward in her chair in anticipation of whatever he had to say.

"He admitted to everything," he said. "Once Detective Morales told him about the button they had in evidence, he completely broke."

"What happened?" Frankie asked.

"He found out his wife was having an affair," Eugene said. "He tracked Asher down. He followed him to the park that night and when he passed through the woods, he confronted him."

"Does that mean he wasn't involved in setting Asher up?" Anna asked. "Someone else was behind that?"

"There isn't anything connecting him to that," Eugene said. "He didn't know what the detectives were talking about. But they are certain that he didn't go there planning to kill Asher. It was the convenience of the location they were in and just the sudden burst of anger he felt when he confronted him that made him do it."

"I had been wondering about that myself," Joe said. "It struck me as odd that everything seemed so planned about the setup except for the murder."

"Me too," Anna said with a nod. "Now that we know about Michael, it makes more sense."

"Whoever is setting up Frankie never intended for Asher to get killed," Bryant said. "They were just trying to get Frankie and Asher to quit looking into the embezzling."

"I have to agree," Marie added. "It sounds like they were just trying to make the scrutiny go away. They possibly still are. That way, they can hide what's going on with the company. They probably weren't even really trying to frame Frankie at first. Just trying to scare her into being quiet until Asher was murdered."

"This is so crazy!" Frankie said. "I can't believe that Melissa's husband killed Asher all while Melissa and the higher-ups were doing all that they were behind the scenes."

"Michael had been following him around for days," Eugene continued. "He had taken a few days off work because he was sick of Melissa's affairs. Asher had been with Melissa right before he headed to the park, which is what made Michael so mad."

"Did he confront him or just kill him?" Anna asked.

"Michael told the police that he was just planning to talk to him," he continued. "He stayed out of sight until they were in the trees because he didn't want to cause a scene and get in trouble."

"He must not have liked Asher's response," Joe said. "Probably set him off."

"Exactly," Eugene said. "It sounded like Asher didn't cower away from him as Michael expected him to and there was a scuffle."

"Michael won that scuffle," Anna said.

"Well, we know how Asher died now," Joe said with a frown. "Where does that leave us on Frankie's case?"

"And what about all this mess with the embezzlement investigation?" Anna asked. "Someone was going to great lengths to keep that under wraps."

"The DA indicated that they would drop the murder charges against Frankie," Eugene said. "They just have to formally do that. Now our attention will need to turn toward the embezzlement issue."

"I was afraid you were going to say that it wasn't over just yet," Frankie groaned. "Where do we even start?"

"It always seems to help when we follow the money," Joe said. "We find where those funds from that account wound up, we find who is behind the embezzlement."

Anna groaned. "I do not have the energy to start that tonight. How about we call it a day and start fresh in the morning?"

"That sounds like a good plan," Marie said. "Frankie, do you want me to come home with you and get you settled?"

Frankie shook her head. "You need rest too, Marie. I'll be fine. Go back to the hotel with Anna and all of you get some sleep. It's been a long day."

"That it has," Anna said with a yawn. "We can all meet back here in the morning."

"Sounds like a good plan," Mr. Matthews said and stood to his feet. "I'll get everything secured here and see you all first thing in the morning."

Anna and the others gathered their things and left the building. They stood together on the sidewalk outside the attorney's office for just a few moments before heading off to separate vehicles.

When she was inside Derrick's car, Anna leaned her head against the window and closed her eyes. The road noise outside her window lulled her into a light sleep, but she jerked awake when Derrick stopped the car a few minutes later in front of their hotel.

"Thank you for driving us around, Derrick," she said before getting out of the car. "We really should think about getting a rental tomorrow, Joe, so he doesn't have to keep being our chauffeur."

"Don't be ridiculous," Derrick said with a laugh. "I haven't had this much fun in years. Besides, your hotel doesn't have much parking."

"Even so," Anna argued. "You shouldn't have to keep on our weird schedule."

"Stop it," Derrick said with another laugh. "It is no trouble at all. I want to do it. I rarely get to spend this much time with my best friend after all."

Anna smiled at him and said, "Still, if we become a burden, please say something."

"Trust me," Derrick said. "I will."

Anna laughed and climbed out of the car with Joe. They met Bryant and Marie in the lobby, and all headed up the elevators to their rooms. After saying their goodnights, they separated and headed off to bed.

"I'm so glad you are all right," Marie said once they were inside their room.

Anna began pulling off her day clothes and changing into an oversized t-shirt and a pair of shorts. "I figured out who killed Asher, so it was worth it."

"I hate that it took you coming face to face with the murderer and being threatened like that to figure it out."

"I'm just glad it's over," Anna said with a sigh. "It was pretty intense."

"I'm sure you're exhausted," Marie said, pulling the covers on her bed back. "Let's get some rest, so we're ready to figure this out tomorrow."

Anna nodded and climbed into her bed. She stared at the ceiling for a few minutes before attempting to close her eyes. However, the moment they closed, her mind conjured up an image of Melissa's body and she jerked them open again. She tried again a few times and was awarded the same result.

With a frustrated sigh, she sat up in the bed and whispered Marie's name. When she didn't get a response, she jerked the covers off her and slid her feet off the bed and onto the carpet. She got down on her hands and knees and felt around for a pair of shoes.

Her hands landed on a pair of heels, and she muttered to herself, "Of course, this would be the shoes I find."

Not wanting to wake her sister, Anna picked the heels up and tiptoed to the hotel door. On her way to the door, she picked her coat up off a chair and slung her arms through it, making sure it had her room key and some cash in the pocket. She only glanced at the shoes when she was outside in the hallway and the door had closed quietly behind her.

"Ugh," she groaned when she realized the shoes didn't match. She reached down and put them on her feet anyway and chuckled. "Oh well, they fit."

She crept down the hallway and stopped at the elevator. Just as her finger went to push the button, she stopped herself.

"What am I doing?" she whispered. "I can't leave like this. Marie would be worried sick."

With a sigh, she turned away from the elevator and turned back toward her room, only to stop again when she spotted a vending machine across the hall. Mindlessly, she walked into the small area and peered into the machine. A smile crossed her face when she spotted a certain bag of chips. Still smiling, she fished money out of her pocket, loaded it into the machine, and waited for the chips to fall into the return bin.

As she waited, she realized a second bag sat behind the first and quickly selected to purchase it as well. She sat down on the floor next to the machine and laid the second bag beside her before opening the first bag and popping a chip into her mouth.

She smiled into the bag and ate another chip. She'd just started pulling a third chip from the bag when a familiar voice caused her to freeze.

"That's some fashion thing you got going on there."

Chapter 25

She looked up to find Joe grinning down at her and eyeing her mismatched shoes.

"Well, you know me," she said as she put her hand over the chips where he couldn't see them. "I'm always up for starting new fashion trends."

He laughed and leaned against the vending machine. "You needed a snack before bed too, huh?"

"Uh, yeah," Anna said, glancing at the bag she was hiding. "Something like that."

"So, what snack did you pick out?" he asked, trying to sneak a peek at the bag in her hand. He gasped when he spotted just enough of it to realize what she was hiding. "Wait a minute! Are you eating my favorite chips without me?"

Anna laughed. "I have to admit. They are pretty good."

"Well, looks like my snack is decided for me," he said and turned his attention to the vending machine. "Uh, oh."

He looked back down at Anna and raised an eyebrow at her. "Please tell me you didn't buy the last bag of my chips."

Anna laughed and picked up the second bag next to her on the floor. "I did. I noticed there were only two left, so I bought one for you for later."

He smiled at her and held out his hand. "Looks like I'm having them for now."

She laughed and held the bag in his direction. He snatched it and plopped down on the floor beside her. After opening it and eating a chip, he grew serious.

"You, ok?" he asked. "I know today was tough."

"Yeah," Anna whispered. "I'll be fine. Just need to get Melissa's face out of my mind so I can go to sleep. Every time I close my eyes, I'm taken right back to her murder, which then reminds me of mom's. I can't sleep."

"There's nothing I could have done to protect you from your mother's death," he said, "but I wish you had let me protect you from seeing Melissa's."

"I know."

He looked at her out of the corner of his eyes. "You going to disappear on me the moment I go back to my room?"

Anna smiled and looked down at her bag of chips. "It crossed my mind, but I can't do that to Marie right now. She's already so worried about Frankie. I can't have her worrying about me too."

"So, how about you let me worry about you this time, then?"

Anna chuckled. "How does that work exactly?"

"How about you start by telling me what's going on in your headspace, and I'll let you know?"

"Oh, trust me," she said. "You do not want to be a part of my headspace."

Joe paused and looked down at his bag of chips. "I know I never talk about it, but that day I lost Merida...the day she died...was the worst of my life. I felt helpless the entire time. From the moment those bank robbers took her to me pulling her out of the car after they had shot her, I couldn't shake that feeling of helplessness."

"I'm so sorry, Joe," Anna said. "I felt the same way when those carjackers killed mom when I was little. There wasn't a thing I could do to change things."

"After I lost her, I poured myself into building that stupid cell phone tracking app of mine," he said. "You can ask Bryant. I completely lost myself. But I was determined never to feel helpless like that again."

Anna sighed and closed her eyes. After a moment, she pushed her head back against the wall and looked at him. "That's exactly why I take off."

"I know it is," he said with a soft smile. "You want to talk about it?"

"They just...left me there," she said. "I was a little kid, and they killed mom and left with the car. I was all alone. I did not know what to do. I just..."

"Felt abandoned?" Joe asked when she didn't finish the sentence.

She nodded. "And trapped."

"So, you take off to prove to yourself that you aren't trapped?"

"Exactly," she said. "The idea of not being able to leave a situation terrifies me."

Joe looked down into his bag of chips again before giving her another sideways look.

"Would it be a reach to say that you push away those close to you so that you don't have to worry about them abandoning you?"

"Ooh, that's getting a little deep there," she said with a teary chuckle.

"I know," he said. "I never want to pressure you into talking about anything you don't want to talk about, but I feel like I need to say something out loud if you want to hear it."

"What would that be?"

"I promise you," he said. "As long as we know each other, there will always be someone to catch you. We will not leave you hanging. Whether it's Claire, your sister, me, or whoever, I swear to you there will be someone around to help you when you need it."

"You sure about that?" Anna asked with a quiet laugh.

"How about this?" Joe said. "If there isn't someone around to help you, I'll at least be around to drive your getaway car when you need to escape."

She laughed and met his gaze for a moment before turning back to pull another chip from the bag. "I appreciate that."

They ate in silence for a few more minutes before Joe said softly, "Hey, do you remember when you and Claire went mudding with Derrick and me?"

"Of course," Anna chuckled. "That was just last week."

"You remember when we parked in the woods? How pretty the sunrise was that morning?"

"It was pretty awesome, wasn't it?"

"It was," he replied with a soft smile. "I'm glad we got to see that."

"Me too."

He looked into his bag and frowned. "Well, looks like I'm out of chips. I'm going to head off to bed."

Anna looked into her bag and laughed. "I'm out, too. Guess I'd better go to bed myself."

Joe stood to his feet and held a hand down for her. She took it and he pulled her to her feet, pausing long enough to stare into each other's eyes again before they headed back to their hotel rooms. She pulled her key out when she approached her room but hesitated when she went to put it in the door.

"Did you know I was down there?" she asked. "Is that why you are out here? To make sure I'm ok?"

Joe laughed. "I wish I had those telepathy abilities, but sadly, I don't. I just wanted some chips."

"Well, thank you anyway."

"Sleep well, Anna."

Anna smiled at him and headed back inside the room. She smiled to herself as she kicked off the heels before slipping back into bed. This time, when she closed her eyes, her mind conjured up the image of the sunrise Joe had mentioned instead of Melissa's face, and she slipped off into a peaceful slumber.

Chapter 26

"What if we trace it this way?" Marie said, pointing at her computer.

Joe frowned at her screen and shook his head. "We don't have access to that."

"What if we—" Bryant started.

"We don't have access to that either," Anna said, not even looking up from her screen.

"I didn't even finish!"

Anna sent an annoyed look in Joe's direction, causing him to chuckle.

"Look," he said. "Unless one of the two of you has thought of something completely out of the box—"

"Which they haven't," Anna added.

"—then we've already thought of it and tried it," Joe said with another laugh.

"Then how are we going to do this?" Marie asked.

"Well, we could always hack—" Anna said.

"No!" Marie and Bryant said in unison.

"Then, what do you suggest?" Joe asked after rolling his eyes at Anna. "It's not like we have other options."

"I'm afraid that is going to have to wait," Eugene said from the doorway. "We have more pressing matters to attend to at the moment."

Anna sighed and closed her laptop screen so she could give him her full attention. He sat down and glanced around at all of them before beginning.

"I just got off the phone with the DA," he said. "They are dropping the murder charges against Frankie."

"That's great!" Marie said. "But I'm sure there is more to the story?"

"Of course," he said. "They implied the FBI is opening a more in-depth investigation into the embezzling situation. Frankie seems to be at the very center of their investigation."

"Well, that's just great," Frankie complained. "Can we just go back to the murder charges? I'm sure that comes with a shorter sentence."

"It will be alright, Frankie," Marie said. "Just like the other, we'll figure out the truth behind the embezzling as well."

"If we can get access to anything," Anna said. "I'd say that's our biggest problem."

"There's something a bit more pressing we need to discuss," Eugene said. "The FBI wants to have a chat with Anna."

"With me?" Anna asked. "Why?"

"They didn't say, exactly," Eugene said. "They just called and said they wanted to meet."

"That's reassuring, considering he called an attorney to speak with me," Anna said.

"Yeah, I'm not comfortable with you going to an interview with the FBI by yourself," Bryant said. "Marie or I need to come with you if this is an official interview."

"It certainly sounded as if that were the case," Eugene said.

"When do they want to meet?"

"Today at three," he said. "Which is the same time Frankie needs to be at the police station to have her ankle bracelet removed."

"Well, that's great," Marie said. "I can't be in two places at one time."

"How about you go with Frankie, Marie?" Bryant said. "You are the one in charge of her bail, so you need to get that taken care of. I can go with Anna."

"What are Joe and I going to do while you all do that?" Derrick asked.

Anna glanced in his direction and laughed when she saw the hopeful look on his face. "No, Derrick. You and Joe are not allowed to get into trouble while we are distracted."

Derrick laughed and picked up a slice of pizza he had sitting in a box in front of him. "I can't make any promises."

"It would be great if the two of you could get us access to the accounts at Frankie's workplace," Bryant said.

"Legally, of course," Marie added.

"Maybe we can find an in with Chris," Anna said with a shrug. "He's already aware of us, so maybe we can use that someway?"

Bryant nodded. "Maybe you two can work on that, then. Figure out how to get close to Chris and hopefully get him to grant access to his systems. If anyone can give us access, it would be him."

"I wonder what he might be up to since Melissa's death," Anna said. "He might be difficult to track down without her."

"Are you doubting me again?" Joe asked and looked up from his computer. "I've already found him."

"Of course you have," Anna laughed. "Do proceed."

"He's scheduled at a fancy golf club here in about a couple of hours," Joe said. "Don't know exactly how that helps, but I at least know where he's at."

"Well," Derrick said with a grin after looking at Joe's computer screen. He took a bite of pizza and sat back in his chair. "It sure would be nice if someone had a client that could get us into that golf club."

"Are you serious?" Anna asked. "You can get him in?"

"Yep. Of course, we'll have to dress the part and do some golfing while we are there," Derrick said. "I can't be embarrassing my client or anything. We wouldn't be able to cause trouble."

"I can be diplomatic," Joe said. "How quickly can we get there?"

"I'll call him right now and I bet he can get us approved and in the door within the hour."

"Sounds like a plan," Joe said. "Derrick, you've certainly come in handy this trip."

"It's nice to feel needed," Derrick laughed. "By the way, Anna, if you have time, you are going to want to see Joe in the outfit I have planned for him."

Bryant shrugged. "Not much else we can do until we know what the FBI is up to."

"And get access to the systems and accounts we need," Anna added.

Marie turned to Eugene. "Unless you have anything else for us right now, we'll head out and get these things taken care of. Meet back up here in the morning?"

"I'll be excited to hear an update on everything."

"I just hope that we have something to update you with," Anna said as they began gathering up their things.

Derrick walked around the table and grinned at her. "Trust me. At the very least, you will get to update your 'Joe Memory Book' because you are going to want to remember him in the outfit I have for him."

Anna laughed. "I'm sure Joe will not share your enthusiasm."

"Ugh, I've seen some of his golf outfits," Joe said. "Let's go get this over with, please."

Chapter 27

"I look ridiculous," Joe said as he looked at himself in the mirror.

Anna laughed, causing him to turn around. She snapped a picture on her phone and laughed again. "This is awesome."

Joe put his hands on his hips. "What do you think you are doing?"

"I'm so using this for blackmail later," she said, her eyes still on her phone. "This is fantastic."

"Blackmail, huh?" Joe said, crossing his arms across his chest. "If I recall, there are a few things—"

Anna jerked her eyes in his direction and almost dropped her phone. He gave her a playful smile and laughed. "I suppose I can let you have one item on your list compared to my fifty."

She held the picture up in his direction and laughed. "This evens us out a bit."

Derrick emerged from the bathroom wearing a rather neutral outfit compared to the pink shorts and heavily patterned shirt Joe was wearing. Joe turned his direction and raised an eyebrow at him.

"So, I get to wear this getup and you get the normal one?" he asked.

"Uh, I need to keep up appearances with my clients," Derrick said. "You will make me look better today."

"Thanks, Buddy," Joe said. "Well, I guess if we are going to get to the golf course on time, we'd better get going."

"Good luck," Anna said. "I'll just sit around here and wait for the FBI to 'interview' me, I suppose."

"It will be fine," Joe said. "You have done nothing wrong. They have to just be interested in what Chris and Melissa have been telling you."

"One would hope," Anna replied.

Joe looked at himself one more time in the mirror and sighed before following Derrick to the door of his hotel room. Bryant followed them out into the hallway, leaving Anna behind in the room.

"Be careful, you two," Bryant said. "Don't be getting into trouble while you're out there."

"Don't you worry about us, Bryant," Derrick said. "I'll make sure Joe is on his best behavior."

"And you don't have to worry about me," Joe said to Derrick. "There is no way that I'm going to jeopardize your clients. You're doing us a favor and if it doesn't work where we can do this quietly and discreetly, we will figure something else out."

"Get going, guys," Bryant said. "We'll meet back at Mr. Matthews's office later this afternoon or evening when we all get finished."

Joe reached into his pocket and pulled out a rubber band. "Here, Bryant. If Anna seems to get nervous, give her this. Tell her it will be alright."

Bryant laughed and took the rubber band from his brother. "You and those rubber bands. I'll give it to her. I'm sure it will make her laugh at the very least."

"She'll be fine, Joe," Derrick said. "Let's go."

"Yeah, let's go see what we can get out of Chris."

Joe and Derrick left the hotel and headed for the parking lot. Once they were in the car, Derrick added the address to the GPS and drove away. Within half an hour, they had pulled into the parking lot of the golf course.

"They have clubs waiting for us in the clubhouse," Derrick said. "I didn't figure you had any handy."

"I certainly didn't expect to be golfing while we were here, that's for sure."

"I just hope you still have some of those skills of yours and you haven't gotten rusty on me."

"Rusty?" Joe asked with a smirk. "Who me? I don't know the meaning of the word."

"Good," Derrick laughed. "Maybe we can make this work, then."

Joe followed Derrick into the clubhouse and looked around at the others milling around. He didn't see Chris yet but knew it was only a matter of time before he showed up. Derrick pointed to the desk.

"I'll go get us checked in," he said. "Stay close in case they need you."

Joe nodded and continued his examination of the room and only returned his attention to Derrick when he stepped back away from the desk and pointed toward an area filled with golf clubs and other gear.

"They said we can pick up our clubs over there," he said. "They have us scheduled to start right before Chris's group."

Joe and Derrick headed over to the equipment desk and were both assigned to a set of golf clubs and a cart. Before they could walk out the door, however, a member of the golf course staff approached them.

"I'm Sean, the manager here," he said. "I'm so sorry, but there has been a little mix-up with the times."

"What type of mix-up?" Derrick asked. "I believe they set us to tee off in about fifteen minutes."

"Yes, that's correct," Sean said. "But I'm afraid we require parties to have four members in them and you and the party just after you only have two apiece."

"Oh, is there something we need to do?"

"Well, I hate to inconvenience you," Sean said. "Mr. Matheson, who set up your time, is such a great client of ours and I wouldn't want to upset him."

"No worries," Derrick said with a professional smile. "You just tell me what you need to do, and I'll tell you if we can accommodate."

"Thank you," Sean said, the relief clear on his face. "Would it be possible to have the pair behind you to pair up with yours? They seem like very nice gentlemen."

Joe turned toward the desk and spotted Chris and another man standing there. Chris made eye contact with Joe and narrowed his eyes, but quickly regained his composure. Joe turned back to Derrick and raised his eyebrows at him.

"Why, that would work perfectly," Derrick said. "It's always fun meeting new people and playing with a larger group. Maybe we can get a few pointers from them."

"Thank you so much for your flexibility," Sean said. "I will let them know you will play with them."

Sean walked away toward Chris and the other man, and Joe and Derrick went back to adjusting their clubs and preparing to take them outside. Completely ignoring Chris, Joe followed Derrick outside and loaded his clubs onto the back of their golf cart.

"This couldn't have worked out any better," Joe mumbled to Derrick. "Now we can get some goodwill in with him."

"Just remember," Derrick said. "I need to make sure I'm playing this as cool as a cucumber. Can't be losing my clients by acting crazy. That would be bad for me."

Joe slapped him softly on the back. "Trust me. I can be diplomatic about this. I won't jeopardize my oldest friend's life. No way."

Before they could chat more, Chris and his golfing partner walked out of the clubhouse and loaded their clubs. Chris's friend came over to shake hands when they finished.

"Thank you for letting us join you," he said. "I'm David and this is my friend Chris. We appreciate you being accommodating."

"Yes," Chris said, again making eye contact with Joe. "We appreciate it."

"Not a problem," Derrick said. "What do you say we get started?"

"Sounds like a plan," David said. "I've heard this is a great course. We normally play at another one here in town. Thought we would try this one out today instead."

"We haven't played on this one either," Derrick said. "I'm looking forward to it."

The four climbed into their golf carts and headed toward the first tee box. They all hit their drives and climbed back into the carts to locate their balls. Joe and Derrick were to the left of the fairway, and Chris and David were to the right, so they quickly split up.

"So, what's the plan?" Derrick asked when he and Joe were apart from the others. "How are we going to do this?"

"I say, for now, let's just play it cool and keep playing," Joe said. "See if we can't get him comfortable with us. I'm pretty sure he recognized me, so he's probably going to be standoffish for a bit."

"So, you plan to turn on the charm and get him to open up to us?"

"Think you can handle it?"

Derrick laughed and got out of the cart to hit his ball. After taking the shot and landing it perfectly near the green, he grinned at Joe. "You obviously don't understand what I do for a living."

Joe laughed and headed over to his ball. When he returned to the cart, he said, "Guess I have the best partner for this job on my team, then."

"I am good at what I do."

They continued their game and engaged Chris and David in small talk every chance they got. After a while, Joe saw Chris's demeanor change to a more friendly stance.

Somewhere around the eighth hole, Chris and Joe were standing near the carts while the others played their latest shots.

"So, what is this?" Chris asked while they waited. "You just come out here and pretend you aren't up to something."

"I'm not up to anything," Joe said. "I'm just playing a round of golf with my friend. Is there something I should be up to?"

Chris frowned at him. "Don't play with me. You and I both know you are with that girl that Melissa had been talking to. The one that has been investigating that stuff against my company."

"I just want to talk."

"I have nothing to talk about," Chris said.

Chapter 28

Chris walked away from him and climbed back into his golf cart. Joe gave Derrick a look when he returned, and they headed off in their cart to find their balls.

"We need a new tactic," Joe said.

"He outed you?"

"Pretty much."

"Let's play a couple more holes and let me get a feel for the other guy."

Joe nodded, and they continued their game. Derrick chatted with David every time they stopped near each other and soon the two had struck up quite a friendly banter.

"What was it you said you did for a living, David?" Derrick asked at the start of the eleventh hole. "Something in real estate, right?"

David nodded. "That's right. Commercial real estate. It's a pretty tough market, right now."

"So, I'm told," Derrick said. He headed to the tee box and prepared his shot. After hitting the ball and locating it, he turned back to David with a smile. "I have a client who is big into commercial real estate. He's been trying to find a new property for months now and just can't find the right spot."

"Really?" David said. "I'd be more than happy to help him if I could."

"Of course, I can't reveal who my client is," Derrick said, "but I'd be more than happy to drop your card off with him. He's been struggling with it lately and could use a good commercial realtor to help him out."

"That would be great!" David said, and fished a card out of his wallet. "I'm always looking for new clients to work with. We have a great selection of properties on the market right now. I'm sure we could find a great fit for him."

Derrick looked at the card and tucked it away in his wallet. "Thanks for this. I'll let him know how great you are."

"You just never know who you are going to meet when you are out on the golf course," David said with a shake of his head. "I'm certainly glad we paired up with the two of you today."

"It was certainly convenient," Chris muttered and headed up to take his next shot.

Derrick gave Joe a wink while he was away. Joe shook his head and watched Chris take his shot. After Chris walked away from the tee box and back toward David, Joe sighed and headed up to take his shot. Derrick moved a little closer to the other duo.

"What is it you do, Chris?" he asked as Joe was preparing to hit the ball. "Didn't you say you are in finance or something?"

"I'm the CEO of a finance firm, yes."

"I have a lot of friends in that industry," Derrick said, maintaining his friendly smile. "Of course, I am in the investment finance industry, so they collide often throughout my line of work."

"I'm sure they do."

"I love the industry I work in, don't you?" Derrick asked and continued when Chris only grunted a reply to him. "I love getting to help others grow their portfolios."

"Helping others is always nice," David said.

"It is," Derrick replied. "Joe and I both are big helpers."

"Let's just finish this game," Chris said and climbed back into the cart.

Derrick climbed back into the cart with Joe, and they headed off to find their balls.

"This isn't working," Joe said when they had pulled away. "We're going to lose him."

"Relax," Derrick said. "I'm just warming him up."

They played another hole before Derrick tried again.

"That was a great hole you had back there, Chris," he said. "You are an outstanding golfer."

"Thanks."

"Maybe you could give me a few pointers?" he asked. "I seem to struggle with my irons. What's your trick?"

Chris studied him for a few seconds with a frown before answering. "You seem to have a bit of an issue with your follow-through, and you hit the ball flat sometimes."

"Ah, yes, I have heard that before," Derrick said. "I'll have to keep that in mind on my next shot."

Joe watched Derrick chat with Chris and mentally crossed his fingers that they were making some headway in breaking Chris down. Derrick climbed back into the cart with Joe after they had all hit their first ball and headed off to find their next shot. This time, instead of Chris and David heading off to find their balls, they followed Joe and Derrick's cart.

"I thought I might give you a pointer or two after you hit this one," Chris said, a smile crossing his face for the first time that day. "Remember, watch that follow-through, and don't hit the ball flat."

"Gotcha," Derrick said and lined up his shot. He made the required adjustments, and Joe nodded in approval when the ball landed in the perfect spot on the green.

"That was great, Derrick," Joe said.

"It certainly was!" Chris agreed. "See, just keep working on those two things and you will be golden."

They all continued the round and quickly finished that hole before heading off to the next. Derrick headed up to the tee first, and David followed along behind him. Chris and Joe waited by the carts for their turn. When Joe didn't address Chris, the man turned toward him and sighed.

"I think I need your help," he said, causing Joe to turn in his direction in surprise.

"How can I help you?"

"I am in too deep," Chris said. "I spent six months trying to ignore the problem and another six months trying to cover it up. Now, I don't know what to do about anything, and I'm in an even bigger mess now than when I started."

"By covering it up," Joe said. "You mean framing Frankie."

"I swear I wasn't trying to frame her...at first, anyway," Chris said. "I just wanted her and Asher to back off."

"You went to a lot of trouble to do that," Joe continued. "Frankie's look-alike. All that fake evidence you created against her. You even set Melissa up."

"I know."

"I have to admit, though," Joe said. "I am impressed with how you somehow used Frankie's number to text Asher to show up at the park the night of his murder. That was impressive. And illegal, might I add. Asher was murdered while you were committing a felony, so that means—"

"Yes, yes," Chris hissed. "I get it. I know what I did. You don't have to remind me. I'm not proud of it. I was just trying to save the company."

"You sure you weren't just trying to save your job?"

"No, I swear!" Chris said. "Good people are working at that company. If word of this got out, no telling what the board of directors would do. They might vote to cut their losses and sell off the company! Then where would all the employees be?"

"So, you are telling me that everything you did was an attempt to save the company and all your employees' jobs?"

"I know how it sounds," Chris said with a shake of his head. "But I swear I was just trying to save the company. I panicked."

Joe sighed and looked at Chris from the corner of his eye. "And now you want my team to save you?"

Chris sighed. "I just don't know what to do at this point. They are investigating the company. I was trying to avoid it, but I...I couldn't figure out what was going on."

"With the embezzling, you mean?" Joe whispered. "How do I know you weren't the one doing that?"

"I wasn't involved. I swear."

"Well, you are in charge, so that certainly puts you in a perfect spot to do that," Joe continued. "If you weren't involved, who was?"

"I don't know," Chris said. "That's what I need your help with."

Joe noticed the others heading back toward them and stopped the conversation. He and Chris teed off and quickly rejoined the group. They didn't get to continue the conversation until they finished that hole and were starting the next.

"Look," Chris said when Derrick and David again walked away from them. "I have 300 employees under me. They all have families. Most do a good job. I need to figure out who is behind this embezzling and put an end to it, regardless of the costs. It's time to do the right thing."

"I have to admit that I'm having a hard time trusting you and believing your sincerity here," Joe said. "You were having an affair with a married woman and she's now dead because of it. Plus, my partner was in a lot of danger when she tried to help her."

"Yes, I'm aware," Chris said, hanging his head again. "I just wanted to protect everyone. It's becoming too much to handle. I need help."

"We just want the truth," Joe said. "But we can't find it if we don't have help from your company."

"What type of help?"

"We need access to your computer systems," he replied. "If we are going to find who is really behind the embezzling, we need access to everything."

"I'll see what I can do," Chris said with a nod. "The least I can do is help you sort this out and hopefully save the company."

"I'm going to be honest with you," Joe said. "Our priority is making sure Frankie doesn't go to jail for something she didn't do. I think you and I both know that she is innocent."

Chris nodded. "I understand."

"But I don't want you to think that we are against you either," Joe said. "We will look at the facts and the data and figure out what's going on. If you or your company isn't up to something, then our work should help you."

"I certainly hope it does," Chris said. "Many people are relying on their jobs and will be devastated if you guys don't uncover the truth."

Joe pulled a card out of his wallet and handed it to him after writing his number on it. "This is Frankie's attorney's card. I've written my cell number on it as well. Check into what type of access you can give us, then call me or call Frankie's attorney. We can get started as soon as we have access."

"I'll do this first thing in the morning," Chris said. "For now, how about we finish this game?"

He stuck out his hand in Joe's direction and Joe shook it. "I'm counting on you to come through on your end, now."

Joe nodded. "And I'm counting on you to come through for Frankie. After all that you and Melissa did to frame her, she deserves a little help from you."

"You can count on it."

Derrick and David returned to the carts and Joe and Chris quickly took their turn in the tee box. When they pulled away to locate their balls, Derrick gave Joe a secret fist bump.

"How did you know anything went down?" Joe asked with a chuckle. "I thought we were being discreet."

"Could tell from both your body language," Derrick said. "You both had been pretty tense throughout this round, and suddenly the tension went away."

"Was it that obvious?"

"It was if you knew what to look for," Derrick replied. "I happen to be an expert at it."

"So, tell me, Mr. Expert," Joe said. "What do you think about Chris? You think he's playing us?"

"I think he's scared," Derrick said. "I think he's really worried he's going to get in trouble."

"Well, hopefully, we can trust him," Joe said.

"Guess you don't have a choice," Derrick said. "By the way, you owe me a beer when we get done here?"

"Why?" Joe asked with a laugh. "Because you helped me get what I needed?"

"Nah," Derrick said and pointed at their scorecard. "Because I whipped you!"

"You are ridiculous," Joe said with a laugh as he looked over the score. "I'm sure there had to be a math error in there somewhere."

"Just buy the beer and quit trying to cheat," Derrick said with a laugh of his own.

"Do me a favor, will you?"

"What's that?"

"Don't tell Anna you won?" Joe said. "She'll never let me live this down. Hell, she'll probably take up golf just so she can try to beat me at it."

"Oh, I'm telling her," Derrick said. "All the times you beat me at stuff and now you want me to go easy on you?"

"Some friend you are!"

Chapter 29

"I might as well give you this now," Bryant said and held out the rubber band Joe had given him. "Joe said to give it to you if you felt worried."

Anna laughed and took it from him. "He hasn't pulled one out this entire trip. I was thinking he'd given up the habit."

"Based on the number of rubber bands I constantly find around our apartment, I can assure you, he has not."

Anna laughed again and pulled the band around her wrist. She smiled at it for a second before growing serious. "So, what are we prepared for, Bryant? I don't even know why they would want to talk to me."

"Yeah, it's hard to prepare when we don't know what they want," Bryant said. "I'm optimistically hoping this is just a routine 'what do you know?' type of thing."

"Pessimistically?"

"Pessimistically, I'm worried they think you did something wrong and want to detain you."

"Well, that's just great," Anna groaned. "Let's try to keep with a version of your optimism, shall we?"

"I'll do my best."

Anna sighed when the cab they had been riding in pulled up in front of the office building they had summoned her to. They climbed out and paid the cab driver before heading up to the door. Before they entered the building, Anna stopped on the step.

"If they keep me in here, please tell Marie that I hid a bottle of the good wine she likes in my bottom dresser drawer," she said. "And tell Claire that I have that outfit I borrowed from her in the back of my closet. Trust me, she'll know which one."

Bryant laughed. "It won't come to that."

"Well, if it doesn't," Anna said with a smirk, "forget I said anything."

"I swear," Bryant said as he held the door open for her. "Between you and my brother, I don't know how Marie and I survive this life of ours."

"You know life would be boring without us around," Anna whispered as they waited to go through security.

"Quiet," Bryant corrected. "It would be quiet without the two of you around."

Anna laughed, which caused the security guard to look up at her and frown.

"Sorry," she whispered and covered the next chuckle with her hand.

Bryant shook his head and chuckled to himself. "Not even in the door yet and already getting us in trouble."

After making it through security unscathed, Anna and Bryant located the right office and were instructed to sit in a small waiting area just outside. It wasn't long before the man who served as Chris's limo driver came to retrieve them.

When Bryant stood up with her when he approached, the man sighed and turned in his direction. "Who are you?"

"I'm her attorney," Bryant said without smiling. "Just in case."

"Well, come along then, 'just in case,'" the man said. "Let's get this over with."

He led them into a small room with a table and a handful of chairs. He motioned to one side of the table and Bryant and Anna took their seats while the man took the seat across from them. Anna crossed her legs and shook her left foot while she waited for the agent to begin their conversation.

He folded his hands in front of them on the table and glanced at both of them before beginning. "For starters, I am Agent Stephens. As I am certain you have surmised, I am currently working undercover."

"Yes, I assumed as much," Anna said with a nod.

"I cannot go into much detail regarding what I have been investigating, but I can tell you it is not pretty."

"What we've uncovered isn't pretty either," Anna said.

"Full disclosure. I have done some digging into you and spoken with your agents back home," he continued.

"Ah, Agents Hoage and Kamera," Anna said and smiled. "We're pretty fond of them."

Agent Stephens raised an eyebrow at her, which caused her to clear her throat. "I take it they didn't share my sentiment."

"They said you and your partner tend to show up amid their investigations," he replied.

"Our paths have crossed a few times," Anna said. "Through no fault of our own, I might add."

"Mmm-hmm."

"Look, it's not like Joe and I go around trying to get on the FBI's radar," Anna said. "We are good at what we do."

"Which is what, exactly?"

"We're private investigators."

"You have a license?"

"We do."

"And you work for someone?"

This time, Anna raised an eyebrow at him. "If you dug into our background to find Agents Hoage and Kamera, you know full well that Joe and I, along with our siblings, own a law firm together."

"Just making sure you were being honest."

"Why wouldn't I be?"

"Look, enough of this," Bryant said. "What do you want with Anna?"

"This is an important investigation," Agent Stephens said. "I cannot have someone coming in and mucking it up."

"However important this investigation is to you, it's even more important to me," Anna said. "One of my best friends is getting framed for it!"

"Have you found proof saying otherwise?"

"We've found a lot of shady stuff going on at that financial firm, that's for sure," Anna said. "And that Chris guy you've been driving around and Melissa have been actively trying to replace evidence we have on file."

"Yes, I am aware of that," he said. "Naturally, we have the limo bugged. So far they have not given you anything top incriminating."

"I assumed they were testing me to see if I was going to go through with what they wanted me to do," Anna said. "The first piece of evidence didn't affect the case at all. Once they knew our attorney had it, they tried a little harder."

"It still was not something significant," Mr. Stephens replied. "You had not yet fully gained their trust before Melissa died."

"I suppose not," Anna said.

"Anything else you need to discuss before I take my client and go?" Bryant asked.

"I just wanted to see if you knew anything else that would help my case," he replied, addressing Anna. "Anything you have discovered outside of what Chris and Melissa gave to you."

"At the moment, no," Anna said. "Is there anything I should know?"

"Just that this is an active FBI investigation you are meddling in," he said. "And that these people are dangerous. You need to be careful."

Anna shrugged. "Story of my life. What else is new?"

"I am going to leave you with my card," Mr. Stephens said and handed a card to both Anna and Bryant. "That way, if you run across something important, you have a way to contact me directly. Keep this information to yourself, however. I am undercover."

"And I am going to leave my card with you," Bryant said, sliding his card across the table to Agent Stephens. "Likewise, if you discover something we should know. Call me. We have someone who will answer our office phone, but it's best to call my cell phone while we are in town."

"So, wait," Anna said. "You called me out here just to warn me to keep my mouth shut? You couldn't have done that over the phone?"

Agent Stephens frowned at her. "I just wanted to feel you out. Make sure you weren't hiding something."

"I don't believe you," Anna said with a frown of her own.

Chapter 30

"Anna," Bryant warned.

"No, Bryant," she said, turning in his direction. "He pulled us out here and away from our investigation. For what? To 'feel me out?' To warn me not to out him? That doesn't make any sense. I could have done all of this with a simple phone call. There was no need to drag us out he—"

"Fine, fine," Agent Stephens said. "I get the picture."

"What then?"

He sighed. "I need your help."

"Why does the FBI always need my help?" Anna asked Bryant. "You would think with all their resources, they could handle things on their own."

"Look, I'm FBI," Agent Stephens said. "There are certain places I just can't get because of that."

"Like inside the financial company's building?"

"Exactly," he said with a nod. "I can't very well pose as a limo driver and get inside the building to investigate things."

"But I can."

He nodded.

"So, your plan is, what then?" Anna asked. "It's not like I have full access to everything."

"Isn't your partner working on that right now?"

"How did you know that?" Anna asked with a frown. "I'm not a fan of us being snooped on by the FBI."

"Look, we're getting desperate in this case," he said. "There just isn't enough evidence or information to investigate things like we normally do."

"So, you bugged our rooms hoping to get something?"

"I bugged you," he said. "Slipped a device in your purse when I stopped you the other night."

"You've got to be kidding me," Anna said. She jerked her purse off the floor and dumped its contents out on the table. After picking out the item that didn't belong to her, she tossed it across the table at him and shoved her belongings back inside. Once done, she looked at Bryant and said, "I believe we are done here."

"Wait, wait," Agent Stephens said. "There's more. Those cards I gave you..."

"Not those too!" Anna fumed. "You have some nerve. We are trying to help keep an innocent woman out of jail. I'd appreciate it if you didn't sabotage us."

"I promise I'm not trying to sabotage you," he said. "I just need your—"

"Help. Yeah, you said that." Anna glared at him.

"Look, I'm sorry," he said. "I'm just trying to figure out what is going on here. If we don't get this figured out, the entire company is going down. Hundreds of people could lose their livelihoods over this."

Anna sighed. "We don't want that."

"Then, help me," he said. "Please."

"I don't even know if we can get back in again," Anna said. "Joe's good at what he does, but it's a long shot. He's going to have to talk Chris into trusting us with his entire company."

"I am just asking for any help you can give me," Agent Stephens replied.

"And what about us?" Bryant asked. "We're just supposed to help you and not get anything in return? That doesn't seem like a fair trade."

"Yeah, you're going to have to give us something that helps us," Anna said.

"Like what?" Agent Stephens shrugged.

"How about you help us eliminate some of our loose ends?" Anna said. "We have several unresolved trails we haven't gotten around to chasing yet. You could save us some time."

Agent Stephens shrugged. "Tell me what they are, then I'll let you know if I can help."

Anna cocked her head. "Not that it matters now, but did Chris pay that security guard to erase the footage of Frankie in the laundry room the night of the murder?"

Agent Stephens nodded. "He was making a payment to that guy the night you and I met."

"So, you've known Frankie was innocent this entire time, and you didn't step in?" Anna asked. "You were just going to let an innocent woman go to jail for murder?"

"This is above Frankie," Agent Stephens said. "It's above the murder. We're talking about the livelihoods of hundreds of people and the customers who deal with that company.

Lots of businesses will suffer too if this company goes down without recovering this money."

Anna sighed. "Fine. I guess that's been taken care of, anyway. What about Chris's accusation about Frankie's intern program? He implied that she's the mastermind behind the entire thing and a plant in their company."

"I cannot comment on that," Agent Stephens said with a frown.

"Are you saying that the intern company is involved?" Anna asked and leaned back in her chair. "That is interesting."

"That is not what I am saying," Agent Stephens argued. "I am saying that the investigation is still ongoing. We don't know who is involved at this point."

"Hmm," Anna said. "I thought you said you were listening in on everything Chris told me."

Agent Stephens hesitated and Anna shook her head. "Did you think I would just forget about him telling me about tracing the money back to the intern company?"

"Fine, fine," Agent Stephens grumbled. "We have been looking into that, but we aren't prepared to say whether they are involved."

"That's good to know," Anna said.

"Anything else?"

"Chris said he had controls in place to stop the embezzling from happening again," Anna said. "Is that true, or is it an ongoing problem?"

Agent Stephens laughed. "Yeah, that's a lie. They are losing money like a leaky faucet."

"How much are they up to at the moment?"

"We're up to at least $20 million," Agent Stephens said. "I'm not at liberty to give you a full amount, nor do I have a completely accurate feel for the amount that's been taken, but that gives you an idea of what we're dealing with."

"That's a hefty amount," Bryant said. "And, complicated to get that much money out of one company."

"Exactly," Agent Stephens said. "We're dealing with a team of people behind this. It isn't just one person or a simple 'putting controls in place to stop it.' It has been happening for a few years now. Whoever is taking the money knows what they are doing."

Anna turned to Bryant. "That's why they've been trying to sweep it all under a rug. They wanted Frankie and Asher off the trail as quickly as possible so they didn't open up a big can of worms."

"Then, when the murder happened, they tried to use it as a distraction to further hide the embezzlement issue," Bryant said. "They were hoping the police would focus on Frankie and everything would just end with her being arrested."

"I'm not sure how that was going to work, considering the embezzlement was still going on," Agent Stephens said. "Still is to our knowledge."

"And you can't trace it?" Anna asked. "You can't demand that they give you access to everything so you can figure out where it's going?"

"There are so many moving parts to this that we can't just sweep in," he replied. "We need to be delicate about the surveillance we do, or we risk scaring off the big fish and only being able to catch a handful of guppies."

"We certainly don't want that."

"Which is why I need your help."

Anna sighed. "Fine. If we run across something that will help with this, we'll let you know. While our priority is helping Frankie, I understand what you're up against. We'll do what we can."

"Thank you," he replied. "I mainly wanted to make sure we will not be working against each other. The last thing we need is an investigation that causes ours to run off the rails."

"We won't let that happen," Anna said. "Can we get you to promise to let us know if you find something that will clear Frankie?"

"I will keep an eye out for that," he said. "Just as long as you keep an eye out for stuff to help me. There are lives at stake."

"Just to be clear," Anna said. "I'm well aware of the lives at stake. My friend is one of them. And, if it comes down to her going to jail for something she didn't do or this company falling, I choose her."

"It is nice to know where your priorities lie," Mr. Stephens said.

"Trust me," Anna said. "My priorities are always with my family. Nothing will change that."

"I understand," he replied. "You have my card."

"Oh, no way!" Anna said. "I'm not taking this thing with me." She pulled her phone out and took a picture of the card before handing it back to him. "There. I have your contact information. We'll be in touch."

Anna stood, and Bryant followed suit. "I assume we are free to go, right?"

"Yes, you can go," he said with a nod.

Chapter 31

Anna was quiet on the way back to the hotel and was still fuming when she and Bryant got back to their hotel rooms. Joe's normally playful attitude changed the moment he sensed her anger. She tossed her purse down on her bed and flopped down beside it.

"What's wrong?" Joe asked. "Did something happen?"

"Anna made a friend today," Bryant said. "Agent Stephens, the agent assigned to this embezzlement case, apparently only stopped her the other day so he could bug her."

"You're kidding!" Joe said.

"Yeah, apparently his warning me to be careful was just a ploy to get me to stop long enough to slip a device in my purse," she said from her spot on the bed. "He knew all about your rendezvous with Chris today because of it."

"That's absurd!"

"I can't believe I didn't think to check for something like that," she said. "I'm so mad at myself and him. Mostly him."

"It's not your fault, Anna," Joe said. "You wouldn't have known that he was going to pull something like that."

"I guess at least it didn't cause us trouble with this case," she said. "And we found it quick enough that he won't get anything else out of us we don't want him to have."

"What did he want?"

"He wants our help, naturally."

"Of course he does."

"If we can get inside the building or get any information out of the company, he wants us to share it with him," Anna continued. "I demanded that he do the same with the information he finds that can help Frankie."

"We didn't promise him anything," Bryant said. "Only said that we would share info with him if he would share with us. We can't help him at all if we can't get access to their computer systems. Speaking of which, how did it go with you today, Joe?"

"Great," he replied and looked at Derrick, who had claimed the armchair in the room. "Derrick was a great help. He was the one who got Chris to open up to us."

"Thank you," Derrick said. "It's great to get the recognition I deserve for once."

Joe laughed. "We ended up getting to play the round with Chris and his partner for the day. Chris recognized me right away but waited to confront me for several holes. He was not interested in helping us at all at first."

"Until I pulled some strings, of course," Derrick said.

"Long story short, after some crafty work on Derrick's behalf, he agreed to help us."

"Seriously?"

"Yep, he has been trying to figure out what's been going on himself and finally decided that he's just in over his head."

"And he's going to let us in?"

"He said he was going to set up something with his IT team and see if they could give us access to everything."

"That's great!"

"You haven't told her the best part yet, Joe!" Derrick said.

Joe grinned at her. "He already called me and wants us to meet him at the office tomorrow morning around 9. He said the IT team will set us up some computers and let us have access to everything under the sun."

"Joe, that's fantastic," Bryant said. "Good job, guys."

The hotel door opened soon after and Marie entered with a newly ankle monitor-free Frankie.

"Yay!" Anna said and stood up to hug Frankie. "It's great to have you back on the law-abiding side of the fence again, Frankie."

"Yeah, I'm relieved to have that thing gone," she said and looked down at her ankle. "Never again. I will not get so much as a speeding ticket for the rest of my life."

Anna laughed. "Well, it's certainly been a day for the rest of us. Let's get comfy and we'll fill you all in."

Joe and Anna took turns filling the others in on their days and when it was all said and done, everyone looked drained.

"I say we don't think about this anymore for the night," Bryant said. "Let's not think about the FBI. Let's not think about the office. Let's just get some dinner and get a good night's sleep. In the morning, we can get up early and plan out our attack."

"I'm certainly game for dinner," Anna said.

"And sleep," Marie added.

"As long as dessert is involved," Joe said with a laugh. "Before bed, of course."

Chapter 32

"Are you sure we were supposed to meet Chris back here, Joe?" Anna asked, looking around at the surrounding alley. "He didn't just want us to come in the front door?"

"He said back here," Joe said, looking down at his watch. "Something about he didn't want to spook the employees by bringing us through security and having to explain why we are here."

Anna frowned and glanced around again, only to jerk her attention back to the door to the office building. Chris opened the door and looked around at them.

"I am so sorry it took me so long," he said. "I got tied up with finding you all a quiet room to work."

"As long as we get access to what we need, it doesn't matter to us," Joe said.

Chris nodded and motioned for them to come inside. Joe led the way, followed by Anna, Marie, Bryant, and Frankie. When they had all made it inside, Chris secured the door behind them and paused.

"I want to avoid going through official channels to get you in and out of here," he said. "I'm glad you brought Ms.

Fritts along with you because that will allow me to eliminate one extra employee from my need-to-know list."

"What do you mean?" Anna asked with a frown.

"Just that Frankie can help you navigate our system rather than another employee," he replied. "I would like to keep this as centralized as possible."

"That's probably a good idea, considering we don't know who all is involved," Joe said.

Chris sighed. "I know I can't make you believe me, but I promise I'm not involved in this."

"I guess we will just have to see where the evidence leads us," Anna said.

Chris nodded and pointed to a secured door just ahead. "I have to use my card to get in and out of here. I plan to log your visits manually so that everything is official, just a little off the record. I have lunch being catered in later, so hopefully, that will eliminate the need for you to come and go."

"What if we need more than one day to track this down?" Anna asked. "This is a lot to do in just one day."

"We can repeat this for however many days necessary," Chris said. "I just want to get to the truth and hopefully save the company."

After he'd gotten them through the secured door, Chris motioned toward a back elevator. Before long, they had ridden to the fourth floor of the building, which proved to be empty save for a conference table, an IT employee, and several computers.

"This is one of our IT techs, Taylor," Chris said, causing the man to look up from the computer he was working on. "He's going to get you all set up on the computers."

"Why don't you and Anna get started with Taylor," Bryant said to Joe, "while Marie and I have a quick chat with Chris."

"Sounds like a plan," Joe said.

He and Anna walked over to the computer Taylor was working on and sat down next to him. Frankie sat across from them and waited for instructions. Meanwhile, Bryant and Marie took the other end of the table. After everyone was settled, Marie pulled out a notebook to take notes.

"Why don't you start by telling us about this company," Bryant said. "That way we have a little background on everything."

"Well, the company started as a small family-owned shop back in the 50s," he said. "Back then, it was Carlee & Goar after the duo who owned it. They built it into a gigantic business over the years and kept it a private company with just them as the sole owners for decades."

"That's impressive," Bryant said. "Most businesses wind up going public after they reach a certain point."

"Yes, as did we," Chris said with a nod. "Eventually, the owners became older and ready to retire, but none of their family were capable or willing to take over the company. Carlee sold his shares to Goar, who continued running it until he passed about eight years ago."

"Is that when the company went public?"

"Yes," Chris said. "Once it went through the probate process and none of the family wanted to continue running the business, a board of high-ranking employees purchased it and took it public."

"Sounds pretty standard," Bryant said. "Was there any animosity toward the drive to take the company public?"

"There were a few standouts that said Carlee and Goar wouldn't have wanted it to go public."

"Like whom?"

"Most are no longer with the company," Chris said. "They left soon after we made the announcement. There is only a handful left at this point."

"Could we get a list of the ones you remember?"

"I can jot down the names I remember," Chris said. "It was so long ago, and everyone seems to be fine with the situation now."

Marie handed Chris a piece of paper and a pen, and he quickly began jotting down names. After he finished, he handed it back to her, and she glanced over it.

"Do you think any of these people might want revenge on the company or the people who work here?" she asked.

"Everyone seems fine with our company's situation but who's to say someone isn't harboring some grief."

"We'll look into it," Bryant said. "How about the board of the company? Anything going on there?"

"Not that I'm aware of," Chris said. "I brought a company hierarchy chart with me in case there is something there you need to look into."

He reached into a briefcase he'd brought with him and pulled it out. Marie took it and looked over it for a few seconds before tucking it away with Chris's list of employees. She looked up at Bryant and shrugged. He frowned in response and looked at Chris.

"Is there anything else you can think of we might need to know at the moment?" he asked. "Frankie can walk us through what accounts to look at, but is there anything else company-related you might know?"

Chris thought for a few seconds before shaking his head. "I can't think of anything else that might help you. Of course, if you run across anything else you need to know, I can address it then."

"Great," Bryant said. "We'll let you get back to work and we'll get started in here. We'll let you know if we have questions or problems."

"Oh, one last thing," Chris said before standing to his feet. "That phone on the desk is your direct line to my office. All you have to do is press the first programmed number and it will come right to me. It also forwards to my cell phone when I'm away from my desk, so you can reach me immediately."

"Thanks," Bryant said, glancing at the phone. "We'll keep that in mind."

Chris nodded and gathered his things and left the room. Soon, Taylor finished with the setup of the computers and was ready to hand those over to them as well. Anna looked up at Marie when she approached her chair and sat next to her.

"Did you hear everything Chris told Bryant and me?" she asked.

Anna yawned and nodded. "Didn't seem like there was much to tell, but yeah, I heard him."

"What have you learned here?" Marie asked.

"Nada, so far," Anna said. "Still waiting for everything to get set up."

"Almost done," Taylor said. He looked over at Frankie and asked. "Do you remember how to navigate the system?"

"Yes, I do," Frankie replied.

"Good," he pointed to a slip of paper sitting to the side of the computer. "I have a login and password written here that will give you access to everything. I've also set up printers here in case you need to print something."

"Thank you, Taylor," Anna said after he'd pointed out the printers on a table in the corner. "We can take it from here if you have everything working."

He nodded and sighed in relief when he stood up. "If you run into any issues, just let Mr. Shepard know. I can be right back up to work on things."

The group waited for Taylor to leave the room before discussing their action plan. Anna and Joe immediately dove onto the computers and started flipping through the programs they found there.

"So, where are we going to start?" Marie asked.

"There is a lot here to look at," Anna said. "They have given us access to everything under the sun."

Joe sighed. "You remember that first case we worked on where we spent all that time going through those accounts and paperwork?"

"Yeah?" Bryant said and raised an eyebrow at him.

"This is gonna be worse," Anna finished for him.

Chapter 33

"Well, that's great," Marie said with a groan. "Where do we start?"

"What do you think, Frankie?" Anna asked. "Start with the original invoice that started all this mess?"

"I bet we could work on more than one thing at once," she replied. "Someone can track that invoice. Someone else can look into some of the other invoices I found."

"What's the rest of the team going to do?" Marie asked.

"How about you and Bryant work on general investigations related to the accounts these invoices flow through?" Joe asked. "That should give us all plenty to do."

"Let's get started," Bryant said.

Frankie spent the next half hour getting them all going with their tasks. Afterward, she sat down at her computer and logged in.

"Wow," she said as she went through the programs. "They did give us access to everything. Some of this stuff is way above what I ever had access to."

"Why don't you show me and Anna what you wound up researching," Joe said. "That way we aren't redoing work you've already done."

"That's a good idea," she said and pulled a chair up between them. She walked them through her research and all the accounts she'd gone through to find the missing invoice. When she reached the end of her search, she sighed. "See, then it starts back over again. I traced it through these accounts and it went right back into a circle and back into the original account."

"What if it didn't, though?" Joe said. "What if we just think it went in a circle?"

"You think it went into a different account?" Anna asked.

"So, I've been thinking about that," he continued. "It couldn't have just disappeared. It had to go somewhere."

"But, where?"

"If I were to attempt this, I would try to disguise it," he said. "Break up amounts, combine invoices, make it difficult to track."

"All right, let's assume they did that," Anna said. "How are we ever going to figure out how many invoices we are dealing with?"

"I might help with that," Frankie said. "When I was looking at this invoice, I realized whoever set up the description on it in the system didn't follow the proper protocol."

"What do you mean?" Joe asked.

"Our descriptions should follow a specific protocol," she replied. "They should put a four-digit number at the beginning of each one that represents which employee set it up, but this one didn't. I ran across another invoice while researching this one that was set up the same way."

"You don't say?" Joe said with a grin. "Well, it seems like our embezzler just gave us a wide-open door into finding which invoices they adjusted or fabricated."

"Can you search for invoices like that somehow?" Bryant asked.

"I'll just write up a quick algorithm to pull them out," he replied, already typing on the computer. "It won't take too long but may take some time to execute."

"While you write that, I'll start looking at these people Chris gave us," Anna said. "Maybe there is something in their online activity or something."

"Good idea."

The room grew silent, and everyone got to work on their tasks. Anna flipped through pages and pages of social media sites and other internet information, hoping to find something that would help them. Occasionally, she would find something that would warrant a quick note, but mostly, her search seemed to come up empty. After about half an hour, she yawned and stretched.

"Anybody find anything?" she asked. "These folks I've looked at so far are pretty boring. Or at least they keep their information off the web."

Bryant shook his head, and Marie looked up at her with a grimace.

"Just a lot of numbers, so far," Marie said. "How's that algorithm coming, Joe?"

"Just about finished writing it, then I got to run it," he replied, not looking away from his computer. "Once it runs, I imagine we'll have a lot more to work with."

Anna sighed and glanced back at her computer, but her phone started ringing and interrupted her. She frowned at it momentarily until she saw Alex's face pop up on her screen.

She walked into the hallway and answered the phone with a smile. "Well, hello!"

"Hello," Alex said in return. "Did I catch you at an ok time?"

"Of course!" she replied. "We're waiting on a program Joe's writing to run, so this is perfect."

"Good," he said. "It's good to hear your voice. I miss you."

Anna sighed in relief and said quietly, "I miss you, too. I feel like we've been away from each other so much lately."

"Me too," he said. "We need to stop that."

"I agree."

Anna frowned when the background noise became loud. "Where are you? It sounds loud."

"Oh, I'm just out at a place where there are a lot of people," he said. "But I wanted to get you on the phone right now to get something on your schedule before you filled in the date with something else."

"Really?" she asked. "What are we doing?"

"I just got an exclusive dinner reservation with that new Italian place you've been talking about," he said.

Anna gasped. "Not Lacorra?"

"That's the one," he said. "I snagged a reservation for Valentine's Day. Are you doing anything that day?"

"If I was, I'm not now."

Alex laughed. "Good."

"You just made my day!" Anna said. "I've been wanting to eat there. Everyone has said it's fantastic."

"So, I've heard," he said. "I figured we were due for a special dinner."

"Special, huh?"

"I guess any dinner's special when you're at it."

Anna's smile widened. "Likewise."

"Hey, listen," he said. "I've got to go, but I just wanted to say I love you and I'll see you soon."

"Hopefully, it's soon," Anna said. "I miss you."

"I miss you, too."

"I love you," Anna said. "Bye, Alex."

"Bye, Anna."

When the call ended, Anna sighed and smiled at the phone for a few seconds before heading back into the conference room. Joe raised an eyebrow at her when she returned.

"Be careful," he said. "You're going to float away with all those heart bubbles around your head."

She laughed and sat down next to him again. "I needed that."

"I know you did," he replied. "By the way, I have the algorithm running. We'll probably start getting some results here in twenty minutes or so."

"Good," Anna said, growing distracted. "That will give me time to look into something."

"What?"

"Oh, it's probably nothing," Anna said. "Alex's conversation just made me realize something I sort of had overlooked before."

She pulled out her list of names and began flipping through screens on her computer again. After she'd found the information that she'd overlooked before, she pointed to the screen.

"This," she said. "So, this guy is a board member, and this woman is on the list of disgruntled employees that didn't like the public company thing. They just happen to have dinner at the same place every couple of weeks."

"How do you know that?" Bryant asked.

"Credit card receipts," she said, giving him a straight look when he narrowed his eyes. "What can I say? I'm thorough?"

"Overlooking the glaring way you found that information," Bryant said, "how does that help us?"

"Well, I mean people can eat at the same restaurants, but their credit cards are being run on the same day within minutes of each other."

"So, you think they are eating together?"

"It can't be a coincidence," she said. "They could be having an affair like everyone else in this company."

"That still makes it interesting to us, considering they've both wound up on one of our lists," Joe said. "Maybe we need to look more into their connection."

"I'll get right on that."

The room grew quiet again, and Anna turned her attention back to her computer. Starting with a general search, Anna began compiling a list of the female employee's family and personal information. After she had dug as far as she could into her information, she switched her focus to the male board member and repeated the process.

When she'd finished, she sat back and looked at the information she found. With a frown, she went right back to the computer and began typing again. Alternating between the list of information she'd come up with and her computer, she continued researching, only to push her computer away and grumble a few minutes later.

"Nothing?" Joe asked, looking up at her from his computer.

"There are just so many angles I have to connect," she said. "Doing it all manually is going to take forever."

"What do you have so far?" he asked.

"Well, I have all their family lines and friendships laid out that I could find online," she said. "I've also been able to get a lot of their properties and other assets sorted out. Now, I just need to find a connection between them all."

"Well..."

"Yeah, yeah, I know," she said. "I could write an algorithm. I was just hoping it wouldn't come to that."

"Well, if it was going to be easy, we wouldn't be here," he said.

Anna rolled her eyes, sighed, and started typing. After a couple of seconds, she looked at his computer and smirked. "Bet I can get mine to run before yours finishes."

"You're on," he said.

"Guys, it is not a competition," Bryant said.

"Says you," Anna said, turning her attention back to her computer and causing Joe to laugh.

Joe watched her work while keeping his other eye on his algorithm. She clicked the button to run it just as he was finishing up.

"Done," she said, sitting back in her chair. "I believe I win this round."

"I don't know," he argued. "That was certainly close. I'm pretty sure mine finished first."

"No, it didn't!"

"Guys!" Marie and Bryant said in unison.

Anna sent Joe a grin, and he laughed before looking at his computer screen.

"Alright, let's see what we have," he said.

He went to work pulling up the information his algorithm had produced and quickly began printing documents. Anna yawned and watched her algorithm run for a few seconds before absentmindedly opening up a new web browser and pulling up the restaurant Alex had booked a reservation at.

For several minutes, she flipped through the images and menu, a smile growing on her face. She was so distracted that she didn't even notice when Marie walked up behind her until her sister said, "Oh, is that the place those people are meeting at?"

"No," Anna said. "I got side-tracked while waiting for my algorithm to run and…" She leaned back and looked up at her sister while smiling. "Alex called to say he had booked us a reservation here in a few months. I was just checking it out. Didn't think I'd get to eat there. It's pretty exclusive."

"Uh, yeah, I'd say so," Marie said and sat down next to her and examined the computer screen. "I hear the reservations fill up weeks at a time."

"Me, too," Anna said with a smile. "I'm excited."

"Looks romantic," Frankie said, coming around the side of the table to have a look herself.

"Mmm-hmm," Anna said.

Marie raised an eyebrow at her. "One girl I graduated college with was just proposed to in that restaurant."

"Oh, is that Lacorra?" Frankie asked with a gasp. "One of my friends got engaged there too."

"Seems like love is in the air there," Marie said. "Do you think..."

A rush of butterflies ran through Anna, and she gasped. "You don't think that Alex is going to propose, do you?"

"Well, you two have been together for three years now," Marie said. "It wouldn't be the most surprising thing in the world."

Anna smiled to herself and clicked through the pictures again. When Joe laid a pile of papers on the table, she sighed and closed the tab.

"All right," he said. "Here's what we are working with. These are all the invoices posted that included that uncharacteristic coding structure."

"Well, looks like we have like 300 to work through," Anna said with a groan. "That's not too bad, I suppose."

"I have more to print," Joe said. "I just pulled out the last six months."

"Six months!" Anna said. "Whoever is doing this has been running this many invoices? That's an enormous amount."

"I'm afraid Frankie is going to have to help us make heads or tails of it," he said. "I'm not sure how they are filtering through the various accounts, but I agree that this is an enormous number of invoices."

Frankie picked up the pile and began looking through them. "Looks like they are all under the threshold, so that could be why they are staying under the radar."

"What do you mean?" Bryant asked. "What type of threshold is there?"

"If an invoice is over $5,000, it must have management approval," she said. "So far, the invoices I've looked at have all been under that amount. It also looks like they are being sent through several departments and accounts, so not one employee is going to be working on all these."

"Well, that's just great," Anna said. "That just widens our net."

"Yeah, but the good thing is that these all have to merge somewhere," Frankie said. "So, while they may seem all spread out, eventually they have to come together."

"Ah, so if the bad guy is really behind these, you think they will all wind up posting in the same account at some point."

"Exactly."

"Well," Joe said. "Guess it's time to get them sorted and traced, then."

"I'll start by sorting them into similar accounts," Frankie said. "All the invoices that ran through the same account will be grouped."

"Then it will be up to us to track down where they all went," Joe said.

"We'll divide out the piles," Bryant said. "Hopefully, it won't take long to see some sort of pattern."

Joe leaned toward Anna. "Bet I find a connection before you do."

"You're on," Anna said with a grin.

"Guys!" Marie and Bryant said in unison, causing the entire room to laugh.

Chapter 34

Anna yawned and flipped through a few more pages of the stack of invoices she was working on before running a hand through her hair. She looked up at the others and sighed when they seemed as unorganized as she felt.

Frustrated, she gathered the invoices back together and shuffled them around to start over with her search. She picked up the first two invoices in her new stack and looked at the totals and information listed on the page.

Beside her, Joe sighed and pushed his chair back. When he stood, one paper in his stack fell off the table and landed near Anna's foot. Absentmindedly, she bent down to pick up the paper and glanced at it before she handed it back to Joe. She froze when she noticed the top number on the page.

"Wait," she said. "Joe, look at this. These two invoices of mine add up to be the same as this item on your account listing."

"Let me see," Frankie said. Anna handed the papers to her, and Frankie spent several seconds reviewing the information Anna had found. "Hmm, this is interesting. It looks like they are coded together too."

"What do you mean?"

"So, both invoices have a description that ends in a three-digit number," she said. "The entry on the account Joe also has that number in its description."

"Sounds like someone is trying to keep track of what they are doing," Anna said.

"It makes sense," Joe said. "Whoever is putting all these invoices in needs to find them again to make sure they get the money for them."

"Looks like they do that by adding codes to the descriptions," Frankie said. "It's subtle, and if you weren't looking for something, it would be easy to overlook. But it's still distinct, so the person behind this could still find everything later when they want to get paid."

"Sounds like it's time to rethink how we are looking at these invoices," Bryant said. "Let's spend some time grouping our invoices by these description numbers."

The room grew silent once more, aside from the shuffling of papers. Within half an hour, they had divided their stacks of invoices into several piles. Anna looked through her stacks and wrote the description codes she found on a piece of paper.

"That's a good idea," Joe said. "Pass that my way when you get done and I'll write mine down so that we have a running list going."

Anna finished up and handed the paper to Joe. While he was writing his numbers on the paper, the door to the conference room opened and a caterer came in with food for the group. She smiled and began setting up, but did little to disturb their work.

"Thank you," Anna said with a smile as the woman finished setting up and prepared to leave. "We appreciate it."

The woman smiled and waved goodbye. Anna headed over to the food she'd brought and fixed a plate while the others finished adding their numbers to the sheet. When she sat back down in front of her computer, she realized the algorithm she'd written earlier had finished its job and was waiting for her to review the information it had gathered.

She took a bite of her food and started filtering through the findings. It wasn't long before her attention was more on the information she was reading than the food she was eating. She was so distracted that she never noticed the others preparing plates and sitting back down to eat lunch.

"Your food is going to get cold if you keep ignoring it like that," Joe teased while taking a bite of the food on his plate.

"What?" Anna asked, looking up at him in confusion. She glanced from her plate to her computer and back to him again. "I think I might have found something."

"Whatcha got?"

"Look at this," she said. "My algorithm turned out some interesting stuff. For starters, it's pulling some family members up that both of our targets have in common."

"So, they might be related?" Joe asked. "That is rather interesting, but might explain why they both work at the same place and have dinner together regularly."

"Yeah, I thought that too until I started looking at this relative." She pointed out a name on her list before clicking to another open tab on her browser. "I started looking into everyone that came up and found something interesting about this one."

"Looks like this one changed their name," Joe said with a frown. "What was it before they changed?"

"Their last name was Carlee," she replied.

"As in Carlee and Goar?" Bryant asked. "The former owners of the company?"

"We would have to confirm that," Anna said. "But what are the odds that this person isn't from the same company?"

"Let's regroup," Marie said. "Anna, you work on figuring out if that person is related to the Carlee person who originally owned this company, and we'll keep working on these invoices."

"I agree with that," Joe said. "We need to get these invoices as narrowly grouped as possible. That way we can figure out where the actual money went after it left this company."

"And, better yet," Bryant said, "who started and accepted payment."

Anna handed her stacks of invoices around the table to the others and went back to her computer. Between taking bites of her lunch, she dug deeper into the relative the employee and board member had in common and soon had built a list of information about them.

With a little luck and extensive research, eventually, she grinned and pushed away from her computer. The others looked up from the work they were doing.

"Well, I can tell you without a doubt that this Carlee relative of our targets and the Carlee family that originally owned this company are the same," she said. "I've confirmed it with online death, birth, and court records."

"Interesting," Bryant said. "So, we have some of the original owner's family members who work with the company in some capacity and are meeting up regularly."

"And all three people are taking steps to keep their true identities a secret," Anna said. "I've had to dig pretty deep to find this information, and it appears they've all done things to hide what families they belong to."

"I don't know what to make of that," Joe said. "That all sounds pretty fishy to me."

"I agree," Anna said. "I think to gauge what's going on, we need to talk with these people."

"I don't think we have anything to lose," Bryant said with a shrug. "Might as well at least attempt to interview them."

"Good," Anna said. "Because I already sent the family member an email."

"Hopefully, they will respond," Bryant said with a nod.

"If not, we'll move on to trying to contact these employees here," Joe said. "This will be a good way to test the water."

"Guys," Frankie said, interrupting their conversation. "I found something."

"What do you have, Frankie?"

"While you have been working on that, I've been merging these invoices," she said, "and tracking them, of course. I've been able to narrow down several of them." She pointed out three of the stacks of invoices in front of her before continuing. "These three stacks have roughly twenty-five invoices in them, but they all wind up filtering through one general ledger account."

"That's a good start," Marie said. "What happens to them after they get to that account?"

"So, they are still separated into three amounts at the point they enter the account," Frankie said. "It's when they leave the account where things get interesting."

"Do they combine at that point?" Anna asked.

"Yes, there is one entry that accounts for all these invoices," Frankie said.

"Now, we're getting somewhere," Joe said. "What happens to them after that?"

"So, I've been able to trace that amount through several other accounts," Frankie said. "It splits back up through a few of them, but winds up joining again in the accounts payable account."

"That seems like a necessary account for it to wind up in," Anna said. "Do you know where the money goes when it's paid?"

"Yep, but that's where I lose it," Frankie said. "I printed a copy of the check that our company sent out, but the company that receives the funds is a bit of a ghost."

"What do you mean?"

"They have it listed on the check, of course," Frankie said, "but I can't figure out what they are or what they do. The only information about them online is that they were established in the 1970s. Other than that, there is nothing."

"What have you found?"

Frankie shrugged. "I have the name of the company from the check. Acclaimed Builders. Other than that, there's nothing. Nothing about them online. No record of them in any type of official capacity. It's like they don't exist."

"Weird," Anna said, turning to Joe. "I would assume Acclaimed Builders is some sort of construction company, wouldn't you?"

"That would make sense," Joe said. "But considering this company isn't expanding locations, I don't see why a financial firm would pay a construction company."

"I also don't understand why a construction company wouldn't have online records with the state," Anna continued. "Are you sure there isn't anything online about them, Frankie?"

"I mean, they are keeping their records active," she said with a shrug, "so they are still an established business. But the information is a shell. The address they have listed is from one of those address forwarding places, and the person listed on the company's information doesn't appear to exist. I can't find any information about them. Also, from what I can tell, we have not been sending out 1099 forms for this vendor, so there isn't even information we can track about them that way."

"There has to be something," Joe said. "Somewhere this company had to set up their organization. Where is all the paperwork related to it?"

Anna shrugged. "It was in the 1970s. Everything would have been on physical paper back then."

"And, if it was a small company, they probably never digitized their records."

"Exactly."

"So, where can we find information about a company that is so off the grid they haven't updated their information since the 70s?" Joe asked.

Anna sat back and thought for a few moments. "Well, you know the library usually has old records of things. Maybe they have something in their newspapers from back then."

"That's a good idea," Joe said. "We could check the microfiche and see if we find anything."

"Good plan," Bryant said. "How about we call it a day here and tomorrow you two can research at the library, and Marie, Frankie, and I can look more into these people?"

"Great," Marie said. "It feels like we are getting somewhere with this, finally. I'm going to call Chris and let him know we are done for the day and that we will work out of the office tomorrow. I'm sure he'll be relieved to have us out of his hair for a while."

Anna and the others began gathering up their paperwork and other items they had brought with them and got throughout the day while Marie made the call. After a quick chat, she hung up and looked up at them.

"He said to hang out for a minute, and he would be up shortly to get us out of the building," she said.

The others went back to cleaning up their spaces and logging out of the computers. They finished up just in time to see Chris walk into the conference room. He smiled at them apprehensively when he approached.

"Hopefully, it's good news that you are leaving so early in the day?" he asked.

"We've made some headway," Bryant said. "There is now some research we need to do away from the office."

"But I'm sure we will need to return the day after tomorrow for more time with your computer systems here," Anna said.

"That won't be a problem," Chris said. "Just call me when you need to visit again, and I'll get you back in."

When Chris headed to the doors, the others followed. Before long, they arrived on the ground floor in front of the exit door at the back of the building. Chris opened the final secured door and stood with it open while they all exited the building.

"Thank you all for your devotion to helping our company," he said. "We truly appreciate it."

"To be fair," Anna said, "we are here to help Frankie. If we help you in the meantime, that is great, but I don't want to misrepresent our devotion here."

"I understand," Chris said with a nod. "Please keep me in the loop, and I'll see you again the day after tomorrow."

They waited for him to close the door before turning to each other.

"I called for us a car earlier," Joe said. "It should be here in about five minutes. I told them to meet us in the parking lot around the corner."

They walked around the corner but stopped when a woman approached them. Anna frowned when she realized the woman seemed to have been waiting for them behind a large tree that was part of the building's landscape.

"You emailed my cousin," the woman whispered when they approached.

"Oh, the person from the Carlee family?" Anna asked. "I emailed someone."

"We would like to meet," the woman said after nodding. "Can we do it tomorrow at noon?"

Bryant looked over at Marie before answering. "Marie and I can meet with you tomorrow. The others have something on their schedule already."

"Great," the woman said and handed him a card. "This is where we would like to meet. It won't take long."

She walked away before they could ask any further questions and sped back inside the building. Anna raised an eyebrow at Joe when she had disappeared.

"Yep, I agree," he said in response. "This case keeps getting more and more interesting."

Chapter 35

Marie looked around the parking lot at the address on the card the woman had given them the day before and frowned when she didn't find any other vehicles. She took a few steps toward the building and gazed up at it while Bryant finished up with their cab.

She frowned at him when he joined her but glanced around again. Together, they looked over the parking lot and building before turning their attention to the rest of the surrounding neighborhood, which consisted mainly of more office buildings, just like the one in front of them.

"I don't know about this, Bryant," Marie said. "This doesn't feel very safe."

"Very secluded," he said. "Tell you what, how about you call Frankie? Tell her you are going to check in with her every ten minutes. If you don't check in within that timeframe, she needs to call the police and give them our location."

"Good idea," Marie said. "I'll set alarms and text her to let her know we are ok. I probably need some sort of code word in case we need her help."

"How about you tell her you are going to text her food names, but if you text her the word 'banana,' you need her to call the police and send them out?"

"I'll call her right now before we go in."

Marie quickly dialed Frankie's number and filled her in on the plan. When she hung up the phone, she turned to Bryant. "I'm glad we had her stay out of this. We wouldn't have had anyone to call for backup if she'd come with us."

"I agree," Bryant said. "Joe and Anna probably wouldn't be able to hear their phones if we called them."

"If they remember to put their phones on silent at the library, at least," Marie said with a chuckle.

Bryant laughed with her. "Yeah, the last time they spent time in a library together they about got themselves banned."

"Eek, that was also the time you and I went off and got ourselves taken hostage."

"Yeah, don't remind me," he said, growing serious again. "How about we don't let that happen again?"

They reached the door of the building and Marie nodded. "Yep, I'm going to text Frankie before we walk in."

After she sent the text off, Marie slipped the phone in her back pocket where she'd feel it vibrate when the timer went off. Bryant took a deep breath and stepped up to the door. He sighed in relief when it opened without resistance, and he and Marie walked through.

"Well, so far, nothing has blown up," Marie whispered. "Now what?"

Bryant looked around the large, open lobby of the building they had walked into. "It looks like this place is abandoned."

"They rarely leave doors unlocked on abandoned buildings, do they?" Marie asked. "Someone has to be here somewhere."

"Maybe there?" Bryant said, pointing to what appeared to be a conference room to the left of the lobby. "It looks like there might be a light on in there."

Marie shrugged, and they walked quietly toward the door. When they reached the doorway, the woman they had seen the day before stepped outside and looked at them in surprise.

"I'm so sorry," she said. "We didn't hear you come in."

"I'm afraid we approach quietly, out of extreme caution," Bryant said.

"That's understandable," she said. "You do not know what we wanted you here for, so I can see why you would be unsettled about this meeting."

"You keep saying 'we?'" Marie said, looking around the room behind her. "Just how many people are here?"

"We didn't see any cars in the parking lot," Bryant added, also looking around.

"Yes, that was cautious on our behalf," she replied. "We parked in the back. Please come into the conference room and I will introduce you and tell you what's going on."

Marie glanced around again before sending a text off to Frankie and resetting her timer. She looked up at Bryant and raised an eyebrow before following him into the room. He walked in front of her and seemed on-guard.

Two men were waiting for them in the conference room when they walked in. Bryant gave Marie a look before turning his full attention to the men. The woman motioned to a pair of chairs that were stationed across the table from the two men, but Bryant shook his head.

"I don't feel comfortable with that just yet," he said. "Why don't you tell us who you are and why we are here before we make ourselves more vulnerable by sitting?"

"Oh, goodness me," one man said. "He stood and immediately approached them to introduce himself. I'm Linwood Nicholls. These are both relatives of mine, Sullivan Gibbons and Evelyn Hutson."

"It's nice to meet you," Bryant said after shaking his hand, "but I'm afraid that still doesn't put me too much at ease."

"It's a little odd for us to be called to an abandoned building in the middle of nowhere by someone we met in a parking lot," Marie said. She stopped long enough to send another text to Frankie. When she finished, she put the phone back in her pocket and said, "I should let you know. We have people who know where we are. I'm checking in with them periodically, and if I don't, they will call the police."

"Understandable," Evelyn said. "How about we try to put your mind at ease? We all come from the Carlee family, which at one point owned 50% of the organization we've all become acquainted with."

"Yes, we'd figured that part out," Bryant said. "That's why our partner emailed you. We are investigating what's been going on there."

"As are we," the man Linwood had referred to Sullivan said. "We are quite concerned about the way our family's old company is headed at the moment."

"I see," Bryant said. "And you think we can help?"

"We just wanted to chat about things," Sullivan continued. "We aren't looking for help or can provide you with any ourselves, but we thought having a chat would be appropriate."

"How about we have a seat so we can go over things?" Evelyn asked.

Marie looked around and frowned. "I still don't understand why you called us to an abandoned building. We couldn't have had this conversation at a coffee shop or something?"

"We like to keep our official meeting about the company away from prying eyes," Linwood said. "This is a building the Carlee family owns that isn't being used right now. We figured this would be a quiet place for us to chat."

"Our family still owns several buildings around the city," Evelyn said. "Some family disagreements have kept us from being able to sell them. So, for now, we rent them out and split up the proceeds."

"Family disagreements?" Marie asked. "What type of disagreements?"

Sullivan shrugged and said, "The type any family of means has over property and such. Everyone has a vested interest in the properties and some feel we should do things with them, and others disagree. We can't force them to sell their half, nor does anyone have the means to buy them out, so we live in a bit of a limbo."

Marie looked at Bryant and shrugged. "It would be easier to take notes if we were sitting."

He nodded and glanced around the room before they claimed the chairs across from Sullivan and Linwood. Evelyn sighed in relief and sat down as well. Marie pulled a notebook out of her bag and prepared to take notes regarding the conversation.

"How about we just start by filling you in on what we've been doing?" Evelyn said. "We've hit your radar if you're emailing Sullivan here."

"Sounds good," Bryant said. "Then we can decide how to proceed."

Sullivan started by pulling a photograph out of a pile of papers in front of him. He looked at it and smiled before passing it across the table to Marie and Bryant.

"This was our grandpa, Dennis Carlee," Sullivan said. "Evelyn, Linwood, and I are all cousins."

"Dennis owned the company with someone named Goar, correct?" Marie asked.

Evelyn nodded. "Benjamin Goar. That's right. He and our grandfather were old friends and opened the company together many years ago."

"Our grandfather and Benjamin Goar grew this company from the ground up," Sullivan continued. "They worked hard to make it what it is today."

Evelyn shook her head. "And now someone is trying to sabotage it."

"I take it you don't approve of what's been going on with your family's old company?" Bryant asked. "Do you wish it was still under your control?"

"Not exactly," Sullivan said. "None of the immediate family ever wanted to take over the business. Honestly, none of us wanted that type of dedication and sacrifice either, so it being sold was the best option."

"But we still feel like we need to protect our grandfather's legacy," Evelyn said. "It would upset him if all that hard work went to waste."

"What do you mean, exactly?" Marie asked. "Go to waste. What are you afraid is going to happen?"

"Well, I'm sure you've clued into that there is currently an FBI investigation," Sullivan said. "It's related to the embezzling situation that brought you to learn of the company."

"Yes, we are aware of that."

"If the leadership team doesn't get a handle on things," Sullivan said, "they will shut the company down."

"And they aren't getting a handle on things," Linwood said. "It's just getting worse. Now that they know about the investigation, the board is furious, and some of them already say that they are thinking about dumping their shares in the company. With all the bad press that we've had recently, it would be at a loss."

"So, that's been your goal in all this?" Marie asked. "Save the company?"

Evelyn nodded. "There are a lot of great people who work there. It would be a shame if they all started losing their jobs over this. Grandpa wouldn't have liked that."

"What have you all been doing to get to the bottom of the embezzling?" Bryant asked.

"We didn't know what was going on at first," Evelyn said. "Something felt off around the place, but I couldn't figure out what it was. That's why Linwood and I had been meeting regularly. We were both digging into it and trying to figure out what was happening."

"It wasn't until your friend found that invoice and started digging around herself that clued us in," Linwood said. "That's when we brought in Sullivan. We knew we couldn't handle it on our own."

"Where has your research led you?"

"I started the same place Frankie did," Evelyn said. "Except I had a lot more access to things than she did, so she couldn't take it as far as me. I didn't have access to the payment system, however, so I tried to focus on who was generating the invoices and how they were flowing around the company."

"What did you find?"

"A lot, unfortunately." She handed a stapled stack of paper to Bryant as Marie sent off another text to Frankie. "This is every one that would have at some point had access to the invoices that were created and moved around."

"Wow," Bryant said, looking through the pages. "This is a lot of people."

"Exactly the problem," she said. "I started looking for patterns. The same people working on every invoice, the same offices handling certain movements, anything I could think of to locate the source of them."

"Did you find anything?"

"For the most part, everything was random," she replied. "One employee might handle one invoice type, but an entirely different employee might handle that type the next go-round. Every time I thought I was getting somewhere, someone would leave the company or things would change up and

I would have to start over again. I discovered odd payments to the company responsible for finding our interns, but never could figure out what that was about."

"Interesting," Bryant said. "We have heard about the intern company payments as well. No clue what that may be about?"

Evelyn shook her head.

"What about the invoices themselves?" Marie asked. "What did you discover about them?"

"I noticed some oddities in the invoices," she said. "They all used coding strategies we used several years ago."

"Is this the number coding system you are talking about?" Marie asked. "We noticed the differences in the way they coded the invoices ourselves."

"Exactly," Evelyn nodded. "They style the codes that these fall into like the ones when the company was still a private company."

"Which was seven or eight years ago?"

"Yes, that's correct."

"Do you think it could be an old employee who is running these invoices?" Bryant asked. "Could they possibly be getting into the system somehow?"

Linwood shook his head. "We've looked into all the employees and none of them have been here that long."

"I've also done some work with the IT department and tracked down the IP addresses on most of them," Evelyn said. "We are certain that the work done on them took place onsite. That may be where the intern company comes into play. They ran most of the activity through machines our interns were using."

"How did you manage that without alerting IT to what you were doing?"

"I asked them to train me how to run certain general reports," she replied. "This was one of them. Once I knew how to look up the information myself, I could do it with any of the invoices I wanted."

"So, none of the same employees have been working on the invoices, the codes being used are old, and you've confirmed that everything is being posted on-site and mostly through the intern computers," Bryant said. "Does that pretty much sum it up?"

Evelyn nodded.

"Wait," Marie said. "If you can see where these invoices originated, what's stopping you from figuring out who was at the computer when they posted. There are cameras posted all around that place. Can't you just check the cameras?"

"I did," Evelyn said. "They were erased."

"Erased?" Bryant asked.

Linwood leaned forward in his chair. "Once Evelyn started figuring out what computers the transactions were being made from, I started reviewing the camera footage. Every time there is a transaction, there is a ten-minute window of time that is erased from the cameras."

"That is plenty of time to make a transaction," Marie said. "What about before and after the missing windows? Which employees were at the computers then?"

"Sometimes the computers were empty," Linwood continued. "Other times the employee assigned to that desk was there before and after the missing time slot."

"How odd," Bryant said. "Could it have been the employee assigned to the desk that made the transaction?"

"That would be a reasonable assumption," Linwood said. "However, it wasn't the same computer every time. It probably filtered through at least twenty different employees in the time we were researching."

"Plus, several flowed through your friend's IP address," Evelyn added. "So, if you are certain she is innocent, I feel it is safe to say someone else is behind it other than the workers assigned to the computers."

"That's very true," Marie said.

"We can prove it wasn't the workers sometimes," Linwood said. "About five of the transactions took place on a worker's computer and even used her login credentials, but she was killed in a car accident a few months prior."

"That's so sad," Marie said with a gasp. "But that means she didn't complete the transactions."

"This is so fascinating," Bryant said. "But I'm afraid it is giving us more questions than answers. Were you able to figure out who was deleting the footage?"

"I brought it up to the IT department," Evelyn said. "Discretely, of course. They said that sometimes that can happen during system updates and when there are issues with the system's connection."

"That's interesting," Bryant said and looked at Marie. "I wonder what Joe and Anna will think of that."

"Hopefully, they can figure out who is behind all this," Marie replied.

"Is there any information you can give us at this point?" Evelyn asked. "We need something to keep us working."

Bryant shrugged. "Honestly, we have little more than you do at this point. Our partners are checking out some leads today regarding the destination of those checks, but we have nothing solid on that yet."

"We would certainly appreciate any information you could give us when you find it," Linwood said. "We are running into a roadblock and running out of options here."

"We need to run any information we share through our team first," Bryant said. "We need to be careful about who we trust."

"That's something we understand very well."

"Speaking of which, why all the secrecy?" Bryant asked, glancing around the room. "You drag us out here. You've been disguising who you are to the others in the company. You meet in secret every month. What is going on?"

"We didn't want to draw attention to any of this," Evelyn replied. "Linwood has been on the board for fifteen years. I started working there ten years ago. Neither of us wanted the extra pressure that would be put on us if the others we worked with knew we were part of the original family. It was just easier."

"So, you've been doing all this in secret to avoid outing your identities?" Marie asked with a frown. She quickly shot off another text to Frankie before continuing. "That still seems over the top."

"We wanted to come and go under the radar as well," Linwood said. "Nobody would have suspected we were investigating things unless they found out what family we belonged to. Then whoever is doing this might have gotten suspicious and changed up what they were doing."

"Well, we are certainly glad that you filled us in on what you were up to," Marie said.

"I'm sure you would have figured it out before long," Sullivan said. "The moment I got an email from you, I knew the jig was up."

"So, you brought us in to plead with us not to out you?" Bryant asked.

"We would appreciate it if you kept our involvement in the investigation to yourself," Evelyn said. "We are just hoping to keep our family's business going for our grandpa."

"He would want us to," Sullivan said with a nod.

"We understand," Marie said and looked at Bryant. "From where I'm sitting, I don't see a reason to let anyone know what you are up to. But, I have to say while your priority is saving the company, ours is helping Frankie."

"That's why we are hoping you will keep us in the loop," Linwood said. "If we can't count on you to protect our business, we will do it ourselves."

"We will discuss it with our team," Bryant said. "But for now, I'm afraid we have nothing to share with you."

"Thank you both for coming to speak with us today," Evelyn said. "We certainly appreciate it."

Bryant nodded and he and Marie stood to leave. "Thank you for giving us all this information as well. We will do our best to help Frankie and the company."

Evelyn walked them to the front door and locked the door behind them when they were outside. Bryant turned to Marie and raised an eyebrow while pulling out his phone to call them a car. After he'd made the exchange on his phone, he looked back up at her.

"Car will be here in ten minutes," he said.

"Good, that gives me enough time to let Frankie know we are alright and to call Anna," she replied.

"Good idea. Joe and Anna are going to want to hear about this."

Chapter 36

Anna sighed and ran a hand through her hair. When she leaned Joe's direction, the librarian cleared her throat and glared at her, but Anna ignored her.

"You find anything yet?" she whispered to Joe.

"No," he replied. "You?"

The librarian snapped a book closed and glared at Joe. Beside them, Derrick chuckled.

"You two always have this much trouble at the library?" he asked. Joe glanced up at the librarian and smirked. "It's Anna. She has trouble written all over her."

"I do not," Anna hissed. "They are all just being ridiculous."

Anna's phone buzzed on the table next to her, and Joe laughed harder. "You have to admit, you are a bit noisy."

Anna rolled her eyes at him and picked up the phone to silence it. "It's not my fault! I'm going to take this outside."

"Good idea," Derrick said with another laugh.

Anna ducked her head as she passed the librarian and answered her phone just as she stepped out the door.

"Took you long enough," Marie said when Anna answered, her voice sounding amused.

"Sorry," she replied. "I couldn't answer in the library. What did you and Bryant find out?"

"We learned a lot," Marie said. "We met with the woman you emailed and the man she's been seeing at the restaurant and their cousin."

"Are you and Bryant both alright?" Anna asked. "That's a lot more people than we expected."

"We were nervous at first," Marie said. "We were outnumbered and the address they brought us to was secluded, but it ended up fine. They are all relatives of one of the original owners and are concerned about what's going on with the company."

"What information did they share?"

Marie spent a few minutes giving Anna a rundown of the information the Carlee family members had given her and Bryant. When she finished, Anna mulled over the situation carefully.

"Hmm," she said after a few moments. "I don't know what to think about that. I'm going to have to talk it through with Joe. Something sounds fishy about that missing footage and all the IP hopping."

"We thought so too."

"Which family did they belong to?"

"The one who sold their shares to the other family," Marie said. "The Carlee family."

"And they took it upon themselves to save the family company, huh?" Anna asked. "They didn't want the ship to sink, I suppose."

"Exactly," Marie said. "At least that's what they claim. They knew their grandpa would have wanted to save the company, so they were doing what they could to save it. Plus, they are worried about the livelihoods of all the employees."

"That's very noble of them."

"They said they wanted to keep their family's dream alive."

"I suppose that makes sense," Anna said. "Do you and Bryant believe them?"

"I didn't clue into them being dishonest," Marie said. "They seemed to be sincere."

"I'm sure there has to be something deeper going on," Anna said. "I'm going to get back to Joe and see if we can figure out a theory. Where are you and Bryant headed now?"

"We're going to go back to Frankie's office," Marie said. "Bryant is talking to Chris now to get us back in. We thought we might do some research into these employees and see if any of them match up with anything going on in the payment system. See if any of these people who worked on the invoices were the same who issued checks for their payments."

"That's a good idea," Anna said. "Joe, Derrick, and I will continue our work here."

"Let's work until dinnertime," Marie said. "Then we can talk about regrouping."

"Sounds like a plan," Anna said before ending the call and heading back inside the library. She sighed when she sat down next to Joe and quickly filled him in on what their siblings had found. When she finished, he sat back and frowned.

"Conveniently, the cameras would shut down at the same time shady transactions were being put into the system," he said. "I'm not buying that."

"Neither am I," Anna agreed. "I think either someone used that time to their advantage, or they planned the outages."

"Either way," Joe continued, "they were going to a lot of trouble to cover their tracks."

"Who would be capable of something like that?" Derrick asked. "In my company, there are few people who could pull off a stunt like that."

"Well, to be honest," Joe said, "it could be anyone in the IT department or anyone with some sort of security clearance in the company. Anyone who would have the capability of knowing about the security system and camera footage."

"Which doesn't come as a surprise," Anna added. "It almost had to be someone high in the company to manage this level of an embezzling scheme. No way a lower-level employee could have gotten away with this for so long."

"And at this level," Joe said with a nod. "But it is hard to narrow down because we can't prove they were forcing the cameras to shut down on purpose."

"Ah, so you're saying they could have been using the timing of system updates to their advantage?" Derrick said. "That would widen the net a bit."

"We can't afford to make assumptions," Anna said. "We have to keep an open mind and keep everyone on our suspect list until we know they don't belong there."

"Including this group of family members," Joe said. "I don't think we should let what they told us to alter our investigation. Just keep it in the back of our mind."

"I agree," Anna said. "Maybe it will help Bryant and Marie figure out something with the invoices, however. We should probably just stick with what we were doing before they called."

Derrick yawned and leaned back in his chair. "I'm not even sure what we are supposed to be looking for if I'm being honest."

Joe sighed and ran a hand across his face before leaning back in his chair as well. "We seem to be shooting at things in the dark, don't we?"

Anna nodded. "We aren't getting anywhere. We need a better plan."

Joe interlaced his fingers and put his hands behind his head. "Recap?"

Anna glanced down at her notes and shook her head. "There's not much to recap, honestly. When the invoices were paid, they went to a construction company called Acclaimed Builders."

"And this company opened in the 70s?"

"As far as we can tell, yes," Anna said. "The only information about it online says it's been open since 1973."

"Here in Atlanta?"

"Yep."

"And nothing else is online about this place?"

"Haven't found anything yet," Anna said. "I've been searching all morning."

"And we've been searching through the newspapers from the 70s all morning for some mention of the company with no luck," Joe said.

"Which brings us back to where we are now," Derrick said. "Nowhere."

"You know, I ran across an article in one paper I looked at that might be helpful," Joe said. "It was talking about an increase in residential construction for the year. It talked about how there had been an increase in it during the early 1970s and was expected to continue. I thought nothing of it at the time."

He paused and sat back in front of the machine he was at and spent some time flipping back through the papers he'd already reviewed. After a few minutes, he stopped and leaned back in his chair again. Pointing at the machine, he continued.

"This article talks about a planned residential build that began in the summer of 1973 right around the location of Carlee and Goar's original building," he said.

"Let me look," Anna said.

Joe moved out of her way so she could read the article for herself. She was silent for a few minutes as her eyes skimmed the article. Eventually, she sat back in the chair and looked at Joe.

"So, we have a big construction project that took place right outside Carlee and Goar's front door right around the time this construction company opened up shop," she said.

"Might be a coincidence," Derrick said with a shrug. "Businesses open up all the time in many industries."

"We have nothing else to work with," Anna said. "I say we look at newspapers from spring and summer of 1973 to see if we can find this company."

"Let's get to work," Joe said. "Derrick, how about you start with March of 73 papers? I'll start with April."

"That leaves me with May," Anna said.

After they had retrieved the items from the film collection area, they grew silent again for several minutes while they filtered through their designated newspaper selections. She had just turned the third page on the newspaper from May 10th when something caught Anna's eye.

"Think I might have found something, guys," she said after reading through the article. She sat back and smiled. "This article tells the story of a side venture the half-owner of Carlee and Goar, Benjamin Goar, took on in May 1973."

"Let me guess," Joe said. "He started a construction company?"

"Yep, Acclaimed Builders."

"You don't say."

"Now that we know that Benjamin Goar owned the company, we should be able to search property records and figure out where the company is located now," Anna said.

Joe nodded and flipped open his laptop. After a few brief minutes, he sat back and frowned. "Well, not sure that it helped us any. Goar had three commercial properties listed in the system. Two have since been demolished, so that doesn't help us any. The third is under the ownership of AB Corporation."

"AB?" Anna asked. "As in Acclaimed Builders?"

"Possibly," Joe said, "but no way to confirm that with the lack of information they have online about the company."

"Maybe we should just go check it out?" Derrick asked. "You said you have an address?"

"Probably the best option," Joe said. "I feel like we are at a dead end again. There just isn't a lot online about this older company."

"Whoever owns it certainly didn't do their due diligence with keeping everything updated, did they?" Anna said. She frowned at the screen of Joe's laptop. "I think you're right. Let's go check it out."

Joe returned the items they had borrowed from the librarian while Anna and Derrick gathered up their computers and other paperwork. Within ten minutes, they were all headed out the door. When they reached the car, Derrick unlocked the doors and smiled at them before climbing behind the wheel.

"I'm going to need a vacation after all this is over with," he laughed. "You two move around too much."

Joe laughed. "This job keeps us on the go."

"I don't know how you both have the energy to keep up with it," Derrick laughed as he started the car and put the address into the GPS. "I'd need a week off every other month if I had to do this all the time."

Anna laughed. "We drink lots of coffee."

Chapter 37

Derrick chuckled as he pulled out of the parking lot, but they grew quiet as he drove. After a few miles, the GPS instructed them to take an older highway that headed away from downtown. As they drove, a ball of worry formed in Anna's stomach as the location became more and more secluded.

"I'm not liking this," Joe said when Derrick pulled off the highway and into a rundown commercial-type setting.

"This doesn't look like the type of place an active business would be," Derrick mused.

Eventually, the GPS led them to a three-story industrial building with several broken windows and an empty parking lot.

"Well, this looks just great," Anna said. "Not a place someone is doing business out of."

"What now?" Derrick asked after he'd parked.

Joe looked up at the building and around the parking lot. "Well, we've come this far. Let's go see if we can poke around. It's probably just abandoned, but maybe we can figure out an address where the company moved."

"We need to be careful," Anna said.

"Agreed."

They climbed out of the car and made their way to the building. One door was missing off the side, and they slipped inside with no issues. There was enough light coming through the windows in the building that they also didn't have any issue seeing.

With glass from the broken windows crunching beneath their feet, the three walked through the building carefully, looking for any signs of life in the space. After milling through a few offices, they came to the center of the building, which was a tall room that was open in the center. Anna looked up at the ceiling and examined the skylights above them.

"Abandoned," Derrick said after glancing around himself. "Now what do we do?"

Joe examined the outer walls of the building. "Looks like there are some stairs over there that lead up to some more offices along the wall there. Maybe we can find something in one of those."

Anna and Derrick followed behind Joe to the stairs and quickly climbed their way to a wide landing that was lined with offices on one side. Joe kept walking and only paused a few seconds at each office to peer inside.

"They appear to be empty," he said. "We may be out of luck, here."

"There are still some more offices up there," Anna said, pointing above them to a smaller landing above their heads. "When we were downstairs, I noted at least one office at the end of that smaller landing up there."

"Let's go then," he said after he'd peeked in the last office on the current landing. "Nothing in these offices."

The second flight of stairs they climbed was narrower than the landing they found themselves on after they reached the top. Joe pointed out a broken section of the landing as he passed and waited to make sure Anna and Derrick safely made it past the hazard.

Eventually, they made it to a small office at the end of the landing and walked inside. Anna smiled when she spotted a file cabinet in the corner.

"Jackpot," she whispered.

"I wouldn't hold your breath," Joe said. "Chances are it's empty as the rest of this place."

"I don't know, Joe," Derrick said as Anna walked across the small space to the cabinet. "This office seems different. It's clean."

Joe frowned and looked down at the floor. "You're right. The rest of the building has debris all over the place. This office has been swept."

"There isn't dust on the desk, either," Anna said as she pulled open the first drawer of the cabinet. She reached in and pulled out a file that was laying in the drawer and grinned. "And the file cabinet isn't empty."

"Jackpot," Joe said and walked in her direction. "What do we have?"

Anna whistled when she opened the file. "These are copies of the canceled checks from Frankie's company. You want to bet they match up with the invoices we've been researching?"

"I bet you're right," Joe said. "Derrick, do you mind taking pictures of these with my phone while Anna and I continue?"

He handed his phone and the file to Derrick, who quickly got to work capturing the documents on Joe's phone. Anna opened the second drawer and found two more folders. She handed one to Joe and opened the other herself. She frowned at the contents.

"What's in yours?" Joe asked as he looked through the contents of his folder. "Mine looks like a bunch of genealogy research. Mostly related to the two families, Carlee and Goar. I've also got some birth certificates in here."

"I have a will in mine," Anna said. "Looks like it's related to Benjamin Goar's estate."

"Anything standing out?" he asked.

"At first glance, no," she replied. "We're going to need to go through it all to see if it's helpful."

"I don't feel comfortable doing that here," Joe said. "How about we get pictures of everything and get out of here? We can go through it all somewhere safer."

"I like that plan," Anna said. "I'll start getting pictures of this will on my phone. Derrick, when you finish, we need pictures of the papers Joe has."

"Just finished with these," he replied and handed Anna back the first folder. "I'll get started on this now."

Joe set about looking around the rest of the office while he waited for them to finish up, taking pictures of everything. Anna snapped pictures of the pages of the will and began collecting the folders and putting things back where they found them.

"You find anything else?" she asked Joe when she and Derrick were finished, and everything was back where they had found it.

He shook his head. "I think we've found everything there is to find here. Let's get out of here."

He led the way out of the office again, Anna and Derrick following behind. Just as he'd stepped over the broken portion of the landing, a loud crash caught their attention up ahead. Anna gasped when she realized the crash had been the stairs to the landing below them falling.

"Well, that's just great," Derrick said. "Now, how do we get down?"

They all looked down just in time to see a man's large arm reach through the opening toward them. Joe reached back across the opening to push Anna out of harm's way, and Derrick wrapped his arms around her waist as the man was trying to grab her.

Sensing that Joe was off balance, the man pivoted his attention in his direction and snagged one of his ankles. Joe fell forward when the man jerked his ankle out from under him and fell partially into the hole. His side hit the landing awkwardly as he fell, but he caught himself.

Anna jerked away from Derrick and grabbed Joe's hand just as the man jerked his leg again, causing Joe to disappear into the hole below them and knocking Anna off her feet. Anna's heart dropped as she felt the building rumble.

Chapter 38

"Joe!" Anna screamed into the hole as the building shook around them. She looked around in panic and her eyes landed on Derrick. "Derrick! Run, grab those folders. This building is coming down. We're going to lose the evidence."

Derrick disappeared back into the office and was back with the folders within a few seconds. Anna had already swung her legs into the opening and was on her way to lowering herself down to Joe when he got back.

"Hold your horses," Derrick said. "What if that guy is down there still?"

"I don't care if he is," she said. "I need to get down to Joe!"

Derrick grabbed her wrist and lowered her down into the opening. Joe was lying unconscious on the landing next to her, and she immediately dropped to her knees next to him. Derrick dropped through the opening and onto the landing just as she was checking to make sure Joe was still breathing.

"Is he alright?" Derrick asked, the panic in his voice clear.

"He's breathing," Anna said, trying to quell her panic. "We've got to get him out of here."

Joe coughed, stirred, and groaned.

"Oh, thank God," Anna said. "Joe, can you hear me?"

He shook his head and finally opened his eyes. He looked a bit dazed, but he blinked a few times and kept eye contact with her. Anna sighed in relief.

"We've got to get you out of here," she said. "This building is coming down."

The building shook again, and a portion of the roof caved in on the opposite side of the building from them. Anna ducked her head and covered Joe's body with her own until the rumbling stopped.

He tried to sit up but laid back when the pain in his side stopped him. "You're going to have to go without me," he said. "Go get help. I'll be fine here."

"You will not be fine here," Anna said. "You are not staying. And I am not leaving you here."

"How do you suppose you get me out of here, then?" he asked. "Are you going to carry me out because there's no way I can walk? I'm pretty sure I sprained my ankle, and I might have a broken rib or two."

"If I need to carry you, that's what I'll do," Anna said. "But I'm not leaving you. Come on Derrick, let's get him out of here."

Anna took the folders Derrick had taken and put them in the bag Joe had been carrying that was still hanging around his neck. She then pulled one of Joe's arms across her shoulder and waited for Derrick to do the same.

"I'm afraid this might hurt for a minute," she warned before she and Derrick pulled Joe to his feet.

He gritted his teeth through the pain and pulled his injured foot up behind him. As quickly as they could, they made their way to the flight of stairs to the ground floor and hustled Joe outside the building and back to the car.

As Derrick was opening the car, another rumble flowed through the building and more of it collapsed. Anna shuddered at the thought of what could have happened had they lingered in the building, but put the scary thoughts out of her mind when Derrick came back to help her get Joe back in the car. They helped him get settled in the back seat but didn't bother trying to buckle him in.

"We need to get him to a hospital," Anna said. "I'll drive."

"No!" Derrick and Joe said in unison.

"The way you drive, you'll throw him on the floor," Derrick said. "Get in. I'll drive."

Anna grumbled but climbed into the passenger seat next to Derrick. She turned in her seat to watch Joe as they drove and sighed in relief when they finally pulled up outside an emergency room. Derrick popped the car in park in the ambulance lane and ran inside to get help.

Before long, emergency crew members were there with a stretcher. Anna followed them inside the emergency room while Derrick ran to park the car. They wheeled Joe through the waiting room, but he stopped them before they pushed him back behind the ER doors.

With a grimace, he pulled the bag he'd been carrying from around his neck and handed it Anna's direction. She teared up when she took it from him.

"Hey," he said. "I'll be alright. Don't worry about me."

"You better be," she replied, and squeezed his hand.

The emergency crew wheeled him behind the doors and left Anna in the lobby by herself. She looked around and noticed a woman behind a window motioning to her. She stepped up to it and the woman slid some papers through the opening.

"Do you think you can fill these out for him?" the woman asked.

Anna looked down at the papers and shook her head. One of the tears she'd been holding in slid down her cheek and she said, "I don't know all this information. I can call...oh, God, I need to call his brother! What am I doing?"

She laid the papers down and started rummaging through her purse just as Derrick walked up behind her. He put a hand on her shoulder and picked up the papers.

"I've already called Bryant," he said. "And I know a lot of this stuff myself, so I can do this paperwork for him."

Anna nodded and took a deep breath. Derrick picked up the papers and pointed to a set of chairs in the waiting area. Anna followed him and sat down in a chair. She stared at the ER doors and twisted the strap of Joe's bag around her fingers while Derrick filled out Joe's paperwork.

"He'll be alright," Derrick said. "He's been through worse. Trust me."

"That doesn't make me feel better."

"He fell out of our treehouse when we were seven," Derrick said. "It was a much bigger drop than the one he just had, and he wound up with a broken leg. That was it. Missed half a season of baseball and was pissed about it, but he was ok. He'll be fine."

"Yeah, well, he's not seven anymore."

A doctor rushed out of the ER doors and Anna tensed in her seat. She relaxed when the doctor sped past them to another family who was waiting in the room's corner. Derrick chuckled.

"I swear, if you don't relax, I'm going to send you back there with him so they can make you calm down."

"You're right," Anna said and ran a hand through her hair before sitting back in her chair. "I'm being ridiculous."

"No," Derrick said, his eyes still on Joe's forms. "You're being a good friend. And Lord knows Joe could use a few of those."

"Yeah, me too," Anna said absent-mindedly. Her eyes pivoted to the doors of the ER entrance when she spotted Bryant bolting through the doors. Their eyes met, and he rushed her direction, Marie behind him and trying to keep up.

"What happened?" Bryant asked when he reached her.

"We found the original location of the business that was receiving those checks," Anna said. "And a lot of evidence." She held up the bag in her hand before continuing. "Whoever is behind this tried to bring the building down with us still inside."

"Are you alright?" Marie asked, her concern suddenly growing.

"I'm fine," Anna said, waving her off. "Joe thinks he has a sprained ankle and a broken rib. Derrick said he'll be fine."

"How did he get hurt?"

"There was a guy there," Anna said. "We didn't see him when we came in. The place seemed abandoned. He must have been hiding outside somewhere."

"He probably saw us pull up or something," Derrick said.

Anna nodded. "And then snuck back in on us when we were snooping around. He jerked Joe through a hole in the landing on the third floor and made him fall."

"Did you get a look at the guy?"

Anna shook her head and teared up again. "It's my fault. He was trying to grab me. Joe had to push me out of the way."

"It's not your fault, Anna," Derrick said. "It wouldn't have mattered who was standing there. That guy was determined to get one of us."

A doctor whisked out the ER doors and called for Joe's family. Bryant took the forms Derrick had filled out and headed over to talk with them. Anna didn't wait to be invited to join. She sped along behind him.

"Are you Joe's family?" the doctor asked when they approached.

"Yes, we are," Bryant said. "I'm his brother."

"Well, good news for you," the doctor said with a smile. "Your brother is going to be fine. It looks like he's got a pretty good sprain and a fractured rib. We sent him back for a CT to check for a concussion."

"But he's going to be alright?" Anna asked. "Can we see him?"

The doctor smiled at her. "He'll be fine. We need to wait on the results from the CT just as a precaution, but he's alert and everything else has checked out just fine. He'll be in some discomfort for a few weeks and will need to use crutches for a while, but he should be fine."

"Great," Bryant said. "When can he go home?"

"Just as soon as the CT comes back clean, so probably an hour or two," the doctor said. "A couple of you are more than welcome to go back and wait with him."

"Thank you, doctor," Bryant said and turned to Anna. "You coming with me or is Derrick."

"Like I'm going to let her worry herself sick in the waiting room," Derrick said with a chuckle. "Go. I'll keep Marie company while we wait."

Chapter 39

The room was empty when they arrived, but soon they were wheeling Joe's bed in. Anna smiled when she heard him protesting.

"Seriously, I'm fine," he said to the nurses. "Just give me some crutches and I'll be on my way. I don't need to stay."

"You're only staying until the CT comes back," Bryant said as the nurses began putting the locks on the bed's wheels. "No way I'm letting you leave before that though."

Joe attempted to adjust himself in the bed, only to grimace and clutch his side. "Fine. But I'm not staying after that. We have work to do."

"I think you've earned a day off," Anna said. She dragged a chair next to his bed and sat down.

"You just want the credit for solving the case," Joe said with a quick chuckle. He grabbed his side again. "Ow."

"Stop it," Bryant said. "You're going to hurt yourself worse."

"Grr," Joe complained. "We don't have time for this. We were just getting somewhere with this case."

"Where was that exactly?" Bryant asked with a chuckle. "We have more questions than answers at this point."

"Well, I'd say we figured out one thing, at least," Anna said. "Acclaimed Builders didn't design buildings very well."

Joe started to laugh but caught himself. "I'm pretty sure that was intentional."

"Considering the giant arm that jerked you through the floor," Anna said, "I have to agree with you. At least you didn't drag me over the cliff with you this time."

This time, Joe couldn't hold back his laughter. "Ow! Stop it. Are you trying to kill me now? Ow!"

Anna laughed and grew serious. "I'm glad you're ok."

"Banged up," he said, "but I'll be fine. That's why we need to get out of here."

Anna rested her chin on the railing of his bed and looked down at him. He frowned up at her and said, "What?"

"This is my fault," she said. "I'm sorry."

Joe shook his head at her and reached over to pick up her wrist. He shook her arm a bit and smiled. "I'm quite sure this little thing couldn't have dragged me through the floor. This is not your fault."

"Still, if I had been paying closer attention—"

"You're being silly," Joe said. "Not your fault. Stop blaming yourself."

"Fine, I won't blame myself if you promise to take it easy for the rest of the trip," she said. "Let me do the heavy lifting this time."

"Depends on what you get us into," Joe said with a smile.

Joe leaned back on his pillow and closed his eyes just as the doctor was walking into the room. Anna looked up expectantly and waited while the doctor read through a report he held in his hand.

"Looks like everything is perfectly normal," the doctor said. "We'll make sure you can get some crutches and get you out of here. I want you to go home and rest, and make sure you check in with your doctor back home here in a couple of weeks."

"Thank you, doctor," Bryant said. "We'll make sure he gets some rest."

Anna leaned back in her chair and pulled Joe's bag into her lap. Within a few minutes, a nurse was coming into the room with a pair of crutches and a wheelchair. Joe took a deep breath and pushed himself up in the bed, grimacing the whole way.

The nurse pointed to the crutches. "I'm sure you know how to use these?"

"Unfortunately, I'm acquainted with them," Joe said. "Had some experience over the years."

"Well, it's just like riding a bike," the nurse said. "Let's get you out of here."

Before long, Joe was in the wheelchair and being wheeled back into the ER waiting room. Marie and Derrick stood up when they saw them all enter the room. Derrick grinned down at Joe in the wheelchair when he approached.

"Ah, yes," he said. "This is a site I've seen many times over the years. Can't say I've missed waiting for you in the ER waiting room, however."

"Just push me out of here, and let's go," Joe said. "You know the drill."

Derrick laughed and pushed Joe toward the exit. Once outside the door, Joe put one crutch on either side of him and used them to pull himself to his feet. Before they could stop him, he'd swung himself onto the sidewalk and was heading to the car.

Bryant shook his head and followed along behind. When they'd reached Derrick's car in the parking lot, Joe sat down in the passenger seat and handed the crutches to Anna, who placed them in the backseat.

"Now what?" Derrick asked. "We can't just go back to what we were doing."

"I need to get Joe back to the hotel so he can rest," Bryant said to Marie.

Marie nodded. "How about this? Frankie and I will head back to her office to continue working on the invoices. Sounds like Anna has a bunch of evidence to go through, so why don't you and Derrick help her with that while Joe rests?"

"I can help, too," Joe said. "I'm not incapacitated, you know."

"How about you help me out by resting so I don't have to worry about you?" Anna asked.

"Oh, kind of like what I tried to get you to do when you had to have surgery in the middle of one of our cases?" he asked, raising an eyebrow at her. "I seem to remember someone being hell-bent on not resting."

"That's different."

Marie groaned. "How about we all just agree that the two of you are stubborn and we can't tell either of you what to do? Then, we can go get some work done."

Anna smiled at Joe, and he gave her a wink before saying, "I'm pretty sure we can agree on that one."

"As can I," Bryant said with a roll of his eyes. "So, how about I ride with you guys to the hotel and Marie you can go pick up Frankie? That way we can save some time dropping people off places."

"Sounds good," Marie said. "Anna, I'll call you once Frankie and I get settled back at the office to check in."

"Be careful, Marie," Anna said and gave her a quick hug. "This is getting a little intense."

"You, too, Anna."

Anna watched her sister walk back toward the entrance of the ER to wait for a car to pick her up before climbing into the back seat of Derrick's car with Bryant. Joe leaned his head against the headrest and closed his eyes, and everyone did their best to stay quiet on the trip back to the hotel.

When they'd parked back at the hotel, Anna grabbed the bag with their evidence and Bryant pulled the crutches out for Joe. He and Derrick helped Joe get to his feet, and they all headed inside the hotel. By the time they reached the hotel room door, Joe looked exhausted.

"Don't think we are going to have any problems getting you to rest," Anna said.

Bryant opened the door and Anna sped around them to get one bed ready for Joe. She pulled back the blankets and fluffed up the pillows before arranging them neatly to give him some support. Bryant laughed when she began stealing more pillows off his bed to add to Joe's collection.

"You are a pillow dragon," he said. "What am I supposed to sleep on?"

"I left you one," Anna said with a chuckle. She went back to arranging the pillows and finished up just as Joe was coming out of the bathroom. He'd changed into a pair of shorts and a fresh t-shirt. Anna moved away from the bed so he could get settled.

"Ah, so much better," Joe said after he'd leaned back against the pillows and pulled the blankets over him. "Hate to say it, but I think you're right this time, Bryant. I need to rest some."

"Told you so," Bryant said. "Anna, Derrick, and I are going to work on this stuff you guys found. You get some rest, and I'll go get you some food when you wake up."

"Mmm, burgers," Joe said, his voice sounding sleepy. "Anna, it's your turn to go get them this time. I got them last time."

Anna laughed. "That you did. I'll make sure you have a good burger when you wake up."

He smiled and closed his eyes. Anna watched him doze off for a few seconds before turning her full attention to the bag she'd laid on the desk when they'd walked in. In a flash, she got to work pulling out the paperwork Derrick had rescued from the falling building.

"I'm so glad you had time to grab these, Derrick," she said. "This would have been a pain trying to make heads or tails of anything if all we had were the images on our phones."

"What is it you found exactly?" Bryant asked. "When everything went south, we never really had time to talk about it."

"If you remember, we'd been working in the library trying to track down the origins of the company that was accepting the checks from those fake invoices," Anna said. "We wound up discovering that Benjamin Goar had opened the company we were searching for as a side business in 1973."

"Well, that's interesting," Bryant said. "So, a company owned by the former owner of the company Frankie works for is now receiving embezzled funds from that company."

"We thought so too, which is why we wanted to check it out," Anna said. "We had just checked out the only address we could find for that business when we were attacked."

"Still no idea who attacked you guys?"

"Honestly, I was too worried about Joe to care at that point," Anna said. "It happened so fast. All I saw was the guy's arm. He was gone by the time I got down to Joe."

"He must have been huge to reach through the ceiling like that," Bryant said.

Derrick shook his head. "When I got down there, I noticed a short ladder tossed to the side of the landing. I bet he climbed up on that and then just shoved it to the side as he made his getaway."

"He had planned ahead," Anna said. "He saw us coming and hid, and he had the place rigged to blow in case we caught him."

"Probably hoped all the evidence you saved would go down with the ship," Bryant said. "Good work on rescuing it, Derrick."

"Now we just have to figure out what it is," Anna said, peering down at the papers she'd pulled out of the first folder in the pile. She handed a stack of them to Bryant. "From what I can tell, it looks like these are canceled checks. I'm betting they match the entries tied to those invoices we've been eyeing."

Bryant looked through them and nodded. "I bet you're right."

"Assuming we now know where the money was going, we now need to figure out who was receiving the funds," Anna said. "And who was sending them out?"

"What's in the other files?" Bryant asked.

"One of them is a bunch of genealogy research," Anna said. "Looked like they relate it to the Carlee's and the Goar's. The other is a will. At first, I thought it was just Goar's will, but a copy of Carlee's is in here as well."

"Having all that evidence gathered together makes me rather suspicious of our friends from the Carlee family who claim they are trying to help," Bryant said.

"Seems suspicious," Anna agreed. "We need to keep them in the back of our mind while we look into this stuff."

"Agreed," Bryant said while shuffling through the invoices. "I don't want to have blinders on that keep us from seeing other possibilities, but I certainly don't want to ignore the fact that they are involved in this."

Anna looked through the folders she still had in front of her and paused for a moment before continuing. "Alright, I say we divide this up. Bryant, I'll give you the wills to review since you're the lawyer and all. Derrick, you look for some sort of pattern with the canceled checks that might tie into the accounts and invoices we've already gathered. I'll try to see if there's something in these genealogy papers."

"Let's do it," Derrick said and took his designated pile from Bryant.

Anna handed the wills to Bryant and settled in at the desk to sort through her pile of papers. For several minutes, they worked in silence until Anna's phone buzzed. She glanced down at it and answered the line when she recognized her sister's number.

"Did you and Frankie get settled at the office?" she asked when she picked up the line.

"We did," Marie said. "Chris wasn't available to let us in, so he had us come in the front this time. Said with it just being the two of us, we shouldn't draw too much attention this go-round."

"He's probably right," Anna said. "You and Frankie were probably not even a blip on anyone's radar when you came in."

"Nobody seemed too curious about us," Marie said. "Have you found anything yet on your end?"

"We're just getting started," Anna replied. "We've divvied up the work and are going through things."

"How's Joe?"

Anna looked over at the bed where Joe was sleeping. "He's sleeping. Demanded food when he wakes up. Specifically, a burger."

Marie laughed. "I'm sure we can accommodate."

"We'll keep working here, Marie," Anna said. "I'll let you know if we run across anything."

"Same here," Marie replied. "There's got to be something in what we have that will break this case. I can feel it."

"Me too," Anna said. "We're so close I can almost taste it."

"Stay safe."

"You, too."

Chapter 40

Anna ended her call and went back to the papers in front of her. Starting with the two owners of the company, Goar and Carlee, she quickly began sorting through the research and built family trees of both families. After she'd arranged all the papers, she sat back and frowned at them.

"Well, I think I have a good idea how the family's worked out, but I have no clue how that helps us," Anna said.

Derrick shook his head. "I'm not finding anything telling in these canceled checks either. An actual person endorsed none of them. They just have the Acclaimed Builders' company stamp and account on them."

Anna looked at a few of them herself and sighed. "Signature from Frankie's company is no help, either. Chris signs all the checks, even the ones that are legit, so him signing these is not a red flag at all."

"I might have found something," Bryant said. He paused and read a portion of the will in his hand again before turning it in Anna's direction. "This language might not make much sense to you, but Goar is specifically eliminating a particular person from his will."

"Well, that's interesting," Anna said. "Do we know who?"

"He has her listed as Gail Marilyn Bazemore and it says she's from Riverdale."

"That's a name I've yet to hear," Anna said with a frown. "Is there anything else about her in there?"

"Not specifically," Bryant said. "The document explicitly eliminates her and any dependents from receiving any type of inheritance from Goar's estate."

"Why would someone need to eliminate someone from their will?"

"Lots of reasons," Bryant said with a shrug. "But basically, they would need to have some reason to make a claim."

"As in be related in some way?"

"Or have a child by that person."

Anna turned back to the genealogy papers and quickly flipped through them. "I'm not finding any record of that woman in these papers."

"Maybe she changed her name or something?" Derrick said.

"That certainly wouldn't be the first time we saw something like that," Anna said. She pulled out a laptop and opened it up. "Keep looking. I'm going to do some research on her."

The room grew silent again, aside from Anna's tapping on the laptop keys and the occasional shuffle of paper. After twenty minutes, a name popped up on her screen that stopped her in her tracks.

"Now, this is a name I've seen," she said and jerked the genealogy papers off the table to find the one she was hunting. She handed it to Bryant when she located it. "Alright, so this person is connected to the woman in the will."

Bryant squinted at the name on the paper. "Susan Woolard. How does she connect to this?"

"Susan's mother is Gail Woolard," Anna said. "Gail married Sam Woolard in 1956 when Susan was three. Sam adopted young Susan two years later."

"That still doesn't explain how they are connected to this case," Derrick said.

"Gail doesn't have a lot of information online, but there is an old court case that I found," Anna said. "It's a paternity hearing."

"You don't say," Bryant said. "Goar, I assume."

"Yep, Susan was born in 1953, which was three years after Carlee and Goar set up shop," Anna said. "The paternity case ended in an undisclosed settlement in favor of Ms. Woolard, who was Gail Bazemore."

"So, you're saying that Gail had an affair with Goar and had his daughter, who is this Susan person?" Derrick asked. "And Susan's information just showed up in this pile of stuff we have."

"If someone is researching the full family history of Goar and Carlee, her being included isn't that surprising," Anna said.

"Nor is it surprising that he excluded her in the will if they had some sort of agreement," Bryant said. "I'm sure her not being included in his will was part of the arrangement of the settlement. He probably signed away his rights to the child as well."

"Do we know where Susan is now?" Derrick asked. "Maybe she's involved in this stuff."

"She passed away about ten years ago," Anna said. "She and her husband, Tom Roberts, were in a nasty car accident and both died a few months later."

"That's sad," Bryant said. "That seems to end our—wait a minute—did Susan have any kids?"

"I didn't think to check since she had passed away," Anna said. She spent a few minutes clicking through a few screens and frowned at the screen when she came up with the results. "She did. Thomas, Rebecca, and Marty. Both Rebecca and Marty would have been minors when she passed. Thomas was older."

"Anna..." Bryant said.

Anna frowned. "What? Did I miss something?" She looked at the screen again and gasped. "Oh, my God! How did I miss that?"

"You just needed that Malone touch to fill in the blank spot," Joe muttered from the bed.

"You be quiet over there," Anna said. "You're supposed to be sleeping."

She turned her attention back to Bryant. "Do you think we could be right on this? Do you think he's her kid?"

"Someone care to fill me in on whatever it is you suddenly discovered?" Derrick asked.

Anna turned in his direction and pointed at the screen. "Gail Bazemore had a child with Mr. Goar who was later adopted by Tom Woolard."

"Susan Woolard," Derrick said. "I've followed you this far. Where do her kids come into play?"

"Susan married Sam Roberts and had three kids, one of which she named Thomas," Anna said.

"Alright..."

"It just so happens that a Thomas Roberts was the name of the head of security who let us into Frankie's company that very first day," Bryant said.

"Oh, I see where this is going," Derrick said. "You think he's trying to avenge his family or something? That he thinks he got cheated?"

"Possibly," Anna said. "We're going to need to do more research."

She picked up her phone. "I'm going to call Marie and see if they can start figuring out how much access Thomas Roberts has to the systems at Frankie's company."

"Good idea," Bryant said. "While they do that, we can work on solidifying his tie to all this."

When her sister didn't answer the line, Anna looked at her phone in confusion. "She didn't answer. I'm going to call Frankie."

When Frankie didn't answer her phone either, Anna looked up at Bryant. "Something's wrong. They should be answering."

"Let's not panic yet," Bryant said. "Let's see if we can call the company directly and get someone to answer."

Anna nodded and waited for him to get through to someone. When he laid his phone on the table, Anna's stomach sank.

"The call didn't go through," he said. "I think we need to assume something's wrong at this point."

Chapter 41

Marie took a deep breath and pushed the button to turn on a computer in the conference room. While she waited for it to spur to life, she pulled some documents out of her bag and laid them on the table next to her.

"I say we start right where we left off," she said to Frankie. "No way to go about this except forward."

Frankie pushed the power button of a second computer and sat down next to Marie. "Where were we exactly? It feels like we aren't getting anywhere."

"We'll find something," Marie said. "I promise."

She logged into the system and pulled up the payment system she had been looking at earlier in the day. Frankie sighed and did the same on her computer. Before they got started, Marie turned to her and put a hand on her arm.

"We're getting there, Frankie," she said. "We just need to keep looking."

"But where do we need to look, and what are we looking for?" Frankie asked. "I feel like we are running out of places to look."

Marie turned back to her computer and frowned at the screen. "You're right. We're spinning our wheels with this. We need to try something new."

"Tell me what I need to do," Frankie said.

"Alright, let's think about this," Marie said. "We have a bunch of invoices here that we know wound up going to that Acclaimed Builders company."

"Right."

"We also know that a lot of employees touched those invoices before they wound up in their account."

"So many that there's no pattern to them," Frankie said. "And even if we wanted to check the computers they ran through to see who was using them, we couldn't because that security footage is missing."

"Also, Chris signs all the checks, so his signature on them isn't helpful either."

"Wait," Frankie said. "Chris might sign them, but who generated the payment? There aren't many people who can do that."

"Ok, maybe that's our angle," Marie said. "Let's see if we can match the canceled checks to payments in the system here and see who issued them."

"I had that system pulled up earlier," Frankie said, turning to her computer. "Let me find it again."

Frankie got to work, but quickly stopped and frowned. "Well, this is weird. It's gone."

"What do you mean?" Marie asked. "What's gone?"

"Well, not gone, exactly," Frankie said, clicking through a few more screens. "Just different."

"What's different?"

Frankie ignored her. "Do you have those images Anna sent you? The ones of the canceled checks?"

Marie opened up her phone and found the images. "What do you need from them?"

"Just let me look at one of them right now," Frankie said and picked up Marie's phone. She studied the check for a few minutes before turning to the computer and clicking through a few items on the screen. After a few more minutes, she looked back at the check on Marie's phone and frowned. "Someone's changed things in our system."

"How so?"

"We have these check copies here," Frankie said, "but in the system, they are different now. The check numbers are the same and the amounts, of course, but the checks are now made out to other companies."

"Who would have the capability of doing that?" Marie asked.

"Nobody should have the capability of doing that," Frankie said. "You can't just change who checks are made out to. That's not ethical."

"But somebody did," Marie said. "Who do you think could have done that?"

Frankie shook her head. "Nobody in the finance department, that's for sure. This would have come from high up."

Marie sat back and thought for a second. "The IT department, maybe? Would they have access to something like this? Or Melissa's department? Chris maybe?"

"This is so high level it had to have been a director," Frankie said. "Chris signs the checks, which means for control purposes, he wouldn't have access to this high-level of the payment system."

"Which leaves who, then?"

Frankie shrugged. "The director of IT might be able to make this type of change. He would be the only person who would make sense."

"They are trying to cover this up," Marie said. "Trying to keep us from finding what we need to find."

"I agree," Frankie said. "But, with these copies, we have proof that they've changed things."

"Which means we have proof that can lead the authorities back to whoever made the changes," Marie said. "Why did they choose now to do it, I wonder?"

"Somehow they figured out we were getting close," Frankie said. "Probably Joe and Anna's escapade at that building alerted them."

"Maybe so," Marie said. "They tried to destroy the evidence and now they are trying to cover their tracks."

Frankie leaned in her direction and whispered. "They may not realize that Derrick rescued the evidence. They probably think they destroyed it when the building went down."

"We need to call Anna and warn her," Marie whispered back. "She needs to know to keep the evidence secure."

Marie picked up her phone and frowned at it when she realized she didn't have service. "That's weird. I don't have any service."

Frankie frowned and picked up her phone. "Me neither. Try the office phone."

Marie picked it up, only to find it dead. "This is weird, Frankie. I don't feel good about things right now."

Frankie looked up at the ceiling and wrinkled her nose. "Hey, do you smell that? Something smells strange."

Marie sniffed the air and gasped. "That's gas, Frankie. We need to get out of here. Something's wrong."

Frankie and Marie quickly gathered their things and headed for the door to the conference room. When Marie pushed on the door, however, it didn't budge. She shoved it again and got the same result before turning to Frankie.

"Someone's locked us in here," she said, her heart pounding.

"Quick, there's a fire escape over on the other side of the room," Frankie said, already turning around and heading in that direction. "Let's get out that way."

Frankie reached the door before Marie and quickly shoved it, but met the same resistance Marie had faced with the door on the other side of the conference room. She shoved again before kicking the door in frustration.

"Great," Marie said. "No phones, no exits, and a room full of gas. We need help, Frankie."

Chapter 42

"But you don't understand," Anna pleaded to the person on the phone. "My sister could be in real danger here. I'm not making something up on a whim."

"Look, if it will make you feel better, I'll have a patrol unit roll by the business and make sure there isn't any sign of distress," Detective Morales said. "We'll even talk to the security guard, but I have no reason to go poking around in a business without some sort of reason to do so."

"But I'm telling you—"

"What you're telling me doesn't even count for probable cause," he said. "You can't just call and tell me that someone might be in danger without actually having any type of proof that they are. Phone lines go down all the time. Cell phones lose service. It happens."

"So, what you're telling me is we're on our own?"

"What I'm telling you is I need more than your word to go bust into a business in the middle of the day."

"Fine," Anna said. "I have your number. I'll call back when I need your help."

"Do not go getting yourself into trouble."

"Don't you worry about me," Anna said and quickly ended the call.

"Not gonna help, huh?" Derrick asked.

"Of course not," Anna complained. "Just like with the evidence we found in the park, Detective Morales is not interested in any help we are trying to give him."

"Thinks he knows better," Joe said from his bed, where he was trying to push himself to a sitting position.

"Stop that!" Anna said. "You just lay there and rest. We'll figure this out."

"What are we going to do, Anna?" Bryant asked. "We have no way of reaching Marie to check on her, but we also don't know if she's really in danger or not."

Anna sighed. "I'll just have to go myself."

"You most certainly will not," Joe said. "They are going with you."

"We aren't leaving you alone, Joe," Anna said. "What if you need something? I'll be fine."

"How about Bryant stays with Joe, and I'll go with Anna," Derrick said. "Then nobody is left alone."

"I would feel more comfortable with that plan myself," Bryant said.

"You better stay in that bed," Anna said to Joe before turning to grab her phone and her purse. "Anything you need, Derrick? I'd like to get going."

"Just the car keys," he said with a shake of his head, "which are in my pocket."

Anna and Derrick sped from the room and headed for the elevator. When the doors didn't open immediately, Anna turned toward the fire exit stairs instead. Derrick groaned and followed her as she hurried down flight after flight.

When they reached the bottom, Anna paused only a second to catch her breath before jogging to the parking lot and Derrick's waiting car. He started the car and threw it into gear as Anna put the address to the office building into the GPS.

As he drove, Anna watched the buildings pass by outside the window and grumbled about the traffic that kept holding them up. However, even with a few slight delays, they reached the building within fifteen minutes.

Derrick parked, and they both climbed out of the car. Anna peered inside the front door of the building before stepping back out of view. She turned to Derrick and said, "That Roberts guy is at the desk. I want to test the waters before I bring you in. Stay here."

"I thought I was here to protect you?"

"If I don't come back in five minutes," Anna said. "Come in after me. He hasn't seen you before. I want to keep you hidden in case I need a distraction."

"Five minutes," Derrick said, pointing at the watch on his arm.

Anna turned back toward the office building and took a deep breath. Trying to maintain a calm and inviting demeanor, she strode into the lobby and up to the security desk. Thomas Roberts gave her a hesitant smile when she approached.

"Hello," he said. "How may I help you?"

"You may not remember me," Anna said, forcing a big smile on her face and a friendly tone to her voice, "I was with some friends of mine when we came and took a tour of your building about a week ago."

"Ah, yes!" Thomas replied. "I believe I remember. What can I do for you?"

"Well, my sister was supposed to be making a stop in here today," Anna said, "but I can't seem to get in touch with her. I was wondering if you might have seen her?"

"I'm afraid not," he replied. "Just been our employees coming in today."

"Are you sure?" Anna said. "I talked to her once today, and she said she was here. Even mentioned checking in at the desk here."

"I'm afraid you are mistaken," he said with a shake of his head. "And I'm also afraid that I'm very busy, so I'm going to need you to go. I can't help you."

He turned away from her and picked up the phone on his desk, thus ending their conversation. Anna sighed and glanced around the lobby for obvious signs of distress, but headed back outside when she found nothing.

Derrick was waiting by the side of the building where she had left him. "No luck?"

"None," she replied. "He was being overly unhelpful. Asked me to leave even."

"That's not a good sign."

"No, it's not." Anna turned to look at the building again. "I'm going to try calling Marie and Frankie again to see if they answer."

She picked up her phone and realized that she had no service. "Well, this is great. I have no service. He must be doing something to block out the cell signals for the building."

"What's the plan?" Derrick asked. "Distraction time?"

"Not just yet," she said. "Let's hit that back-alley Chris took us into. See if we can get in that way again."

Derrick followed her around the side of the building and frowned when she slipped into a small, darkened alley. She walked to the door and pulled on the handle, but it didn't budge. With a frown, she looked around the alley for another option. Finding none, she began digging through her purse.

When she pulled out a small pen-like device and turned back toward the door, Derrick raised an eyebrow at her. "What is that thing?"

"That is a lock pick," Anna said, her attention already on the door. "It's going to get us inside this building. It's an electric lock, so all I need to do is short out the system."

She worked on the lock for a few moments before hearing a satisfying click. This time when she tried to pull on the door, it swung open freely. They walked in the door, and Derrick let it close quietly behind him.

She looked up and down the hallway around them and sighed in relief when she didn't find anyone. She glanced at the elevator first, but turned away from it, opting to head down a short hallway to her left.

"Where are we going?" Derrick whispered when she opened a door to a darkened room.

"When we were here last time, I figured out that this is a security room," she said. "I should be able to tap into their security feed with my phone. That way if something goes down, we'll be able to have a copy."

"Well, that's just great," he grumbled. "I'm starting to not like this job at all."

Anna chuckled and looked around the small room and located the server that belonged to the video surveillance system. After digging into her purse, she pulled a small clip out and attached it to the main cord running into the server.

She then pulled a second cord from her purse and plugged it into the clip. After hiding her cord as much as possible, she attached the other end of it to her phone and opened a few apps on the screen.

Once satisfied her phone was recording the surveillance camera's output properly, she bent down and tucked the phone behind some of the other servers' cords to better hide it. When she stood back up, Derrick was looking at her with wide eyes.

"What?"

"Do all girls keep that kind of stuff in their purses?" he asked. "I've always wondered what kind of stuff goes into those things."

Anna laughed. "I could live off the contents of my purse for three days in a pinch. I come prepared."

"I'll remember that."

Anna crept back toward the door to the security room and opened it until she could look down the hallway in both directions. She stepped back inside and closed the door to give Derrick some instructions.

"I don't want to take the elevator," she said. "It makes too much noise, will take too long, and might put us in danger."

"Yeah, I don't want to be trapped in an elevator with you," Derrick said. "I do like you, but not that much. You'll have me climbing out the top of it."

Anna laughed. "Thank you for making this not seem as stressful as what it is. I really appreciate it."

She opened the door again and looked down the hallway quickly before stepping out into it. She motioned for Derrick to follow her, then turned to point at a doorway at the end of the hallway. "The stairs are that way. Marie and Frankie should be on the third floor."

Derrick nodded and followed her down the hallway. They crept up the stairs, being careful to watch for signs of others in the stairwell as they went. It wasn't until they reached the second-floor landing that they saw any signs of life in the building.

As they were passing the door that led into the second floor, Anna peered into the small window. The room behind the door was another conference room, much like the one they had worked in on the third floor. A single employee sat in the room.

Anna jerked away from the window, only to move to the side to get a better peek. The employee stood up and stretched before picking up a coffee cup on the table in front of them and heading out into the main section of the building. The room stayed quiet after the door to the conference room closed behind them.

"Alright, let's go now so they don't hear us on the stairs," she whispered.

She and Derrick quickly climbed the stairs, and about halfway up, Anna wrinkled her nose. She turned to Derrick and said, "Do you smell that?"

He frowned. "That smells like gas, Anna."

"Alright, no more trying to be quiet," she said. "Let's go."

Chapter 43

She sprinted up the remaining stairs and reached the door to the conference room. To her horror, she found a thick chain wrapped around the handles and secured by a lock. In a panic, she peeked inside the window and banged on it when she spotted Marie and Frankie lying on the floor nearby.

"Marie!" she screamed. "Derrick, we have to get this door open."

"Move back," he said.

She turned to find him holding a fire extinguisher and stepped out of his way just as he was bringing it down on the lock that held the chain in place. After a few hits, the lock broke and the chain loosened from the door.

Anna jerked it out of the way and slung the door open, immediately rushing to her sister. Marie stirred when she touched her shoulder.

"Oh, thank God!" Anna said. "Marie, can you hear me? We've got to get you out of here."

"There's gas," Marie mumbled. "We...tried to stay low...so we didn't breathe it in. I feel dizzy."

"Stop talking," Anna said. She grabbed her sister's arm and threw it over her shoulder. "Derrick, can you get Frankie?"

Anna maneuvered Marie to her feet as Derrick was picking up Frankie. Together, they all headed back to the stairs and got all four of them to the landing on the second floor.

Anna nodded to the conference room they had passed earlier. "In here. We need to get some help."

They pushed through the door and deposited Marie and Frankie in the first chairs they found. Anna immediately dropped to her knees in front of Marie and looked at her.

"I'm fine," Marie said. "Really. Just need to catch my breath."

"You need oxygen," Anna said. "Real oxygen. Derrick, we need to get an ambul—"

"Well, well, well," a voice suddenly said from the other side of the room. Anna looked up to see Thomas Roberts standing at the door with the IT manager they had met on the first day behind him. "If it isn't our little group of trespassers. Where do you have the rest of your team stashed?"

Anna glared at him. "What are you trying to do here? We were onto your game, so you decided to just kill us? Was that the plan?"

"I guess I should have tried harder," Thomas said. "Seems like the lot of you are difficult to dispose of."

"There's still time," the IT manager said. "They can't call anyone. Nobody knows they're here."

"Yes, people know we're here," Anna said. "They'll look for us."

"Well, then we'll just dispose of them, too," Thomas said. "Besides, by the time they get here, you'll already be gone, so it won't matter."

"You will not get away anytime soon, so why don't you and your friend have a seat with the others?" Thomas said. "Let's have a fun little chat before we get down to business."

Before she stood to her feet to move to a chair, Anna reached into her purse and palmed the small container of pepper spray Alex had given her. She then sat next to Marie in a chair and pulled the purse into her lap to hide it. Derrick sat next to her. While Thomas talked, he looked around the room.

"I'm going to need to get rid of all the evidence you found on me," Thomas said. "You be a little dear and tell me where it is and maybe I won't have to hurt you too badly."

"Oh, a quick death, huh?" Anna said. "Yeah, I don't think so."

"Maybe if I rough up that sister of yours, you'll tell me what I need to know."

"You're going to kill us all anyway, so what does it matter?"

"I didn't figure you'd be the type that would want your sister to suffer."

"Guess you don't know me that well," Anna said, allowing her voice to take on an evil tone. "Say, before you get to all the torture stuff, why don't you fill me in on what exactly is going on around here?"

"Why don't you tell me your theory while Daniel here clears the building," Thomas said. "There's a dangerous gas leak, after all. Would hate for anyone to get hurt."

Daniel rolled his eyes and grumbled. "Why am I always the one doing this stuff? Why can't you do it yourself?"

"Because that's what I pay you for."

Daniel rolled his eyes again and headed out the door. Anna heard the distinct sound of the door lock when he left.

"So, where were we?" Thomas asked. "Ah, yes, you were telling me what you know."

"Well, I know you are a descendant of the original owner Benjamin Goar," she said. "It appears your grandmother had an affair with him."

His eyes darkened, and he cursed. "That SOB is the reason my mother and father died. She was his daughter, but when she was in the hospital with no chance to pay for the treatment she needed, he just let her die."

Anna's eyes softened. "That's horrible. She couldn't get the care she needed following the car accident she and your father were in? And that's why she died?"

"He could have paid for it easily," Thomas said. "But he refused."

"I'm so sorry," Anna said. "But that doesn't give you the right to kill us."

He ignored her and circled the table in the conference room. "I might have forgiven him. My mother was in terrible shape and my father had already passed. She might not have made it even with the treatment. But what that man did to my sisters was unforgivable."

"What did he do, Thomas?"

"I tried to get them," he said. "To raise them myself. They were the only family I had left. But he made sure that didn't happen. He made sure the state took them and sent them off to live elsewhere. I've never been able to find them again."

"Family is really important," Derrick said, cluing into Anna's attempt to keep Thomas talking. "I can understand your anger."

"Is that when you enacted your revenge by embezzling the money from the company?" Anna asked.

Thomas shook his head. "I wanted to wait him out. I wanted him to die. I did all the research. Had all the evidence. I was part of that family. By law, they owed me a portion of his estate."

"But when he died, you found he had specifically excluded your family from his will," Anna said.

"It was ludicrous! He tricked my grandmother into letting him remove their daughter from his will. It wasn't fair. I deserved that money. I deserved our portion of his estate."

"So, you took it?"

"I only took what was rightfully mine," Thomas said. "I took the funds that would have been given to my family."

"Did it make everything better, Thomas?" Anna asked. "Is everything alright now?"

"It will be once I hop on a plane later," Thomas said. "I will not rest until I find my sisters. They need to know I didn't stop looking for them."

Daniel returned and unlocked the conference room door. Thomas looked up at him when he walked in. "Building's clear."

Daniel sat at the conference room table and waited for instructions. Anna nodded in his direction. "So, what is your deal with all this? Just some tech junky along for the ride? Looking for an easy paycheck?"

"It was a hard deal to pass up," Daniel shrugged. "This company has paid me crap wages for years. Time to get a little for me."

"And all it took was being a sell-out?"

"Hey, I am not a sell-out!" Daniel said, jumping to his feet. "They could afford to lose some money. It didn't hurt anybody."

"I think Asher would beg to differ if he were still alive," Anna said. "And Melissa."

"They didn't die because of us," Thomas said.

"You tried to use me as a scapegoat," Frankie said, speaking for the first time since they'd arrived in the room. "I can't say that I approved of that."

Anna met her eyes and found them clear and alert. Marie also seemed more alert than when they had entered the room.

"You should have thought about that before you poked your nose in our business," Thomas said.

"There is just one thing that I'm confused about," Anna said. "Is the company that hired Frankie and the other interns involved? I just couldn't wrap my head around those payments you sent to them."

Thomas laughed. "You really had everything figured out, didn't you? Nah, I included no more people than I had to. I just paid them a little extra to ensure they sent us interns that weren't looking for long-term commitments."

"I see," Anna said, her eyes narrowing. "You didn't want the interns you were using for your schemes to stick around long enough to figure out something was going on. Frankie just impeded your plan."

"Stupid thing," Thomas said, glaring at Frankie. "Causing all that trouble. Of course, it made it easy for me to blame you for everything. With all the attention on you, I almost had enough time to make my final arrangements and get out of this place."

"So, you were using things as a distraction," Anna said with a shake of her head. "It wasn't just Chris trying to distract the board of directors. You were trying to keep the focus off you as well."

Thomas shrugged. "The opportunity presented itself nicely, so why not. I don't care what happens to this stupid company after I leave. I got my money. Now I just need to go find my sisters."

"Do you think your mother would be proud of the son you've become?" Anna asked, maintaining eye contact when he glared at her.

"Enough of this," he hissed. "If the building is clear, we need to get rid of them. Then we can burn the building down."

"There is no way you are going to get away with that," Anna said with a chuckle. "Burning the building down won't hide your crimes."

"Well, you will be dead," Thomas said. He looked around the room and located a pipe laying on the floor. He grinned when he picked it up, dragging it on the ground loudly as he walked in their direction. "And I'll be on a plane to Tahiti to hide out until I have a new identity."

"You did seem to forget something," Anna said and looked up at the security camera behind her. "All this is on camera. The police will have you in custody before you get to the airport gate."

Thomas's eyes widened as he looked at the red dot glowing on the security camera. He turned Daniel's direction and glared at him. "You were supposed to take care of that."

"I'll erase it," Daniel replied. "Just like I did with all the other security footage. Don't worry. Just do what you need to do."

"Why don't you go do it now, so we don't have to worry about it later?"

"Fine."

Daniel stood to leave the room again and Thomas watched him. While Thomas was distracted, Anna whispered to her sister, "Marie, can you run?"

"I think so," she whispered back.

"What about Frankie?"

"I'm good," Frankie replied.

"Good," Anna whispered. "On my signal, run down the stairs and get out of here. Find help."

"What do you want me to do?" Derrick whispered.

"Follow my lead."

Anna stopped talking the moment Thomas turned back in their direction again. He laughed at her. "Planning an epic escape there? I'm pretty sure your ship is sinking and there aren't any lifeboats left."

Anna didn't reply as Thomas headed their way with the heavy pipe he held in his hand. He looked at Marie first, followed by Frankie, and then chuckled. Turning to Anna, he said, "Guess I'll just start with you and your guy friend over here. Doesn't seem like they are going to be much of a challenge."

From his pocket, he pulled a pair of handcuffs and headed in Derrick's direction. "Let's just get you out of the way first, then we'll get started there, Anna."

When Thomas turned Derrick's direction, Anna motioned for her sister and Frankie to make a break for it. Thomas spun back in their direction just as they were leaping toward the staircase. With his attention on Marie and Frankie, Anna jerked the pepper spray canister upward and sprayed him in the face with it while being careful to keep it away from Derrick.

Thomas screamed and fell to the ground while rubbing his eyes. "It burns! It burns!"

Anna kicked the pipe Thomas had dropped from his hand in Derrick's direction and he picked it up. Before they could move away from Thomas, Daniel sprinted back into the room.

"What in the world?" he yelled. "What did you do?"

Derrick stood to his feet and held the pipe up. Daniel turned to run, but a large group of FBI agents stopped him. Agent Stephens followed in behind them and waited until Thomas and Daniel were subdued.

"Well, I suppose you could help me out after all," the agent said after walking up to Anna. "Can't say that I approve much of your methods, but we have suspects in custody."

Anna looked up and tried to smile at him, but he looked at her sternly and said, "What did I tell you about being careful?"

"They tried to kill my sister," she said. "They admitted to everything. It's on camera."

"Yeah, too bad they erased everything a few seconds ago," Agent Stephens said.

"We'll just have to get them to repeat themselves," said an agent as he hauled Thomas to his feet. Daniel sighed and let them put cuffs around his wrists.

"Yeah, I would think again about that," Anna said. "I figured they would try to erase the cameras, so I linked my phone into their system before we even headed up here. There's a copy of everything downstairs."

"Where at?" one agent asked. "I'll have a tech team copy it over."

"First floor," Anna said. "Server room by the back elevator. It's hidden behind some wires in the second server cabinet on the right."

Agent Stephens looked at Anna and shook his head. "You are something, you know?"

"Yeah, I know."

Chapter 44

Anna looked around the room, grateful they were all in one piece. Medics had checked Marie and Frankie out at the office building, and she and Derrick had escaped without a scratch. Joe seemed to be on the mend as well, and he and Bryant had met them all at Mr. Matthews's office. Now they sat waiting to plan out the rest of the case.

"So, is that it, then?" Joe asked as he used his crutches to spin himself back and forth in his chair. "Frankie is clear and free, and it's time for us to go back home?"

"Pretty much," Eugene said. "They already dropped the charges against Frankie and agreed to remove them from her record. I also talked to Agent Stephens about the embezzling case, and it looks like there won't be any charges for that either."

"Thanks to all that evidence Anna rescued from that abandoned building and the security cameras," Frankie said.

"I can't take credit for all that," Anna said. "Derrick went back for those files."

"It was still your idea," Derrick said. "I'll let you take credit for that."

"Well, I don't care who takes credit," Frankie said. "Thank you all for everything. I can never repay you all for helping me out of this mess."

"No thanks or repayments are necessary," Bryant said. "We're all family, and we take care of each other."

"Still, thank you all," she said.

"Are you coming back home now, Frankie?" Marie asked. "Please tell me you're coming back home."

"I have to finish up a few loose ends around here, but I've already scheduled a truck to move my stuff back the week after next," she said.

"That's a relief," Marie said. "You want me to stay and help you?"

"Nope. I want you to get back home and start helping me find a new apartment," she said. "I already have some leads on jobs, but I need a place to stay when I get back."

"You're always welcome to stay with us for a while if you need to," Anna said. "We'd be happy to have you."

"Thank you, Anna," Frankie said. "But for now, I just want all of you to get out of here and get back home. You all need to rest, and I can't be holding you up here and messing with your practice."

"You don't have to tell me twice," Joe said with a laugh. "It's almost Christmas, Bryant. You know mom is up in that kitchen baking a ton of cookies."

"Mmm, cookies," Anna said. "You think she'll let—"

Joe stopped her with a laugh. "Are you fixing to ask me if my mother is going to make cookies for you? She'll probably make more for you than she will me!"

Anna laughed and then looked around the room. "Well, guys, I say we get back to the hotel and get us a flight out of here."

"I'm already way ahead of you," Joe said. "I've got tickets ready for us to pick up for a flight this afternoon."

"Thank you again for all your help, Mr. Matthews," Frankie said, as they all gathered their things. "I appreciate everything you did for me."

"I can't say that I did much," he said. "They did it all, but you're welcome. If you need anything else before your time here is finished, just let me know."

Anna and the others headed back into the parking lot and split up one last time. They divided up into two vehicles and headed back toward the hotel. Soon they were back in the hotel's parking lot.

"Well, Derrick," Joe said. "I'm sure this is where we are parting for this trip, isn't it?"

"Nah, I'm walking you up to your room to make sure you make it alright," he said. "I'll give you all a proper goodbye there."

Joe chuckled and shook his head at him. They all climbed out of the car and headed inside. Once they were on their floor, Joe pulled a key out of his pocket and opened his hotel room. Derrick gave him a quick hug before stepping back.

"Man, I always hate these goodbyes of ours," Joe said. "Seems like it's a zillion years between visits."

"I'll have to come back this summer for a visit," Derrick said. "Pop in on vacation or something."

"Yeah, make sure you do," Joe said with another smile. "I'm going to get in there and get my stuff together. It's going to take me twice as long as everyone else while on these things. See you, Derrick."

"See you, Joe," Derrick said with a smile. "Stay out of trouble."

Joe laughed and walked into the room, leaving Derrick and Anna in the hallway alone. Derrick turned in her direction and hugged her. "Well, take care of him for me, will you?"

Anna laughed. "Does this mean I passed this test of yours?"

Derrick pulled away from her and frowned at her playfully. "What test?"

"The test you've been putting me through all week," she said and folded her arms across her chest. "The one where you are making sure I'm not wrecking your best friend's life with this crazy venture of ours."

"I don't know what you are talking about," Derrick said, a playful smile on his face, "but if I were testing you, yes, you would have passed."

"Well, thank you," Anna said. "You passed mine as well."
"Wait, what?" he asked. "You were testing me?"
"You did involve yourself with my best friend, after all."
"Who? Claire?"
"Mmm-hmm."
"Don't know what you're talking about."
"Right."

Derrick laughed before growing serious and nodding toward Joe's door. "Seriously, Anna. Take care of him for me."

"I will."

"See you around."

Anna smiled at him as he walked away and then headed toward her hotel room to gather her things.

Chapter 45

Within an hour, they were at the airport preparing to pick up their tickets. When they stopped at the desk, Joe looked at his bag and said, "You know what. I'm checking everything. Take it all. No way I'm going to hop around on these crutches while trying to keep a carry-on bag with me."

Anna chuckled and helped him get his bags on the belt and carried his flight papers for him. After going through security and finding their gate, Joe slunk into a chair, exhausted.

"I'm not moving," he said. "They need to wheel me onto the plane."

Anna laughed. "Hopefully, we will get home in record time so you can get some rest."

"Remind me to have you stop at the gift shop on the way out so you can get me a little bell," he said.

"Why?" Bryant asked. "So you can ring for me every time you need something?"

"Exactly! I'm milking this for all it's worth."

When they called his name over the intercom, Joe groaned and pushed himself to his feet. "You've got to be kidding me."

Anna watched him swing toward the gate's desk and talk with the attendant behind the table. After a bit of a back and forth, the woman shook her head and handed him a piece of paper. When Joe turned their direction, Anna could see the frustration all over his face.

"Well, this doesn't look good," Bryant said. When Joe approached, he asked him, "What's going on?"

"Well, apparently, they overbooked our flight," Joe complained. "They bumped me."

"They bumped you?" Anna asked. "That's ridiculous. We are flying together."

"That's what I told them," he said, "but it didn't matter."

"Give me that ticket," Anna said. "I'm going to go talk to her myself."

Joe handed her the new ticket and grumbled. "Good luck with that."

Anna walked back up to the woman and passed the paper across the desk to her. "Excuse me, you bumped my friend from this flight, but we are all flying together."

"As I told him," the woman said, "there's nothing we can do. The flight is full, and we had to bump two people."

"But, why him, though?" she asked. "He's on crutches and needs help getting around. How's he supposed to get to the next gate on time? We have a layover before we head home."

"We have wheelchairs," she replied. "We can have an attendant help him. We bumped him specifically because he is on crutches. The next flight can accommodate him. This one can't."

Anna's attention was suddenly pulled away from the woman she was talking to and to the woman who was standing next to her at the desk. The woman started crying.

"Please," she said. "You don't understand. I'm going to miss my daughter's wedding if I don't get on this flight. The next one won't have me landing before her wedding is over."

"I'm so sorry," the attendant said. "We didn't have any volunteers to move flights. We don't have an option."

Anna sighed and turned back to the woman she was working with. The woman raised an eyebrow.

"Can you get me on his flight?" Anna asked.

"Sure can," the woman said.

"Fine. Do it."

The airport employees quickly explained to the other woman the situation, and she immediately swept Anna into a big hug. "Thank you. Thank you. Thank you."

"Seriously, it's not that big a deal," Anna said. "I'm trying to make sure my friend doesn't have to wait alone in the airport."

"Still, you do not know how much better you just made my life," the woman said.

Anna smiled. "You're welcome."

The woman handed Anna her a new ticket and returned Joe's. Anna gave her a small smile and turned back toward her group. Joe was grinning at her when she returned.

"So, how did it go?" he asked.

Anna sat down next to him and handed him his ticket back. "Well, you don't have to wait by yourself now."

He chuckled. "Well, that's a bonus, at least."

"We can get them to bump us, too," Marie said. "That way we all stay together."

"No way!" Anna said. "You guys get home. I'm sure you are both dying to get home to Eddie and Allie."

"What about Alex?" Joe whispered.

"Well, I'd be excited to get home to him too, but I haven't been able to get ahold of him again," Anna whispered back. "It's getting annoying."

"I'm sure there's a reason," he replied, growing serious.

Anna sighed. "I hope so."

Within a few minutes, the doors to the flight opened, and the attendants began calling passengers onto the plane to load. The woman with whom Anna had switched tickets gave her a big smile and wave when she boarded.

Bryant looked at his ticket and said, "Well, I hate to leave you two at the airport, but this is us. Try to stay out of trouble, will ya?"

Joe laughed. "Not sure what you think I'm going to do with my leg all messed up. I don't even have a carry-on bag, so I have nothing to do either."

Anna laughed. "I have a pair of earbuds. We can listen to music together while we wait." She looked up at Marie and grinned. "We'll be good. I promise."

"How did they talk us into this, Bryant?" Marie asked as she stood and collected her bag. "Whose idea was it to open a business with our younger siblings? They must have hypnotized us or something."

Anna laughed and grinned at Joe. "You know they love us, right?"

"Yep, couldn't live without us."

Bryant laughed and shook his head before walking away toward the plane. Marie leaned down to hug Anna before following him. When the doors to the airplane closed, Anna sighed and pulled out the promised earbuds. She handed one to Joe and put the other in her ear.

"I hope you have a long playlist," he said. "Otherwise, we are going to be listening to the same songs a bunch of times during this sudden four-hour delay of ours."

"Four hours?" Anna said, jerking the ticket into her hand. "I have to sit in this place with you for four hours? What was I thinking!"

Joe laughed and smiled at her. "Well, I, for one, am quite pleased with the situation. Much less boring of a wait now."

"Oh, you owe me for this one," Anna said with a laugh of her own.

He picked one crutch up and shook it a bit. "Hey, I kept you from having to use these things for a couple of weeks. That has to count for something."

Anna looked at the crutches and chuckled. "Good point. Guess we're even. For now."

"WE'D LIKE TO WELCOME you all to Richmond International Airport. The current time is 9 PM and the current temperature is..."

"It's about time," Joe said as he stretched next to Anna. "I'm glad we were on this flight instead of crunched up on one of those little ones. My body would have been killing me."

"Yeah, the extra legroom is rather nice," Anna said. She looked around and stretched while waiting for the flight attendants to let them leave the plane. When the traffic started moving, she sighed in relief and hurriedly helped Joe get off the plane.

They headed toward the baggage claim area and Anna found a seat for Joe to wait. "You stay here. I'll get our bags and then I'll go get us a car."

Joe smiled up at her when he sat down. "I don't think you're going to have to do that."

"Why not?" she asked and turned around. She gasped when she spotted Alex standing by the baggage claim. After sending Joe a smile, she dropped her bag by him and made her way to Alex as fast as her feet could carry her. He engulfed her in his arms the moment she reached him.

"What are you doing here?" Anna asked, after wiping a happy tear from her cheek and kissing him. "I didn't know you were going to be waiting for us."

"Remember, you texted me to let me know you were headed home?" he asked. "I was here when that plane landed and Marie told me what happened. I came back to get you myself."

"Well, I'm glad that you did!" she said. She turned around and looked at Joe. "Hey, I was going to make sure he got home alright. Do you mind if we take him?"

"Of course not," Alex said.

Anna looked at the conveyor belt when it moved. "Looks like our bags are coming."

"Great," he said with a smile. He smoothed the hair around her face and kissed her again. "You grab those off and I'll go pull around the car."

She smiled when he walked away and looked back at Joe, who gave her a thumbs up. Her eyes headed back to Alex again, and she frowned when she saw something fall out of his pocket. She took the few steps in his direction to retrieve it for him.

"Hey, Alex," she called after him. "You dropped this."

She held it up, and he frowned. "Nope, not mine. Must be someone else's."

He turned away from her and continued heading toward the door. She looked at the item and frowned. She examined it while she waited for their bags to pop out on the conveyor. When she had them off the belt, she pulled them back over to Joe, still looking at the paper in her hand.

"Well, I see you enjoyed your delightful surprise," he said. "I have to admit that I didn't see that one coming."

"Neither did I," she said, still looking at the paper.

"What is that?"

"It's a flight ticket," she said. "From Boston. I thought Alex dropped it, but he said it wasn't his."

"Thought?"

"No, actually," she said. "I saw it fall out of his pocket."

"You're saying he just lied to you?"

"I don't know."

"Why would he lie about traveling?" Joe asked with a frown. "Does he know anyone in Boston?"

"Well, my dad is in Boston this week," Anna said with a frown.

"You think he went to see him?" Joe asked, his eyes widening. "Like Eddie did when he propos—"

"Don't you dare get that far ahead of things," Anna said, her own eyes widening. "There is no way I want to put that thought in my head just yet."

She put the paper in her pocket and smiled a bit to herself. When Alex returned, she gave him another kiss. He squeezed her before taking the handle of her bag from her.

"You two ready?" Alex asked. "Let's get you out of here."

Anna pulled Joe's bag and Alex took hers and their carry-on bags to his car. After getting them all settled in the car, Alex drove to Joe's apartment and parked by his door. Joe looked at Anna in the mirror before getting out.

"Well, Anna," he said. "See you at the office?"

"Not tomorrow, you won't," Anna said with a laugh. "I'm sleeping in."

"Slacker," Joe said with a laugh. To Alex, he said, "Thanks for the ride home."

"Anytime," Alex said and got out to get his bags out of the car. While Alex pulled Joe's bags to the front door and made sure he got in alright, Anna moved to the front seat. Alex pulled her in for a soft kiss when he returned.

"You ready to go home and go to bed?" he asked.

"I am," she said with a tired smile. "It's been a long week."

"I'm sure it has," he replied and pulled out of the parking lot. "Oh, and when I said home and to bed, I meant mine."

He stopped at the stop sign and Anna pulled him toward her for another kiss. "I might be tempted to just stay in it."

He grinned. "Wouldn't hurt my feelings a bit."

Also By

Don't miss out on the other stories in The Hartman and Malone Mystery Series from

Paige H. Perry!

- *When World's Collide—A Hartman and Malone Story/Prequel*
- *Trial By Sabotage ——A Hartman and Malone Mystery #1*
- *Forgotten Promises ——A Hartman and Malone Mystery #2*
- *Count the Lies ——A Hartman and Malone Mystery #3*

Visit our website at www.paigehperry.com to learn more about the series, the characters, and upcoming release dates.

www.ingramcontent.com/pod-product-compliance
Lightning Source LLC
LaVergne TN
LVHW091528060526
838200LV00036B/523